A DREAM OF EMPIRE: OR, THE HOUSE OF BLENNERHASSETT
BY
William Henry Venable

A DREAM OF EMPIRE: OR, THE HOUSE OF BLENNERHASSETT

Published by Silver Scroll Publishing

New York City, NY

First published circa 1920

Copyright © Silver Scroll Publishing, 2015

All rights reserved

Except in the United States of America, this book is sold subject to the condition that it shall not, by way of trade or otherwise, be lent, re-sold, hired out, or otherwise circulated without the publisher's prior consent in any form of binding or cover other than that in which it is published and without a similar condition including this condition being imposed on the subsequent purchaser.

ABOUT SILVER SCROLL PUBLISHING

Silver Scroll Publishing is a digital publisher that brings the best historical fiction ever written to modern readers. Our comprehensive catalogue contains everything from historical novels about Rome to works about World War I.

I.: AN ECCENTRIC VISITOR.

It was the first of May, and the sun had passed the noon line in a bright sky, causing the shadow of Peter Taylor to fall east of north and infusing his substance with the delightful languor called Spring Fever. Leaning upon an idle spade, Peter watched the lazy motions of a negro slave whom he had directed to trim a level lawn ornamented with flowerbeds. The English origin of the overseer was revealed by his looks and in his speech.

"Scipio, 'ave you 'oed the corn?"

"No, boss, but I's jes' gwine to ten' to it right away."

"Well, make 'aste. Daniel and Ransom can 'elp you, and tell Honest Moses to get the south patch ready for the watermelon seed."

Scipio received his orders submissively, and, shouldering a hoe, sauntered toward the cornfield, and was soon hidden by a clump of young weeping-willows, the sunny green branches of which trailed to the darker verdure of the sward. Screened by the drooping foliage, the shirking menial cast his body on the grass to store up energy for anticipated toil.

Meanwhile, the taskmaster, having issued commands to his black subordinates, felt justified in neglecting his own duties, in a dignified way, by seeking a shady retreat in which he lingered contemplating the charms of Nature and the pleasing results of his own skill as a landscape-gardener. The prevailing aspect of the surroundings was wild, though several acres of cultivated land, including a fine lawn with gravelled walks and drives, attested that much labor had been expended in reclaiming a portion of savage Nature from its primeval condition. The plantation occupied the upper end of Blennerhassett Island. Standing on a knoll, with his back to the "improved" grounds, Peter took in at a sweeping glance a reach of gleaming water which flowed between woody hills overhung by a serene sky. He saw the silver flood of the Ohio River which, coursing southward, broke against the island, dividing its broad current into two nearly equal streams. He admired the meadow slopes of Belpre, on the Ohio side, and the more dimly seen bluffs of Wood County, on the Virginia border. The tourist of to-day, standing where the gardener stood on Blennerhassett Island a hundred years ago, sees in the northern distance the iron framework of the Parkersburg bridge spanning the river, so far away as to show like a fairy web in the air. Beyond, as if issuing from the heart of the hills, the river blends with the purple mist.

Having "bent the quiet of a loving eye" upon the river and its delightful valley, the Englishman turned his ruddy face toward the chief building on the island, a frame structure of odd appearance, painted in dazzling white save the window shutters, which were vivid green. The mansion consisted of a main edifice fifty feet square and two stories high, with a peculiar portico in front, projected not in straight lines, but forming a semicircle, embracing within the curvature of its outstretching arms a favored area of dooryard. The proprietor of the estate had chosen the site and designed the plan of this his residence with the double purpose of indulging a fancy for architectural novelty and of providing against disaster by lightning and earthquake. Never did it occur to him that fire and flood were the elements he had most reason to fear: each of these ruinous agents was destined, in turn, to devastate the island.

In the rear of the fantastic dwelling, and not far from it, stood a row of log cabins for the negroes who served on the place, and a cluster of barns and stables abundantly stocked. All the houses were new, and the adjacent cultivated land showed many signs that it had not long been tilled, or even cleared. The rank soil retained its quick fertility, as could be seen in the thrifty growth of peas, beets, radishes, and early potatoes, flourishing in the "truck-patch." The plum and the peach trees had cast their bloom; the cherry blossoms were falling like snow; the flowers of the apple loaded the air with fragrance; the red-buds were beginning to fade; the maples and oaks, just starting into leaf, hung full of light green tassels.

The vegetable close had irresistible attractions for the gardener, and this drew his laggard steps from their idle excursion, back to the freshly spaded spot enriched by leaf mould, and carefully picketed against the incursions of scratching hens. Here he busied himself in planting lettuce seed, forgetful of Scipio, who lolled sleepily in the shadow of the willows.

The drowsy bondman was just sinking into slumber, when his attention was aroused by a plashing noise followed by the sound of whistling. Glancing in the direction of the disturbance, his eyes fell upon the ungainly figure of a man who was stooping at the water's edge. The negro got upon his feet, and approached the stranger, who at first took no notice of him, being absorbed in puzzled observation. A cut of lean meat, encircled by a row of stones, lay immersed in a pool caused by an eddy in the river.

"Danged if I can make out what this hunk of raw beef is put here for," soliloquized the visitor. "The minnies are nibblin' it away. I wonder if this here Mr. Bladderhatchet means to feed all the fish in the Ohio on beefsteak. Hello, Cuffey, what do you want?"

"I's not Cuffey, sah; I's Scipio."

"Well, I's Byle, Plutarch Byle," said the stranger, raising his gaunt, gawky figure to a posture which, though far from erect, revealed a stature so much above the average height that the negro stepped back a few paces and stared with astonishment. Plutarch Byle's feet, hands and head seemed somewhat too large for his trunk and limbs, but were quite in harmony with the big joints of his knees, elbows and wrists. His attitudes were grotesque and his gestures awkward. Light, curly hair covered his head; his nose was long and inquisitive; his eyes, big, blue and good-humored; his mouth, incredibly wide, with shrewd, mobile lips, which habitually smiled. A tuft of yellow beard on the end of his sharp chin, gave his face a comical expression resembling that which caricature bestows on Uncle Sam. His voice was pitched in a high key, and was modified by that nasal twang supposed to indicate Yankee origin; but a habit of giving his declarative sentences an interrogative finish, might denote that he came from the mountain regions of Pennsylvania or Virginia. A pair of linsey pantaloons, a blue hunting shirt with a fringe of red and yellow, moccasins of tanned leather and a woollen hat were his chief visible articles of dress.

Scrutinizing Scipio's features as he might inspect a wonder in a museum, Byle interrogated him:

"Potterin' about for greens, I reckon? Do you belong here, Africanus?"

The only information drawn from the slave was that the proprietor of the island had bought him in Virginia.

"Bought? Consarn my bones! How much did he give for you? Look here, Sambo, if I was a Roman general, like you, and in your fix," said Byle, pointing with his left thumb over his right shoulder and winking, "I'd skite over to the Buckeye-side of the water and forget to pay for myself. Don't you know what the Ordinance of '87 says? 'No involuntary servitude in said territory.' I agree with John Woolman, that niggers are our feller-creatures."

Turning abruptly, the tall man moved with long, slow strides in the direction of the white house with green shutters, talking continually, more to himself than to the perplexed negro who followed at his heels.

"Wonder how things are growing in the front yard? By gum! that's a fine Italian poplar! Guess the old Coot's at home. Maybe that youngster is one of the little Bladderhatchets! Say, sonny, come this way."

The sentence was addressed to a lad, who, bounding from the portico, ran nimbly toward the intruder. The boy was prettily attired in a military costume, and wore a toy sword at his side and a gay feather in his cap. He was followed by a brother smaller and much less jaunty.

"What might your name be, now, bub? By crackey, you've come out in full blossom, haven't you, like a red-bud bush? What do you say your name is?"

"Dominick."

"Dominick, hey? I've seen many a young dominick rooster, but I never saw one with finer feathers than yours. Suppose you flap your wings, and crow for us, like a fighting cockerel."

"I'll not crow; I'll stick my sword through you!"

"Jerusalem artichokes! He wants to kill me with his tin sword! Dominick, I give in. If your pappy is about the house, tell him to come out; a gentleman wants to ask him something."

Before a summons could be served on Mr. Harman Blennerhassett, that person appeared emerging from a wing of the long porch. Being extremely near-sighted, he could not distinctly see the man who awaited him until the distance between the two was diminished to a few steps. The uninvited guest without ceremony opened conversation.

"How d'ye do? I am Mr. Byle—B-y-l-e—Plutarch Byle. Of course everybody knows you by reputation, Mr. Bladderhatchet—"

"Blennerhassett."

"It's a prodigious long name, ain't it? Too long, in my opinion. You can have it shortened by law. I'm told you're from Ireland. You don't look much Irish, nor you haven't a bad brogue. I s'pose you've got your naturalization papers all right. This administration is rather easy on foreigners, especially French, for Jefferson has Frenchy notions. President Adams was rough on emigrants—maybe too rough; he wanted to sock it to them hard by acts of Congress. What is your opinion of the Alien and Sedition laws? I favor them; I'm a Federalist to the marrow-bones. I don't reckon you're a United Irishman, Mr. Blanner—"

"Blenner, if you please—Blennerhassett. I belong to the order of United Irishmen, but I presume your errand here is not to discuss politics. Your looks denote that you affiliate with—shall I say, the common people, the humbler class? What is your business here, my good man?"

"Rattlesnakes and brimstone! Me your good man! Me of the humbler class! Why, Squire B., we have no humbler class on our side of the Ohio. But you needn't apologize; I'm not huffy. You're new to the country and your blunders are excusable. I happened along this way—"

"My time is valuable, I must ask you to be brief. What do you want?"

"You're a bigger man than I calculated to see; you're a large-sized citizen, full six foot, I should guess, and you stoop consider'bl in the shoulders, like myself. The Byles are all built that way. But your feet are smaller than mine, and I should think you'd feel awk'ard in such toggery as them red breeches and shoe buckles."

"You are impertinent," snapped Blennerhassett, turning from his rude critic. "If you have nothing to tell or to ask that is of any importance, make off, for I can be detained no longer."

"Hold on, neighbor; I've heaps yet to tell, and lots more to ask. The first thing I noticed particularly when I landed was that puddle up there, with the hunk of raw meat soaking, and I would like dangnation well to know why you put that meat in that puddle?"

Annoyed beyond endurance, the lord of the island would have hurried away, but he was diverted from his intention by the unexpected conduct of his guest, who, suddenly dropping on all fours, fell to examining with the liveliest interest a wild plant which had forced its stem up through the sod.

"Do you know what that is?" asked Plutarch of the two boys who stood near their father, perplexed by the dialogue to which they had listened. They shook their heads, when, glancing up at Scipio, the questioner repeated, "Do you know?" and not waiting for a reply, "That's snakeroot; smell it!" He plucked a portion of the herb, rubbed it between his thumb and forefinger and thrust the bruised substance first under his own nose and then beneath the reluctant nostrils of the disdainful Master Dominick.

Mr. Blennerhassett was himself a botanist, or desired to be considered one, and his eagerness to become familiar with the flora of his vicinity so far overcame offended formality, that he also got down on his knees and directed his imperfect vision to the pungent specimen. The two men, each an oddity, presented a ludicrous picture as they knelt on the grass, their heads almost in contact, and their long noses only a few inches above the object of their scrutiny.

"Yes, Virginia snakeroot, and I couldn't expect it to sprout up in this open place. This is a different thing from the Seneca rattlesnake-root; there's more cure in an ounce of this than in a pound of that. I'll wager five shillings to a sixpence that I can name you nine out of ten of the medicines and dyestuffs growing on this island."

"If that is the case," said the Irish recluse, scrambling to his feet, "I shall be glad to avail myself of your knowledge. There are many vines, shrubs, and trees flourishing here, the names and qualities of which I greatly desire to learn and many herbs which perhaps—"

"I'm your man, neighbor; I'm your man. There are three things which I calculate I do know by experience: the first is fish, the second is game, and the third is yarbs."

"What is the third?"

"Yarbs. Anything that grows wild. I'm acquainted with pretty much every critter that has seed, flower, leaf, bark or root. I fish a good bit, and I doctor a good bit."

"You doctor, fish and hunt," repeated Blennerhassett, his attention now completely captured; "I myself prescribe simple remedies and I am fond of the sports you mention, though a defect of vision interferes with my shooting."

"If you like," proposed Byle, "we will prowl around this very afternoon and study physic together. I call the wild woods God's apothecary shop."

Blennerhassett was convoyed to the depths of the island forest, where the strangely assorted pair conversed intimately on the virtues of pleurisy-root, Indian physic and columbo. Byle discoursed on the high price of ginseng, and the new method of preparing that specific for the Chinese market; recommended the prompt use of succory to cure a snake bite, and the liberal application of green stramonium leaves to heal sores on the back of a horse. He advised Blennerhassett to acquire an appetite for custard apples, which, he said, regulated the bowels.

On returning from the excursion, Blennerhassett hurried into his library, lugging a basket filled with botanical specimens; and Byle prepared to leave the premises. Before starting, he beckoned the gardener, who sulkily responded to the sign. The pertinacious visitor was proof against repulse. No social coolness could chill his confiding ardor. He took Peter's arm, and with a backward jerk of the head declared interrogatively:

"The Mogul is sort of queer, isn't he? A screw loose somewhere, eh?"

"Well," responded Peter cautiously, "yes and no; he is queer and he isn't queer. He has plenty of book learning and plenty of money, and a fool can't get much of either. Folks say he has every kind of sense but common sense."

"At first he didn't want to be sociable. I asked him a civil question about a public matter, and he shut up like a clam. Now can you tell me, as man to man, why the deuce that hunk of beef is put to soak in that puddle, up at the head of the island?"

Peter chuckled in the contemptuous manner of a practical man, without sympathy for speculative genius.

"That's one of his chemical experiments. The man is always up to something of the kind. The carcass of a dead 'og was dug up on the place, and his Honor noticed that it had turned into something like tallow, and he takes the notion that the water here has power to change flesh into solid fat—hadipocere, he calls it—which he thinks may be used to make candles."

Byle listened to the solution of the lean-meat mystery with waning attention, for before the explanation was concluded his roving eye caught glimpses of an apparition more interesting than the gardener's dry sarcasm. He discerned, through openings in the boscage fringing the river bank on the Ohio shore, an object like a scarlet flag flying rapidly along.

"Greased lightning! What strange bird is that coming down the river road? A woman on horseback, sure as Easter flowers! Two of 'em, one in red and one in black. Don't they make them animals cut dirt? I wouldn't miss this sight for a hogshead of tree-honey. Why, it beats a Pittsburg horse-race on the Fourth of July!"

"Oh, it's mamma! It's mamma and Miss Evaleen coming back from Marietta," shouted Dominick.

A gang of colored men, led by Honest Moses, poled an unwieldy scow to the Ohio shore, took the dashing equestriennes on board and ferried back to the island.

The announcement that their mistress was approaching caused a general flurry among the servants, male and female, and several of them, headed by the boys, hastened down to the landing to receive the ladies. Byle was not the man to let slip such an opportunity of taking a look at the paragon, whose charms of person and brilliancy of mind he had heard many tongues extol; and he did not hesitate to join the family group on the river bank. His curiosity was amply rewarded by the vision of fair women which he beheld.

Madam Blennerhassett stepped from the ferryboat, beaming smiles of motherly fondness upon her children. She wore a riding-habit of scarlet cloth embroidered with thread of gold, and a snow-white hat, adorned with long plumes of ostrich feather. The rich attire did not blind Plutarch to the natural beauty of "the woman herself." She was of regal stature, graceful bearing and animated face. Her buoyant step, her rising bosom, her clear, rich voice evidenced the vital glow of maturity in a woman still young—a June rose blooming in May.

Byle, pressing nearer, noted that the madam's hair was brown; her eyelashes long; nose, Grecian; lips, ripe red. When he had fixed her image on his mind, and was meditating the propriety of making friendly inquiries concerning the purpose and results of her excursion to Marietta, her large, calm eyes searched his countenance with a look of offended dignity, which caused his tongue to cleave to the roof of his mouth. Speechless for the moment, but not blinded, Plutarch withdrew his optics from the imperious dame, and took an instantaneous brain-picture of her companion, a light-footed, quick-glancing girl about eighteen years of age, whose arrival put little Harman into an ecstasy, and gave manifest delight to the servants. Her blithe manner and cheerful voice won Byle's complete approbation, and led him to describe her as one who "'peared not to know there was a valley of the shadder of trouble here below."

Madam Blennerhassett instructed Moses to take care of the horses, and side by side with the winsome maiden walked from the landing to the house, followed by a retinue of servants.

Thus abandoned, Plutarch Byle plodded his way to his skiff, pushed the light craft from the sandy beach, ensconced his gaunt person on the rowing bench, seized the oars, and pulled up stream, saying to himself.

"She's the compound extract of Queen 'Liz'beth and Cleopatry; but why didn't she take a fancy to a good-looking Federalist like me, instead of throwing herself away on a near-sighted United Irishman with silver shoe-buckles?"

II.: A NOTED CHARACTER ARRIVES IN PITTSBURG.

On the last day of April, 1805, more than the usual number of guests crowded the bar-room or lounged about the open door of the Green Tree, a popular tavern on the bank of the Monongahela, in Pittsburg. The proprietor had found difficulty in providing refreshment for the swarm of hungry mechanics, farmers and boatmen who elbowed their way to a seat at his famed dining-table. To the clatter of dishes was added the clamor of voices making demands upon the decanters, which yielded an inexhaustible supply of rum, whiskey and peach brandy.

In the throng of bar-room loafers was a swarthy boatman, wearing a leathern waistcoat, who, on being jostled by a stalwart roysterer carrying a long rifle, poured out curses and slang epithets, swearing he could whip any man in the tavern or in the town. The challenge was no sooner uttered than the offender for whom it was meant called out to the landlord:

"Here, Billy, hold my shooter a minute until I pitch this Louisiana rat into the river."

"Don't mind him, Mike; he's drunk."

"Drunk or sober," blustered the quarrelsome boatman, "I swear I can whip the best man in Pittsburg or in Pennsylvania."

This sweeping defiance elicited laughter and derision.

"Give him the heft of your fist, Mike!" cried one.

"Bruise the snout of the Mississippi alligator!"

Thus incited, Mike Fink, the recognized champion of Pittsburg, disposed of his rifle, doubled up his fists, and stood ready for assault or defence.

"Fair fight or rough and tumble?" said he, appealing to the crowd.

"Fair fight," growled the boatman and tossed a fiery dram down his gullet. But fair fight in the accepted sense of the phrase was farthest from his intention. Quick as a flash, he drew from his belt a dirk, and would have stabbed his antagonist, had not a bystander seized his uplifted arm, while another wrenched the weapon from his grasp. The ruffian's comrades hurried their dangerous leader from the inn, and guided his steps to the river and aboard a large new flatboat recently launched.

A flourish of bugle notes and the noise of wheels announced the arrival of the mail-coach from the East. Everybody went out to hail the lumbering vehicle, which, drawn by four horses, came bowling down the road in a dust-cloud of glory. The driver cracked his whip with a bang like a pistol-shot, and firmly holding in his left hand the four long lines, brought his team to a sudden halt in front of the tavern.

Only two passengers alighted from the stage, clambering out at the front, a mode of egress requiring agility to avoid awkward slips and tumbles. The first to step down was a handsome young man, who held his head proudly and looked about him with easy self-possession. A fashionable suit of clothes and a hat in the latest Philadelphia style proclaimed him a man of "quality." But aristocratic as were the mien and attire of this fine gentleman, he ceased to be the chief object of attention when his fellow-traveller emerged from the pent darkness of the coach and sprang to the pavement.

Every eye fastened on the second stranger. His was an individuality sure to command deference. Though of slight figure, he bore himself with a lofty air, which lifted his stature and magnified its proportions. Not one of those tarrying to behold the man could resist the feeling that his was a dominating spirit, a will and personality not to be ignored or slighted. A careful scanning of his externals discovered that his form was symmetrical, though the head seemed disproportionately large; the brow was high and sloping; the nose, rather sharp; every curve of the mouth, clear cut and delicate; the eyes, black, bright and piercing. Such was the man who, attired in a suit of black broadcloth, with buff vest, ruffled shirt, and white stock, and with hair tied in a modish queue, revealed himself to the gaze of the throng in front of the Green Tree.

The spectators observed as he descended from the coach that his feet were small, and were fitted to a nicety with polished boots of the finest leather. No amount of gaping, gazing and inquisitive side remark embarrassed the newcomer. Perhaps his dark eyes emitted a sparkle of gratified vanity as he glanced about him, distributing a gracious bow among his unknown fellow-citizens. Addressing the innkeeper, he asked:

"Can you inform us whether Judge Brackenridge is in town?"

"Yes, sir; we are going that way," politely replied a stripling, who stepped forward, followed by another youth with a law book under his arm. "This is Harry Brackenridge, the judge's son."

"Surely? and your name is—?"

"Morgan Neville."

"Son of Colonel Presley Neville?"

"Yes, sir."

"Indeed! The particular friend of Lafayette." Young Neville blushed with proud pleasure.

"Yes; father was his aide-de-camp."

"I know," said the stranger, smiling, as he turned to ask young Brackenridge, "Is the judge at home?"

"We expect him home to-morrow from a trip to Washington College."

"Your new Western college, eh? Judge Brackenridge is a promoter of learning and literature. Allow me to make you acquainted with Mr. Arlington, of Virginia." The Southerner saluted the students and, inclining his head deferentially toward his travelling companion, said:

"I have the honor of introducing you to Colonel Aaron Burr."

Diverse were the effects produced on the listening spectators by Arlington's words. At the sound of the notorious name some shrank as from the hiss of a coiled serpent. Others drew near, as if eager to manifest partisan sympathy for the renowned leader, whose pistol had ended the life of Alexander Hamilton ten months prior to the time of this visit to Pittsburg. The unfledged lawyers whom his favor had distinguished were of his faction. They manifested their fealty and gladness with boyish exuberance, by delighted looks and words expressive of esteem and reverence. Burr was importuned to dine at their houses, but he excused himself on account of business affairs which required prompt attention. However, he accepted an invitation to visit Colonel Neville on the following day.

Dinner over, the newly arrived guests sought the general supply agent, with whom Burr had contracted by letter for a boat, intending a voyage down the Ohio. The vessel was ready and that very morning had been brought from the shipyard to the landing.

"You will find her a first-class flatboat, Mr. Burr—strong and tight—sixty foot long by fourteen wide—four first-rate rooms, and as pretty a roof as you ever set foot on anywheres. There's a fellow here from down Mississippi I've spoke to—a number one pole and a letter A oar—Captain Burke Pierce by name—and he'll manage her for you, Mr. Burr, and provide his own crew."

"Where can I find this Captain Pierce?"

"I'll take you to him right away. He's down on the boat now. A mighty good hand is Burke, tough as a bull, swims like a muskrat, but he has one failing—only one so far as I know—he will drink, and when he's drunk he's vicious. But they all take their whiskey, these boatmen, and so does almost every landsman, for that matter—and Pierce is no worse than the rest. But here's the point: cap had a row at the tavern, and his crew took him down to your boat to sober off."

"Why there?"

"Well, I thought you'd ask that. I gave them leave to go to your boat out of regard to you. I told him if he'd whistle together five or six experienced poles and a good cook, like as not you'd hire him to take charge of her for you and steer her down the river; see to the kitchen, beds and everything."

Inwardly remarking that the agent had presumed beyond his commission, Burr was conducted to the boat, within which he found half a dozen rough rivermen seated around a table, playing poker. Their redoubtable chief rose with a civil salutation not to be expected from one of his station. He was a stalwart fellow, of swarthy complexion and strongly marked features. A broad yellow belt confining a leather doublet was buckled around his waist; the legs of his coarse blue woollen trousers were stuffed into the wide tops of heavy Suarrow boots, and his head was covered by a broad hat, such as were worn by Spanish traders on the lower Mississippi.

"That's your man; that's Burke; born and raised on a broad-horns. Speak for yourself, cap; this is Mr. Burr, which I told you about."

The boatman spoke for himself in surprisingly good language, with an air combining the bold and the obsequious. For a fixed sum, payable in weekly instalments, he proposed to give his own services and to hire the additional help necessary to navigate the boat, under the general control of the owner. To this arrangement Burr finally agreed, notwithstanding an instinctive repugnance which he had felt on first seeing the letter A oar, who was tough as a bull and who had but one failing. As the captain received in his palm an advance payment, he called upon his men to witness the contract and to vouch for his character, and pledged word and honor that, by six o'clock on the evening of the following day, the boat would be in readiness for the voyage.

Relieved of present care, Burr returned to the tavern, where many citizens, incited by various motives, waited to pay him their respects. The rumor of his arrival had spread over town, and speculation was rife concerning his movements. What could be the noted politician's object in coming to the West? Was he flying from persecution? Could he be suffering remorse? Or was he merely making a tour of observation for commercial reasons?

Burr's reticence gave little satisfaction to the busybodies who sought by direct question to verify their several conjectures. All comers were received with a hearty handshake and were entertained with urbane speeches. Not the humblest caller was slighted. It was late in the evening when, having affably gotten rid of his last visitor, Burr proposed that he and Arlington should retire. They were well content to make the best of the scanty accommodations of the one sleeping-room to which they were both assigned.

After a disturbed night's rest Burr awoke early and called his drowsing companion.

"Rouse up, Mr. Arlington. Shake off this downy sleep."

"Downy sleep!" answered the Virginian, yawning and stretching; "the only down of this couch is shucks and corn-cobs."

The two men had scarcely finished breakfasting when a committee of local officials called to invite them to see the sights of growing Pittsburg.

The "Emporium," as the Gazette called the town, had a population of about two thousand. Most of the buildings were of logs; a few of stone or brick.

Burr listened with every appearance of intense interest to animated accounts of the academy, the old Dutch church, the ferries, the shipping-yard, Suke's Run, and Smoky Island. The party sauntered along muddy thoroughfares—Southfield Street and Chancery Lane. They strolled through Strawberry Avenue and Virgin Alley. They viewed the ruins of Fort Pitt, stood on the site of historic Du Quesne, and paused to gaze up at the garrisoned post of La Fayette, over which floated the flag of the Old Thirteen. During the tour Burr kept up a sprightly conversation. His guides took pains, at his request, to introduce to him the young men of Pittsburg, and those who had the favor of being presented felt themselves enrolled among his devoted adherents. He carried their hearts, not by storm, but by irresistible sunshine.

At the appointed time the visitors were warmly welcomed at Colonel Neville's, where they were gratified to meet Judge Brackenridge. The four gentlemen spent an hour in lively political and military talk, over a decanter of Madeira. Under the mellowing influence of wine and good company, the judge, with Scotch curiosity, made bold to sound Burr in regard to the purpose of his Western trip.

"We are going out West to witness the 'Rising Glory of America,'" was the evasive answer. "I am eager to explore that domain of which the author of 'Bunker Hill,' has sung so sublimely:

'Hail, happy land,

The seat of empire, the abode of kings,

The final stage, where time shall introduce

Renowned characters and glorious works.'"

Flattered to hear his own verse recited by the ex-Vice-president, the judge returned a quick response:

"It is seldom that a poet lives to hear his own prophecies fulfilled. The 'renowned characters' are entering upon the stage; I dare say the 'glorious works' will be accomplished according to prophecy."

The conversation returned to general themes: prospects of trade, routes of migration, growth of western towns, literature, and education. A passing comment on the recent purchase and organization of Louisiana led Colonel Neville to ask:

"When did you last see your former comrade-in-arms, General Wilkinson?"

"Not lately. I thought I might meet him here in Pittsburg. Is he not due here?"

"Yes, he is on the way from Philadelphia, but he travels with his family, and is liable to many detentions. His barge lies at the wharf, to convey him to Fort Massac."

"So I learn," said Burr. "I fear I shall miss him. He is a jovial companion."

"A bon-vivant," ejaculated the Judge. "Few men enjoy a convivial occasion with his gusto, or have the constitution to indulge as he does. Gossip charges him with living beyond his purse. Some ill-natured rumors assert that he allows the rites of Bacchus to interfere with the duties of Mars."

"Bacchus is a gross and vicious god. But your gossips traduce Wilkinson. He is a brave man and a fine officer," said Burr with an emphasis of finality.

"O undoubtedly! Apropos of the wine-god, Colonel Burr, do not fail to tie up your boat at Bacchus Island, you and Mr. Arlington, and call on my friends the Blennerhassetts. Harman Blennerhassett is an agreeable man, though peculiar, and his wife is charming."

"A fine woman, is she?" responded Burr.

"Both beautiful and opulent. A sultana, sir!"

"Then, gentlemen," said Burr, rising with glass in hand, "let us do ourselves the honor of drinking the health of Madam Blennerhassett."

When, at six o'clock in the evening, the travellers went down to the boat, not a soul did they find on board. Seven o'clock came, but no Captain Pierce, no minion of his. Burr made inquiry of the agent, the tavern-keeper and others, without obtaining information concerning any of the missing men.

Much incensed, he and Arlington were compelled to lodge another night in the best bedchamber of the Green Tree.

III.: PILLARS OF SMOKE.

On the morning after their provoking delay, when the travellers again appeared at the boat landing, impatient to resume their voyage, Aaron Burr was in a mood not to be trifled with. It scarcely mollified his anger to discover on the deck of the boat the slippery crew that had disappointed him.

"Here we are, sharp on time," bawled Captain Pierce audaciously. "How soon do you want to start?"

Burr, stepping aboard the vessel, confronted his plausible employee, and said in a tone of stern reprimand:

"You will be of no use to me unless you obey orders to the letter. You make a bad beginning. Why were you not here twelve hours ago?"

"I didn't agree to shove off before this morning. We were to come at six——"

"At six last evening. You broke your word."

"What was the use of lying?" said Arlington contemptuously.

The boatman lowered upon the Virginian, and muttered to Burr: "Then I must have heard wrong. I thought you said six o'clock this morning. I'll take my oath on a pile of Bibles."

"Produce the Bibles," suggested Arlington.

Burke ignored the sneering remark, and continued his protestations to Burr. "I mean to do the fair, square thing, as these men will tell you. Ask them. They know Burke Pierce keeps his promises."

"Enough; I hope you do. Don't disappoint me again. Put the boat in motion."

Under the captain's directions, all the hands but one bestirred themselves. The exception, a burly knot of muscles, with stubby beard and purple nose, instead of joining in the work, stood idle, chewing tobacco, ostentatiously. Without a word Burr stepped lightly in front of the impudent roustabout, and, delivering a blow, with the dexterity of an expert boxer, knocked him into the river, amid the jeers of his associates, and of the concourse assembled on the shore to see the boat off.

This prompt stroke of executive policy had a salutary effect. Recalcitrant subjects had warning that the little man wearing the queue and the small, shiny boots, could not be bluffed.

The boat, once in midstream, was easily managed by the use of long, spiked poles, and, now and then, of an oar. The captain kept his station at the stern of the uncouth craft, handling the steering-pole. The two travellers, standing upon the roof of the ark, admired their pilot's skill, and freely exchanged comments regarding him. To their murmured conversation, the steersman seemed dumb, deaf and indifferent; nevertheless, he gave the closest attention to every word, and his sense of hearing was as keen as that of a wildcat.

The scenery along the upper Ohio River is pleasing in any season of the year; no wonder that, in early May, the travellers were enchanted by its picturesque beauty. To this day, in many places, the hills, vales, and woods on either bank, retain almost the original wildness of primeval Nature. The river winds among high limestone hills, which are carved in frequent deep ravines, by tumbling brooks, or trickling rills. Low, green islands rise magically upon the forward view of the voyager, then vanish in the receding distance, like fairy worlds withdrawn.

The real and the imaginary became strangely blended in Arlington's mind. He could hardly distinguish the substantial from the visionary, while he gazed on cloudlike bluffs in Ohio and dim highlands in Virginia. The boat drifted on without sound or jar, and he easily fancied himself at rest on a surface of water, while the woody shore swam by in slow panorama.

Chester Arlington was the son of a wealthy citizen of Richmond, and a graduate of the College of William and Mary. He had studied law, and was beginning life on his own account. Entrusted with a commission to collect some claims held by his father against a merchant in Cincinnati, he was on his way to that metropolis of the Miami country. His acquaintance with Burr dated from a day in the middle of April, when the two got into the same coach to journey from Philadelphia to Pittsburg. A difference of twenty-five years in their ages was cancelled by the art, which the elder possessed, of maintaining perpetual youth. And Burr's genial conversation won his companion's confidence and friendship before they had crossed the Alleghanies. Thus it came about, that the Virginian had been invited to share the conveniences of the flatboat, a courtesy which he had accepted, on condition that he might share the expenses.

Toward the close of the fourth day of the voyage, as the two sat on the top of their drifting domicile, smoking cigars, they fell into a discussion concerning the Great West, and the prospects of new States and Territories.

"To me," said the Virginian, in the slightly florid style habitual to him, "this wonderful new country into which we are sailing is attractive beyond my power to express. This river, the Oyo of the Indian, La Belle of the romantic La Salle, excites my imagination and recalls interesting legends and historic facts. How many keels have plowed these waters—the canoe of the Iroquois, the peroque of French explorers, the batteau of early English traders, the boats of the Spaniards coming up from the Gulf region."

"The boat of the Spaniard has not yet abandoned our western waters, Mr. Arlington."

"No, not yet. Twenty years have not elapsed since the first white settlement was made on the soil of Ohio, at Marietta, a town we are now approaching."

The smokers lapsed into a silence of many minutes. Burr resumed conversation abruptly:

"Arlington, you are not a Federalist?"

"Could you imagine that a son of my father, Major Arlington, would hold the principles of Adams and Jay?"

"You are not, you say, an admirer of Adams, the arch-Federalist. Do you worship his successor? Are you an unconditional Jeffersonian?"

"No, I am not. It seems to me that Jefferson aids the cause of centralization, with the same motive that moved Adams, but with less boldness. What do you think, Colonel Burr, of the temporizing policy of the administration in regard to Spain?"

"In regard to Spain?" echoed Burr, blowing a ring of smoke from his lips, "what do you think, yourself?"

"I think it infamous! It disgraces this nation to submit to exactions and insults from the

Spaniards. Why don't the Government declare war, and conquer Mexico?"

"Would you be in favor of that?" asked Burr, lightly touching the ashes of his cigar with the tip of his little finger—so lightly that the ashes did not fall.

"Would I be in favor of it? I am in favor of it. Are not you, Colonel Burr?"

The politician again barely grazed the cylinder of white ashes with his little finger.

"We must not be rash."

"I feel that I am rash to talk so positively, but how can there be a difference of opinion on a subject like this? Why don't Congress declare war?"

"Is it your belief that, if war were declared, there would be difficulty in raising volunteers in Virginia?"

"Not the least. Thousands would enlist."

"Would you enlist, Mr. Arlington?"

"Yes, sir, I would."

Burr's little finger tapped the burnt out inch of his cigar, and the frail ash fell, crumbling to fine powder, which the breeze bore away. The touch recorded a point won.

"Suppose that Congress and the President, disregarding the wishes of the people, and refusing to declare war, force the country to submit tamely to the insults of Spain, do you think it possible that independent men might take upon themselves the responsibility as a private business enterprise, and march against the Dons in Mexico?"

After a thoughtful pause, the young man replied:

"Yes, some would. Many would. The warfare might not be regular, but, in my view, the object would justify extraordinary means to a patriotic end. What is your own feeling on that phase of the subject, may I ask, colonel?"

"I wish to learn the sense of my fellow-citizens. You may express yourself to me with perfect freedom."

"Why not? We are discussing a public question."

"Certainly. But your idea, that an expedition against Mexico, conducted as a private enterprise, might prove popular and——"

"That is your idea, sir, not mine. However, I see no objection to adopting it, providing the Government is in the secret, and tacitly permits an expedition."

"Oh, surely! That is understood," responded Burr, and fell pondering.

With quick whiffs he revived the dying fire of his cigar, leaned back in his chair, and lost himself in reverie. What were his meditations? Perhaps he mused of the past, the half century of crowded events in which he had borne a conspicuous part. Did his memory fly back to the far off, sad days when, a lonesome orphan boy, in a Puritan school, he penned sympathetic letters to his sister? Or was recollection busy with the scenes of the Revolutionary War, in which he served his country nobly and won proud laurels? He recalled his part in the march to Canada and in the assault on Quebec, not forgetting his own heroic exploit of carrying from the fatal field the body of his slain general, Montgomery. He thought of the retreat from Long Island, and of the credit he gained as aide-de-camp to Putnam; he retraced each step in his military career, reflecting on his rise from the command of a regiment to that of a brigade, remembering how his distinction as a brave and able officer reached its culmination in the battle of Monmouth. Perhaps, through his mind ran the events of his political history, his transition from the field to the bar, thence to the State Assembly of New York, to the Senate of the United States, and finally to the Vice-Presidency.

These memories and a myriad more came thronging to his quickened consciousness as he sat smoking. The retrospective visions rose before him, not as vague memories—they seemed living realities as they reproduced events more recent. At last one vivid picture—nay, was it not an actual scene?—one set of vital images, usurped his brain and would not vanish or fade. It showed a grassy ledge guarded by rocks and forest growths, in a secluded spot overlooking the Hudson. There stands himself confronting his political rival and partisan foe; the figures speak and move; a ghastly tragedy is imminent. Yes, imagination compels the repetition—the men are placed—Burr takes deliberate aim, touches the trigger, the fatal bullet pierces Hamilton's breast and the slain Federalist falls heavily, his face upon the sward. But before he falls, his pistol, which he had resolved not to fire, is accidentally discharged, sending its ball eight feet over the head of his antagonist and cutting off a leafy twig from an overhanging bough. Burr's attention is strangely affected by the fate of the green branch which he heard the bullet sever, and, as he sees it come wavering to the ground, he cannot resist the fancy that he beholds an emblem of his own ruin—a symbol of his future self—a living thing cut off from its nourishing stock as he was destined to be from a nation's sympathy and support.

The gloomy retrospect, the dismal forecast, were too painful; by a strong effort of the will, Burr strove to expunge the past and illuminate the future. Rising, he took a brisk turn or two, pacing the deck. His cigar had gone out; casting it into the river, he lit a fresh one, and again sat down. The kindled roll diffused its searching perfume and wrought a soothing change of mood. By some subtle chain of new associations Burr was led to think of the words of Milton's hero in Paradise Lost:

"The mind is its own place, and in itself
Can make a heaven of hell."

He puffed at the long cigar, and began to build a future out of rolling smoke. Toppled fortunes may be rebuilt; lost reputation may be retrieved. There are new worlds to discover, to conquer, and to possess. What may not be achieved by genius and courage? What to undertake, what to dare and do! Shall he span the Ohio with a bridge, and dig a canal around the falls? Would he find success by settling in some rising city of the West, and resuming the practice of law? Or might he not reasonably hope to be returned to Congress from one of the new States? Or to secure from the President an appointment as Minister to a foreign court, perhaps that of St. James? Better than these schemes and more independent, to embark in a stupendous land speculation in Louisiana, and open a splendid way to riches and power.

The wavering blue nebulæ of intoxicating clouds rise and float, and fashion their fragrant columns into grander castles of smoke. The Mississippi Valley is spacious and fertile, Louisiana is a wide domain, but why limit the scope of enterprise to these? Why not conquer Mexico, make

New Orleans the capital of a magnificent empire, and possibly annex the southwestern States of the severed Union. Myself the emperor of the richest realm on the globe, my daughter the crown princess and prospective queen Theodosia!

Such was the gorgeous dream, the cloud-vision, the unuttered soliloquy of Aaron Burr, the political bankrupt, as he sat smoking on the deck of a flatboat, drifting down the devious current of the Ohio.

IV.: PLUTARCH BYLE MAKES A NEW ACQUAINTANCE.

The boat had reached a point a few miles above Marietta, when an incident occurred to interrupt the resumed dialogue on the Spanish question. A skiff was seen to push off from the Ohio shore, and move rapidly in the direction of the flatboat, urged on by the long, powerful oar-strokes of a man who, even in distant perspective, appeared larger than life-size. Instead of hailing the crew of the passing vessel, as was customary, the man gave no sign that he was conscious of the existence of any other craft than his own fast-gliding skiff. However, he steered straight for the boat, hove alongside, sprang on board with surprising agility, and, having fastened his light boat by a chain to a timber of the flat, stalked deliberately to the stern where Captain Pierce was stationed with steering-oar.

"I saw you coming down and I thought maybe you'd like to buy some fresh fish. I've got a thirty-pound cat in the boat; I caught one last week that weighed one hundred and three pound."

"Don't want any fish. Wouldn't take 'um as a gift."

"You're welcome not to, captain. I suppose a man has a right to hop on board and ask a civil question. Whose boat is this, anyhow, and where bound?"

No attention being paid to the question, the nonchalant intruder went on: "What plunder are you loaded with? Salt or whiskey, or pork or butter, I reckon? Or maybe you carry passengers? Is it a family of emigrants? I see two chaps on the upper deck; who are they? What might your name be, captain?"

The helmsman relieved his irritation by delivering a volley of oaths.

"You 'pear to be out of sorts, captain. Sour stomach, likely. Better take a dose of saleratus."

Hearing a strange voice, the cook, who was the captain's trusted confidant, came out. He was recognized by the ubiquitous Byle.

"Abe Sheldrake! as sure as ham is hog's flesh! Abe, if there's an onrier man than you on earth, the bottomless pit is shaller."

The cook stood speechless, and the tall man sauntered leisurely through the several apartments of the boat, calculating their dimensions and inspecting the furniture, and pausing occasionally to handle such articles as appealed to his curiosity. He passed through the kitchen into the dining-room, and thence through both the sleeping-chambers, finally emerging from a door at the bow of the boat, after which he ascended to the roof, where he accosted Burr and Arlington.

"How d'ye do? My name is Byle; Plutarch Byle—B-y-l-e. I can't call your names, gents, but no matter. We all belong to the same human race. I thought you might be a little bored-like with your own talk—so long together you know—and I hopped on to cheer you up. George Washington used to say to his nephew, 'Be courteous to all, but intimate with few,' and George was half right. I admire a mannerly man. How goes it?"

The familiarity of this overture puzzled, but did not offend the travellers, who conceived that chance had thrown into their presence an original whose company might afford them an hour's entertainment. Arlington politely offered the visitor a chair.

"No, thank you, stranger. I've been setting in the skiff all day, fishing, and I'd rather stand up and stretch my bones."

The gentlemen thought, when they saw Mr. Byle throw back his arms, and gradually straighten up his towering body, that the length and thickness of bone he had to stretch were extraordinary.

"I've got a lot of mussel shells in my boat for Mr. Blennerhatchet. Would you like to see 'em? 'Union-idea,' he says they are. He's a queer customer, that Blennerhatchet."

"You know him then?" asked Burr.

"Know him! I know him like a book. I know him better than I do you. He is not so good-looking as either of us, by ginger. I can't make out why the Rose of Sharon ever took to a near-sighted United Irishman."

"The Rose of Sharon?"

"I mean his old woman—Mrs. B. She's a perfect lady. Pretty! Pretty as a sassafras tree in October! I didn't just catch your names, gentlemen. I like to call a man by his Christian name. It seems more sociable. That's one thing I like about the French—sociability. They go in for liberty, equality and brotherhood. But I don't take any stock in their skeptical notions. I'd as soon eat poke-root and sleep on pizen-vine as read Voltaire and Rousseau. Tom Payne is no better. What's the latest news from Washington? Is Tom Jefferson going to make war on Spain? It ain't war we want; it ain't more territory we want; we need a closer union, and a strong tariff."

"You appear to be a politician, Mr. Pyle."

"Byle—B-y-l-e—Plutarch Byle, if you please. Yes, it's my notion that every citizen ought to be a politician. I'm a John Jay Federalist—a centralizer. Which side are you on?"

"I'm not concerned in politics at present. We are lawyers, not politicians, Mr. Arlington and I."

"Arlington? That's not a bad name. Where do you hail from, Arlington?"

"From Richmond, Virginia," said the young man good humoredly. "This gentleman is a citizen of New York."

"New York City? Porcupines and wildcats! You don't say! There's where Alexander Hamilton lived—the greatest man that ever lived in these United States, except Washington. I suppose there was a heap of excitement in New York when Alexander Hamilton was killed—murdered, I might say. Did you ever see Alexander Hamilton?"

Burr looked steadily into the eyes of the Great Inquisitive. "Yes," he replied, "I was very well acquainted with Mr. Hamilton. He was a fine man."

"You're right there, stranger! Give us your hand on that! I'm proud to shake with a man who has seen Alexander Hamilton."

The enthusiastic Byle extended his prodigious palm and grasped the delicate hand politely proffered him. Arlington looked on in astonishment.

Burr, wincing at the vice-like grip of his new acquaintance, placidly responded: "Yes, there are few men more worthy of esteem than was my admirable friend Mr. Hamilton—whom I shot."

Byle was struck dumb. He could only open his cavernous mouth, and gasp. His heavy hand relaxed its hold, and dropped as if paralyzed. For a moment he stared at Arlington. Then he recovered his powers sufficiently to articulate.

"You shot him? You—you aren't——?"

"Yes, I am Aaron Burr."

Plutarch Byle turned on his heel and with three strides carried his leaning tower of a body to the edge of the deck. Scrambling precipitately down the boat's side, he stumbled into his skiff, undid the chain, grabbed his oars and fairly shot away, as if pursued by flying pestilence. He directed his course northward and quickly ran the bow of his skiff against the river bank. Then plunging his right hand into the water, he rubbed and scrubbed it vigorously, using sand for soap.

"Dog-fennel and skunk-cabbage! I don't believe there's water enough in the Ohio River to take out the wicked smell of that murderer's hand!"

V.: IN THE LADIES' BOWER.

The Byle episode put Burr in a merry mood, quite diverting his thoughts from Mexico and the future to the happenings of the hour. A reckless spirit of frivolity took possession of him, and he astonished his fellow traveller by the ebullience of his humor and the play of his extravagant fancy. He mimicked the speech and grotesque gestures of Plutarch, and laughed over the ludicrous finale of the encounter with that free-spoken genius.

"Mr. B-y-l-e, Byle, is exquisite! It is worth coming a thousand miles by stage coach and flatboat, to meet so droll an adventure with such a nondescript amphibian. He has a prodigious gift of gab, plain and ornamental. Did you take note of his metaphors? 'Rose of Sharon' is good.—By the way, we can't be far from the Bower of Bliss. We must tie up our Argo there as Brackenridge recommended, and go in quest of those exotic and visionary Blennerhassetts."

"What do you know of them, colonel, further than we learned in Pittsburg?"

"But little. They stopped in New York for a few months, after arriving in this country, ten or twelve years ago. The man is a barrister, educated in Dublin. He claims to be a descendant of King John. The lady is a daughter of the governor of the Isle of Wight, and a granddaughter of the late Brigadier-General Agnew, who was killed in the battle of Germantown."

"A British general, you say?"

"Oh, certainly—a violent royalist."

While the gentlemen were thus chatting, the boat drifted lazily on, following the windings of the current. The broad Ohio glowed like liquid gold, in the slant sunshine of mid-afternoon, and the interplay of shade and color, shifting from object to object along the shores, gave the varied scenery an ethereal beauty almost supernatural. The distant, forest-crowned uplands, seen dimly in the direction toward which the ark floated, looked as unsubstantial as clouds. A delightful, spicy fragrance exhaled from the blossomy thickets which fringed the river margin.

Burr took a deep breath, and began to hum a half-remembered verse advising youth to "gather the rose whiles yet is prime."

"Yonder is Bacchus Island," said Arlington, pointing down stream.

"I suppose you are right. The Western Navigator locates the spot somewhere about here. But beware of illusions, my friend. I begin to doubt the testimony of my senses. Perhaps yonder prospect is a mirage, and Byle was only a goblin of the mind. This interminable river is enchanted. I sympathize with La Salle's conviction that the Ohio runs to Cathay. Maybe we have sailed round the globe and are now in sight of the Indies. Or we have come to Arabia. Does not the vision resemble some Mohammedan Isle of the Blest—one of the happy seats reserved for blameless souls such as yours and mine? I shall expect to discover the rivers of clarified honey, the couches adorned with gold, and the damsels having complexions like rubies and pearls, as the Koran promises."

Arlington laughingly replied in the same extravagant vein.

"Colonel, you have eaten of the insane root. This island belongs to the Hesperides, not to the East. The best luck we can hope for is to steal one or two golden apples.

"That may prove a risky adventure even for a bold Virginian. If there is a dragon to slay I leave the bloody business to you. I stick to my Oriental paradise."

"Very well; golden apples for me and pearl-ruby damsels for you. But I am scandalized that a Puritan Senator permits himself to dream of Mohammed's heaven, and its honey and houri felicities."

"Mr. Arlington, you are the first and only anchorite that Virginia has produced. You will grant that it is in character for a Senator to pay his devoirs to a sultana. Something too much of this. See there over the willows; that must be the house."

They both gazed forward, and caught glimpses of the secluded mansion, gleaming, snow-white, through forest vistas. Burke Pierce, who knew the private wharf, steered to the landing, and the boat was moored fast to a huge sycamore tree.

The travellers disembarked, and following a path which wound among mazes of shrubbery and early blooming flowers, came to the semicircular plot of green sward fronting the piazza.

"The place is marvellously beautiful!" remarked Arlington.

"A new Garden of Eden!" answered the other.

On approaching the main entrance, they heard, within, the twangling music of a harp.

The hall door was decorated with a large, bronze knocker of curious design. A tap of the falling hammer on its metallic plate, brought to the threshold a jet-black maid-servant wearing a gaudy turban. She ushered the visitors into a spacious drawing-room and took their cards and a note from Judge Brackenridge, to her mistress.

The guests while waiting could not fail to be impressed by what they saw around them. Walls, ceilings and doors were unique in their decorative effects. The furnishings of the apartment were elegant and sumptuous. There were rich hangings at the windows and costly Persian rugs on the floor.

Soon was heard a swish and rustle of brocade on the stairs, and, a moment later, the gentlemen rose to meet Madam Blennerhassett, who came in, smiling a cordial welcome. She was dignified, even stately, in her demeanor, and looked, not indeed the ideal sultana, but rather every inch an empress.

Burr was at once upon his mettle. No levity, nothing of the jester, no trace of ennui lingered in his manner. The presence of the magnificent woman transfigured his body and called up all his social resources. His eye kindled its sparkling fires, his lip took a deeper glow of vital red. These manifestations were spontaneous, almost involuntary, though he was conscious of an obscure design.

"Gentlemen, it hardly needed this note from Judge Brackenridge to insure you a welcome here; you do us a great honor by seeking out our lonely island home." These words, though addressed to both the visitors, were meant for the elder and more distinguished guest, who replied suavely:

"Madam, we made bold to invade the privacy of these grounds in the hope of forming the acquaintance of a family well known by reputation."

Returning a formal bow and a look of appreciation, the lady continued:

"I regret that you do not find my husband at home; his affairs called him to Farmers' Castle, just across the river, but I am expecting him to return at any minute. You must not go without seeing him. Of course, you will take dinner with us."

The wayfarers, having come ashore for idle adventure and recreation, were easily persuaded to linger. Burr tactfully advanced to the borders of familiarity by giving Madam Blennerhassett an embellished report of the encomiums which Brackenridge had bestowed upon her and her ancestors. He was lauding the name of Agnew, when a sound from the vestibule suspended his eloquence, and quickly thereafter the figure of a graceful girl appeared in the entrance to the drawing-room. The maiden paused a moment, a glowing picture in the deep doorway. She was a peerless blonde, blue of eye, scarlet of lip—and her fair head and face were so aureoled by locks of sunniest yellow, that she seemed to radiate light and warmth. Her exceeding loveliness smote through Arlington's nerves and set his southern blood tingling.

"Ah, Evaleen, did you enjoy your ramble?" asked the hostess, affectionately, as she rose to receive the young lady. "Colonel Burr, this is my very dear friend, Miss Evaleen Hale."

The American Chesterfield made a courtierly obeisance.

"Permit me to introduce Mr. Arlington, of Richmond."

"Miss Hale, gentlemen, like myself is a sojourner in a far country. She comes to us from Boston."

Having complied gracefully with the demands of convention, the maiden, in wilful abstraction, busied herself with some wild flowers which she had just gathered in the woods.

"Where did you leave the boys?" inquired madam, referring to the lads Dominick and Harman.

"They are out of doors, making a cage for a young squirrel which I had the luck to catch. But the lively creature bit me; see here, Margaret!"

Evaleen held up a dainty hand, on the whiteness of which the teeth of the captive had left a small purple wound. In her playful carelessness, she let fall a sprig of wind-flowers and two or three violets. Arlington gallantly picked up the flowers.

"What peculiar violets," said he, as he offered to return them.

"Yes, they are of a variety found only on this island, I am told. You may keep them if you like."

"I presume, Mr. Arlington," said Burr, "that you understand the language of flowers. When I was of the sentimental age I knew the floral alphabet and could convey all manner of covert messages through the agency of pinks and pansies and rosebuds and all the sweet go-betweens of Cupid's court. The blue violet, I believe, signifies modesty, does it not?"

The question was accompanied by a look at Miss Hale, who made no reply, not appearing to notice the appeal.

"Our native Western plants," said the hostess, "have no poetical association. The Indians were devoid of sentiment. It is only in Persia and such romantic lands that they make roses and lilies talk. But this island is rich in its flora. Before you resume your voyage you should take time to visit a beautiful spot which Miss Evaleen calls her Violet Bank. It is on a bluff overlooking the river, only a short walk from here."

At Burr's request, Mrs. Blennerhassett was induced to talk of her island home and of her husband's pursuits. It gave her evident relief of mind to narrate the story of her life's trials and vicissitudes since her marriage. She spoke with less reserve than was wise, and notwithstanding the reverence with which she alluded to him, the consort she unconsciously described seemed at best the prince of Utopians. That he was wealthy and lavish could not be doubted. The wife's unguarded revelations gave Burr food for speculation. Many pertinent questions by him elicited answers which he locked away in the safe of memory.

The minutes flew rapidly—an hour went by, yet the master of the house came not, and at length Madam Blennerhassett renewed her suggestion that an excursion to the edge of the island might prove pleasant.

"We shall see him return from the Ohio shore; at least, I hope so."

She reminded her guests that she was an Englishwoman, accustomed to long walks, and, with the buoyant energy of an Artemis, led the way to the near green wood.

"I will pilot ahead with Colonel Burr, and you, Mr. Arlington, shall be taken care of by Miss Hale, who is as familiar as a dryad with these glades. How romantic! Virginia and New England wander together on a solitary island in the Ohio."

The elevated level of ground upon which the party halted lay open to the sunshine, and it was completely covered by a thick bed of wild pansies.

The view from this fragrant knoll surpassed expectation. While the admiring spectators were gazing across the river, now on the village of Belpre, now on the farther off rude fortress aptly named Farmers' Castle, there came floating by a long, slender craft, rigged somewhat like a schooner, and displaying from its mast the flag of the United States. The music of a violin, faintly heard, was wafted across the water from the deck, upon which could be seen a bevy of ladies, a few dancing, others waving handkerchiefs to those watching from the island. By means of a field-glass which Mrs. Blennerhassett handed him, Burr could bring out plainly the forms and faces of the passengers. His attention was immediately fixed upon one striking figure—that of a woman in black, who stood apart from her fellow-voyagers in a pensive attitude, gazing into the sky. A cheer arose from the boat's crew, and the report of a small cannon boomed and echoed along the woody shores; yet Burr still held the magnifying lens before his eye, and a certain agitation was observable in his behavior.

"That," said he, handing back the glass, "is General Wilkinson's barge. He is bound for St. Louis, to take possession of his domain as governor of Upper Louisiana and commander-in-chief of the Army of the West."

For a time the four stood gazing in silence at the receding craft. Then Madam Blennerhassett, speaking aside to Miss Hale, asked:

"How long does the captain intend to remain with you in Marietta? I understand he has orders to proceed to the general's headquarters for duty."

The answer was spoken softly and with a rising blush, noticing which, Arlington was disquieted by a feeling much akin to jealousy.

"We do hope he may stay with us at least another fortnight."

"In that case we will expect him to spend a few days here. I wonder what detains Harman? He may have crossed over while we came through the grove. Perhaps we shall find him at home waiting for us."

With sauntering steps the four returned through the twilight of the woods, breathing the scent of new leaves and now and then stopping to pick a stem of sweet dicentra or a white addertongue. Soon after they reached the house dinner was served in a style distinctively English. During this meal, and afterward, when the cheerful party repaired to the drawing-room, Burr, as was expected of him, assumed the leadership in conversation.

The affluence and the brilliancy of his discourse seemed appropriate to the splendor of the surroundings. He did not monopolize the talk, and never failed to return an appreciative response to any remark or question. To the ladies he gave the most deferential attention. Arlington, a peer in the social realm, felt piqued to admit himself outrivalled by an undersized widower who was a grandfather.

The conversation, in which Miss Hale now more freely participated, flowed afresh in livelier and more sparkling stream—ripples of wit and humor—foam-bells of nonsense. The Geneva clock in the room across the hall struck nine—struck ten—but its musical warning was not heard. Nor yet did the lord of the mansion make his appearance. Madam Blennerhassett concealed the secret uneasiness she felt, and did all she could to contribute to the pleasure of the occasion by every delicate art of hospitality. She sang a Scottish song, she spoke piquantly of the amusing phases of life in a new country, and of her husband's need of congenial literary associates.

"He is compelled more and more to depend upon his books. Would you like, colonel, to look into the library for a moment?" Burr promptly rose and followed his queenly hostess into the adjoining apartment.

The couple left together in the drawing-room verified the homely adage, "Two is company." Arlington might have said, "My blood speaks to you in my veins," but he could not consistently quote Bassanio's other words, "Madam, you have bereft me of all speech." From the presence of Evaleen he received access of eloquence; the two were conscious of a silent interchange of sentiments more meaningful than any spoken word. While Evaleen sat listening with responsive interest to some frank personal disclosures of the young man's hopes and ambitions, her attention was diverted by a slight sound on the porch. She glanced up, and saw, or thought she saw, an ugly face staring at her through a window-pane. Her sudden pallor and dilated eye were observed by Arlington, who asked in a tone of gentle solicitude:

"What is it?"

"I saw a face at the window—a man staring in."

Arlington immediately left the room and, softly opening the door, stepped out upon the piazza and looked searchingly in every direction. Not a sign could be discovered of the prowling eavesdropper whose shadowy features had frightened Miss Hale.

"I may have been mistaken," she said, when Arlington came back, "but I am almost certain that I saw a hideous face at the window."

The effect of the incident was to give the conversation of the two a somewhat more intimate character, and the gentleman's manner assumed an air of protective regard which the New

England beauty did not repulse. Her resiliant spirit soon regained its wonted gaiety.

Meanwhile, what had Aaron Burr found to interest him so long in the sanctum sanctorum of the lord of the island?

Blennerhassett's study was both library and laboratory, containing philosophical apparatus, musical instruments and books. The shelves were piled with scientific works and standard editions of the ancient classics. On the wall hung a large oil portrait of a man with an amiable, meditative face, not wanting in agreeable features, yet not indicative of force. Burr scanned the indecisive mouth, the handsome, trustful eyes, the low forehead, at the middle of which was parted the slightly curling mass of brown hair. While her visitor was studying the picture, the lady stood at his side, perusing him.

"Well, what is your verdict?"

"A noble face! A noble face!" he repeated, turning to her with an expression subtly suggestive that his interest was passing from the flat, dead canvas of the absent husband to the breathing, beautiful woman he was addressing. "A noble face; but one fact puzzles me. Madam, pardon my candor. I cannot understand how your husband contents himself to spend an obscure life in this out-of-the-way spot, when his education, talents and fortune qualify him for a career so much more ambitious and useful. I am at equal loss to conceive how a lady of your distinguished birth, breeding and accomplishments could consent to exchange the splendid opportunities of social life in lofty places for the domestic quietude of a rural home, however luxurious. Things cannot make us happy, human associations only can do that. Is it possible that you are satisfied with your present limited sphere?"

"No," she replied, speaking low, "nor is he." She glanced at the portrait. "We have had quite enough of this self-banishment. We grow discontented and would gladly dispose of the estate."

"Madam, you are not unacquainted with the world. You derive your blood from a noble source. The granddaughter of General Agnew inherits all advantages that women covet—rank, wealth, culture, beauty—and you have a husband who appreciates you." When in the enumeration of her endowments Burr pronounced the word beauty, the lady's eyelids drooped and a perceptible constraint came over both the woman and the man—he not feeling sure he had chosen a safe approach to her favor—she in doubt whether to invite or to repulse further personal compliment. It entered his consciousness that she might become part of his political plan—might somehow abet his magnificent purposes. In the pause which succeeded his appeal to her self-love and ambition she once more scanned the mild, meditative countenance beaming from the pictured canvas.

A mesmeric influence drew her eyes from the portrait to encounter those of Aaron Burr, regarding her with a gentle look of wistful melancholy. The color deepened in her cheeks, and her bosom labored with an inaudible sigh.

"Ah, madam, you should give your husband back to the world of great actions suited to one in whose veins runs the blood of a king. How I wish he were here that I might tell him so in your presence. Give him my profound regrets. We have tarried too long."

Madam Blennerhassett never forgot this tête-à-tête with Burr; but an inexplicable qualm kept her from mentioning it to her belated lord on his return from Farmers' Castle. It was nearly midnight when the two visitors reluctantly took leave of the ladies and stepped out into the diffused light of the May moon.

"Pretty late," called out Burke Pierce familiarly from the stern of the boat where he stood, ready to resume his piloting.

No tattling breeze carried to the ears of the ladies the comments spoken by Burr as he stood in the moonlight on the roof of the vessel, beside Arlington.

"Exceedingly fine women, are they not?"

The Virginian made no reply. He was pinning to the lapel of his coat a tiny bunch of violets, and his face was turned from his fellow-voyager.

"Both are ladies of decided individuality. They are amazingly beautiful, too, and possess unusual force of character, especially the captain's lady."

"Damn the captain."

"So say I. You stole a march on him in the Hesperian Garden, and we both escaped the jaws of the absent Dragon."

Soon after their guests left the house Madam Blennerhassett and Evaleen Hale, standing by an open window in a chamber upstairs, looked out toward the wharf. They heard the voices of the watermen and the noise made in shoving out from the gravel beach. Then came silence, and they knew the ark was adrift, bearing away two passengers whom they could not easily forget, but expected never to meet again.

"How delightful he is!" mused the madam, speaking more to herself than to her friend.

"Do you think so?" returned Evaleen abstractedly.

"Perfectly captivating! A brilliant mind! I am charmed with him, are not you?"

"He is pleasant enough, but too bold, too audacious, isn't he?"

"Not, I think, Evaleen, for a person of his age. We expect more freedom in elderly men."

"Elderly! Why, he can't be more than twenty-five!"

"Twenty-five! My dear child, he has a married daughter!"

"Oh, you are speaking of Colonel Burr! I hate him."

VI.: DOCTOR DEVILLE AND HIS LUCRECE.

"Behold this Ohio city of the Gauls. Volney's ruins of modern date—new oldness—fresh decay—dilapidation to begin with! I am proud of this consummation of American enterprise!"

This irony was uttered by Burr to Arlington as the two men stood taking a first look at Gallipolis, a poor village, consisting of a dozen miserable log houses patched with clay and occupied by a score of wretched French families. The travellers had walked up a steep bank to the natural terrace on which the forlorn dwellings stood.

"Shall we go back to our boat? Have you seen enough of Palmyra? Here are the palaces, but where are the citizens? Ecce Homo! One inhabitant turns out to receive us."

The person to whom Arlington's attention was thus called was a small, nervous gentleman, about sixty years old, who came forth from a whitewashed cot, and, taking off a scarlet cap, saluted the strangers, whom he had eagerly watched from the moment of their landing.

"Pardon, messieurs. Permit that I speak. May it be convenient should one passenger more be accommodated in your polite boat? I much wish to go to Cincinnati, for one of my business very special. I have courage to ask ze bold favor by my necessity professional to come to mon frère."

"Ours is a private boat. Do you say it is to meet a brother that you wish to go to Cincinnati?"

The old man's countenance fell. "Monsieur, accept my apology. Permit me to speak my explanation. Pardieu, I deceive not. When I speak I shall not indicate ze son of my mother, but I shall indicate ze brother in medicine, Monsieur Goforth, ze physician celèbre. Pardon. Pardon that I detain you so long."

Disappointed, the old man turned toward his modest domicile, at the door of which stood a petite maiden awaiting the issue of the interview. Immediately descrying the damsel, Burr remarked aside to Arlington:

"Another alluring petticoat. Tree nymphs or naiads haunt every island and green bank."

"Père," asked the girl anxiously, in a gentle voice, so clear that every word she spoke reached the ear of Burr, "may you go with them?"

The father shook his head.

"Non, chérie."

He went up to his daughter, who impulsively kissed him, as if to solace his disappointment. He seemed about to enter the cottage, when, like one suddenly recollecting a neglected duty, he wheeled round and again approached the strangers.

"Do me ze honor, messieurs, before you depart to enter in my poor dwelling and drink with me one glass of wine."

An invitation so naïvely extended could not be declined. Burr felt a kindly impulse toward the cordial sire and was not averse to wasting a few stray glances on mademoiselle.

"It will give us great pleasure to accept your hospitality and also to have your company as our guest on the boat. There is room, and you shall be accommodated."

The doctor's spirits rose. His face shone with gratification.

"Your courtesy lift my heart. I shall never forsake to do you ze friendly service. Is it convenient now that we present us. I am your servant, Eloy Deville."

Having imparted his own name, the flighty Frenchman waited not for the completion of the ceremony he had proposed, but, taking on trust the respectability of the strangers, he hastily led the way to his cottage. Burr noticed that he was attired in a tight-fitting suit of brown cloth, clean and well pressed but threadbare and redeemed from shabbiness only by the stitch in time. The feminine apparition vanished from the threshold as the travellers approached, but the father, ushering them in, placed chairs beside a small table, and called out cheerily: "Lucrèce, ma chère enfant une bouteille de vin." The girl promptly obeyed by carrying in a salver on which were a flask and three tiny wine-glasses. She glided to the table upon which she set her light burden, keeping her head demurely bowed and her eyes cast down bashfully.

"Messieurs, permit that I you present my daughter, my aide chirurgeon." Thus introduced, Lucrèce, raising her head, bestowed a modest smile of welcome on her father's guests and divided between them a coy courtesy.

She could not elude the pardonable glances cast upon her by the strangers—glances which left in their memories the form and face of a dainty brunette with large and very brilliant black eyes. Her waist was slender, her hands and feet were nimble and delicate, and her dress fitted her so neatly that she looked the personation of trimness.

"This wine is not original of Ohio. No, no. Ze cask was from Bordeaux, very old, very old—he has fourteen years. Presented to me by my countryman, Comte Malartie. I speak ze truth. From this very cask I have ze honor to drink also ze health of ze General St. Clair, and at one time of Daniel Boone. Eh bien! Long have I suffer in this wilderness; it is fifteen years that Eloy Deville was ze fool to leave France, to leave my native Lyons, and seek ze Terre promise—to find ze tree of natural sugar, ze plants also with wax candles for ze fruit, ze no work, no tax, no war, no king—ze paradise on ze ground! Oui, sold I not all my property—take ze ship, take ze wagon, ze flatboat—en route pour Gallipolis! Ah! mon dieu! ze damn fever kill ma femme; you see ze old Frenchman in ze poverty; voilà sa richesse! une cabane, un verre de vin—et ma bien aimée—ma pauvre fille—ma Lucrece!"

To justify his grievance, the excited man sprang up and ran to a drawer, from which he took an old French map of the Seven Ranges of the Ohio, representing as cleared and inhabited lands large tracts of unbroken wilderness. This chart had been used by speculators to induce French families to migrate to the Ohio Valley.

"See!" continued Deville explosively; "ze scoundrel Barlow cheat my honest poor friends—he print here no veracity—he draw here only to deceive! Look on this place I put my finger"—he tapped the paper angrily—"you see ze Premiereville—ze Premiereville? Eh? I come to Premiereville—no street—no house, only ze forest tree! Messieurs, my little axe make ze first log in ze city, in Premiereville, where we drink now this wine."

The doctor's preparations for the trip down the river were quickly made. Half the population of the village, led by Lucrèce, flocked to the boat-landing to see him safely off. After the passengers had gone on board, and while the damsel stood waiting their departure, Burke Pierce, leering in her direction, threw her a kiss and as the boat was pushed off began to sing a ribald song. Deville did not witness the insult, but Arlington, with quick anger kindling his chivalrous blood, strode up to Pierce.

"You ought to be flogged, you filthy cur."

The boatman scowled and clenched his fists, but did not attempt to strike the imperious Southerner.

"Cur? I'll remember that!" he muttered, and swaggered away. "I'm a dog, a filthy cur! But I'll have my day!" he growled to Sheldrake.

The loquacity of the French doctor seemed accelerated by the motion of the boat and the breezy freedom of its deck. Unlike most of his Gallic brethren who left their native land to come to America in 1790, he was in sympathy with the Revolution, and had rejoiced at the falling of the Bastile. By chance a copy of the Marseillaise Hymn had reached him, and snatches of this he would sing, keeping time to the music with his own springing steps as he marched up and down. The cry of "Liberté, Egalité, Fraternité," often broke from his lips. When Burr opened to him part of the plausible scheme against Mexico he eagerly volunteered to join any expedition gotten up in the name of freedom. He proffered his services as surgeon, and asked with amusing simplicity what would be the emoluments.

"Sacré!" exclaimed he. "Il faut vivre! Let us destroy ze Spaniard. Vive l'amérique! Vive le Général Bur-r-r! Vive Eloy Deville!"

The tedious passage from Gallipolis to Cincinnati required almost a week's time. On the last day of the voyage, soon after breakfast, while Burr and Deville were enjoying the morning sunshine and discussing the French Revolution, Arlington heard a knock on the door of his room, in which he sat writing a letter.

"Come in," he shouted, hurrying to pen down the sentence that was in his mind. The door opened, and Burke Pierce thrust his head and shoulders into the room. Arlington glanced up from his writing and saw a flushed face and a pair of bloodshot eyes.

"You know what you called me up at Gallipolis?"

"Yes—dog."

"I'm a dog, eh? a filthy cur?"

The Virginian made an impatient gesture and dipped his quill into the ink. The drunken boatman after a moment's pause said:

"I want you out here in the kitchen."

Arlington paid no attention to the insolent speech, but went on with his letter writing.

Pierce, without closing the door, stepped back into the narrow quarters in which Sheldrake did the cooking, and a minute later reappeared with two long butcher knives, which he flung down on the table, in front of Arlington.

"Take your choice."

Arlington picked up both the ugly weapons, one in each hand, and stepping to a window, tossed them out into the river. The contemptuous act raised the fury of the captain to the point of frenzy; he seized a stick of firewood and rushed forward. Arlington parried the stroke, closed in, and grappled his assailant. The noise of the scuffle brought to the place Sheldrake and others of the crew. Summoning all his strength, Arlington hurled Pierce backward over a chair with such violence that the ruffian, falling on his head, was rendered senseless. The Southerner stood on the defensive, expecting to be attacked by the others, as he would have been, had not Burr strode into the room, followed by the French doctor. The colonel's sudden appearance on the scene prevented further turbulent demonstrations. The three passengers repaired to the deck, leaving the drunken captain to be revived by his faithful henchman, Sheldrake.

Arlington in few words told how he had been challenged, not stating any cause for Burke Pierce's animosity.

"Wanted to butcher you without provocation! Has the fellow gone mad?"

"Mad from drink."

"This fellow's bellicose propensity," said Burr, "must be punished. I shall have him arrested by the first magistrate I can find."

"Not on my account, colonel. He'll sober off. Your unctuous agent in Pittsburg allowed that when cap is drunk he's vicious."

"Sacré!" burst in the doctor, "not always a gentleman shall be able to observe formality in a quarrel with ze savage. I who tell it you was one time attack on this very river by three red devil in ze canoe. See here, ze scar on my head! Ze wild gentlemen make no ceremony—he yell, and he shall right away take ze scalp with his knife. Pardieu! By good chance I shoot ze one impolite Iroquoix—and ze two, his second, paddle away!"

"We must beat our swords and pistols into scalping-knives and bludgeons," remarked Burr, banteringly. "The code of honor is not observed by Indians or Western boatmen. Mr. Arlington, you may be compelled to adapt yourself to the customs of the country."

VII.: CONSPIRACY.

Near Yeatman's Cove, at the foot of Sycamore Street, Cincinnati, stood a commodious tavern, built with some reference to architectural effect. Being directed to this resort, the party from the boat climbed the slope of the levee, ascended a flight of wooden steps, and entered the vestibule of the inn, a long, narrow corridor which the landlord considered very imposing. The first objects to attract attention in this public haunt were life-size wax-figures of two men fighting a duel. One of the figures represented Burr with an aimed pistol in hand, the other Hamilton staggering forward mortally wounded. To Arlington Burr remarked as they passed by the waxen show:

"The artist makes me a beauty, don't he? What boots! What eyes!"

Seldom had genial Grif Yeatman welcomed guests more desirable and less like one another than were the strongly individualized men who came from the flatboat to his tavern to take temporary lodging before hunting up the several citizens they wished to meet.

Burr's arrival in the embryo Queen City of the West was noised from house to house, and within an hour many citizens had called to shake hands. The suave New York politician had partisan adherents and personal friends in the Buckeye State. Among these was John Smith, whose acquaintance he had made in Washington—the Hon. John Smith, one of the first two senators representing Ohio in Congress.

Burr procured a fine saddle-horse, and after bidding good-by to Arlington set out to visit the Senator who lived some twelve miles from town. The solitary horseman was not sorry to leave behind him the raw metropolis, the dirty streets of which were lined with log cabins and dingy white frame houses. Beyond Deer Creek the horseman spurred eastward along a black loamy wagon road, trotting through groves and half-cleared fields until he passed a small hamlet bearing the great name Columbia. Beyond this cluster of habitations lay Turkey Bottom, so named on account of the wild flocks which made it their resort. Burr selected the most distinctly marked of the several discernible trails and traces in the mazy wilderness before him. Uncertain wheel tracks indicated that the backwoods farmers, whose cabins were never less than a mile apart, took various routes, according to their fancy or the exigencies of the season. At one place a tree, recently blown down, lay across the bridle-path, and, while guiding his horse around this obstacle the rider saw a brown bear lurch off, swaying its head in sulky humor.

The grandeur of the primeval solitude impressed Burr more profoundly than he had imagined possible. The solemn majesty of the brotherhood of lofty trees around and above him inspired awe. A sense of bewilderment stole upon him. "Am I lost in the woods?" he wondered, looking around for signs of human life. So strange did everything appear that he was in doubt whether the log house not a hundred feet ahead of him was an actual structure. The house was real, and in the dooryard he saw a human being busy about some task. He rode up and asked the way to Senator Smith's.

"Smith? You mean Elder Smith?" gossipped a woman, pausing from her soap-making, near an ash-hopper. "Some do call him Senator, and some call him Preacher, but most call him Elder Smith or else plain John."

"Does he preach?"

"Yes; some Sundays; generally he only exhorts. Turn to your right after passing that wild-cherry, and you will see the Miami; follow along up stream, and you can't miss sight of the mill and the still-house. They belong to him, and so does the big store at Columbia. John Smith is the richest man in these parts, but he isn't proud and stuck up. When you come to the mill they'll show the way to the house. A mighty fine house it is."

Burr thanked the woman and spurred on. "Smith is worth the trouble of coming out for to see. No broken reed, but a pillar of state and church is this same senator, elder, farmer, merchant, miller and distiller." Thus meditating, the fisher of men followed the road by the cherry tree and along the river, and soon reached Smith's lonely dwelling, a new farmhouse, constructed of hewn logs and having a huge stone chimney. Dismounting, Burr stepped upon the porch and knocked at the door. The summons was answered by Mrs. Smith, who, though a senator's wife, was country bred and untaught in artificial usages. She received the urbane stranger with a timidity amounting almost to trepidation.

Her husband had gone to the woods to cut a wagon pole, and pending his return Burr waited in the front room of the log mansion, and made a heroic effort to melt the ice of reserve which seemed to congeal Mrs. Smith's flow of speech. Seldom had he failed in the winning art of conversation, especially with women. Ladies were his favorite pursuit, if not his prey. But Elder Smith's wife proved unapproachable by language of tongue or eye. Talking to her was like talking to a lay figure with vocal and locomotive organs.

Luckily or otherwise, an unexpected diversion was in store for Burr—a rôle which he did not anticipate devolved upon him, and required him to play his part in a dramatic scene with a character much more sympathetical than Mrs. Smith. From the moment he crossed the threshold to enter the plain parlor he had been conscious of a fugitive fragrance, scarcely perceptible, which he recognized as the scent of Parisian musk, a perfume much in favor with the exquisite beaux and belles of that day. The telltale odor was reminiscent of past gallantries, and it served in a subtle way to herald the coming of a person whose appearance suggested knowledge of the gay world. Not uncurious to steal a glance at the strange visitor, a woman, tastefully arrayed in sable robes, entered unannounced from a cozy side-room. An unbidden blush betokened her surprise and emotion. Burr blenched slightly, but neither the red signal nor its effect was observed by Mrs. Smith, who, glad to shift the task of entertaining Colonel Burr, introduced him to Mrs. Rosemary.

"You will please excuse me; I'll send a boy to the woods for Mr. Smith. Make yourselves at home; we housekeepers in the country have a good many chores."

Like the practical Martha that she was, Dame Smith, cumbered with much prospective serving, hastened to the dining-room to set the table. On her exit from the parlor she closed the door behind her, not having the slightest suspicion that chance had made her house a place of clandestine meeting.

"Salome! Can it be you?"

"It can, if we are not both in a delirium. I did not expect ever to see you again. Who could induce Aaron Burr to come to Ohio?"

"Perhaps an irresistible attraction—some spell of bewitchment. You must inform me. What brings you to this wandering wood like a lost Una?"

"Business. I came a passenger on General Wilkinson's barge. We had a delightful voyage, a May festival, gaiety, music, dancing."

"Do you recollect passing Bacchus Island?"

"Yes. Why do you ask? We floated by the interesting place one heavenly afternoon. We saw four persons looking at us from a high bank—two couples that seemed strolling lovers. I wondered if either of the women could be the beautiful Madam Blennerhassett. We were dancing on the deck—that is, the other ladies were; I do not now dance."

"I grieve to see that you do not, Mrs. Rosemary. I did not even know that you had become his wife; these mournful robes tell me you are a widow."

"You did not know? Do you care? You grieve to see me a widow? Ah, me! Men are consistent. Let me explain the cause of my coming West. I own ever so much land near Cincinnati and a whole block of town lots, bequeathed to me by my late husband. George was kinder to me than I deserved. When I read his will I cried. I went to my lawyer in Philadelphia and asked what I should do to realize most on this Ohio property. He advised me to come here, and have the title examined, and learn the real value of the land, and he gave me a letter to Senator Smith, who, he said, was a good man, one who knows about law and deeds and everything. So I am here. These pokey people are very obliging; they insisted I should lodge with them until my affairs were settled. Now you have my story—tell me yours. As for my bereavement—my heart history—why speak of that?" A film of tears dimmed her eyes as Burr made answer in soothing words.

"I am to blame. Let us not pain ourselves by talking or thinking of death or mourning. I dreamt lately of you as you now appear. How beautiful and brilliant you look in black, Salome. Pardon me, Madam—, I knew you by that name in the past, and you must not be offended if I recall."

"Ah! do not recall. I am willing for you to let bygones be bygones—if—you—desire. Do you like this black gown better than the blue brocaded one I wore that evening at Princeton?"

"How can I decide? You always dress in perfect taste. Whatever you wear is pretty, and you, I am sure, are lovelier than ever."

Smilingly the young widow sighed, then in a listening attitude, with finger on lip, whispered, "Sh! Our hostess!" and changing her voice continued in a tone of conventional languor: "Yes, the weather is very fine. We were remarking, Mrs. Smith, how sweet and pure the atmosphere."

"Well, yes; the air seems fresh and healthy, but we have a touch of malaria now and then in this Miami Valley."

Hon. John Smith, having chopped down a hickory sapling to make a coupling pole, put his axe-craft to further use by cutting off a forked bough, crooked by Nature, in the exact shape for a pack-saddle. Satisfied with these forest spoils, the rustic statesman returned to his house, where Burr met him with a cordial grasp and a ready tribute of adulation.

"My dear Senator, this is like greeting Cincinnatus on the pastoral side of Tiber, where he dwelt in domestic peace with his wife Racilia."

The salutation gratified the Member of Congress, for he was susceptible to flattery, and knew enough of Roman history to understand the allusion to Cincinnatus, though he had never before heard of Racilia. He valued the evidence of Burr's esteem, implied in the pilgrimage the latter had taken the trouble to make, and no effort was spared to load the colonel with proofs that his visit was appreciated.

In Washington, Burr had known Smith only slightly and officially as one of the senators from Ohio. In the retirement of a lonely farm hourly companionship fostered intimacy. Conversation forgot constraint; the two freely unfolded to each other their thoughts, feelings and hopes, and a community of ideas was gradually established between them. Burr encouraged personal revelation and solicited confidential opinions. He affected warm interest in the details of Smith's affairs—farming operations, grinding of wheat and corn, profitable sales of whiskey, and growing trade at the Columbia store. Neither the piety of the preacher nor the patriotism of the senator could quell in Smith the cupidity of the fortune-builder. Adroitly did Burr shift the trend of discourse to suit his own ends, leading the elder by plausible arguments to accept as logical the sophistry of self-love and greed. The word business was stretched to cover a multitude of sins; the new dictionary of self-aggrandizement concealed a spurious gospel of intrigue and treason.

Spoken words are but breath, and who can report all that passed between the tempter and the tempted? Or who can be sure that the craftiness of the guest was greater than the cunning of the host? The nebulous emanations of Burr's mind were rounding into a definite world of purpose. He invoked the aid of the Hon. John Smith to set the new planet revolving. Conspiracy was planned in the woods and fields of a quiet farm in the valley of the Little Miami.

Burr, yielding to persuasion, protracted his stay almost a week, being feasted and lodged in the country house. Many were the spoken confidences and frequent the "fair, speechless messages" which passed between him and Mrs. Rosemary, as occasion offered, while they lingered at the home of their common friend and counsellor. On the day preceding that of Burr's departure, a bright Sunday, they accompanied the Smith family to a religious service held in a maple grove, near the Miami. The devout farmers, who, with their wives and children, came many miles to the place of worship, observed with solemn eyes of approbation that Burr studied his hymn-book and small gilded Bible, and that the demure lady by his side, dressed in mourning, looked the pattern of saintly piety. While going home from the camp meeting, supporting Mrs. Rosemary on his arm, Burr spoke feelingly of himself, his hopes, and secret plans. Then it was that he told his lovely partner about his contemplated Southern empire which, he declared, would be an elysium for women. Then it was that he gallantly offered to invest to her advantage any portion of the cash she might realize from the sale of her deceased husband's estate. She hung on his arm confidingly and promised to consider his words.

Sitting on the porch in the Sabbath twilight beside Salome, Burr softly intoned his regret that in the morning he must part from her. Sportfully he drew from her finger a diamond ring. "Do you want it back after all these years?" she murmured. "No, dear, you shall have it again in a moment." He turned to a window, and with the sparkling stylus incised some delicate characters upon a pane of glass. Then he returned the ring to its owner, who, after perusing the inscription, looked round into his face, her own radiant with happiness.

The window-pane remained unbroken for nearly a century, and the writing on it was always shown to strangers visiting the old historic homestead. The cutting diamond traced two names upon the glass—those of Senator Smith's transitory guests. Many a sentimental girl, pausing over the double inscription, and mildly condemning Burr, has wondered whatever became of Salome Rosemary.

VIII.: DIAMOND CUT DIAMOND.

Bearing in mind his hours of cautious interview with the elder and minutes of furtive dalliance with the widow, Burr rode back to Cincinnati, and regretful that he had lost the companionship of Arlington, resumed his housekeeping and his journey on the flatboat, which he now christened Salome.

Burke Pierce was retained as captain, notwithstanding his late atrocious conduct.

"I didn't know what I was about," he asseverated, in self-exculpation; "I was full of Monongahela, and there's a quarrel in every pint of that and manslaughter in every quart."

Burr, whose prospective foray in Mexico would require the service of all the dare-devils who could be enlisted, did not scruple to conciliate this outlaw, nor to give him an inkling of warlike preparations against the Spaniard. Pierce, flattered by this confidence, readily volunteered to lend his aid at any time to whatever enterprise Burr might propose, and, like one of the tools of Brutus, he was ready to say, "Set on your foot; I follow you to do I know not what." Yet he knew more than might be supposed, of the history, official rank and designs of his employer. To the soothing counsel, "You must not bear malice toward that young Virginian; remember, he is one of us." Burke replied with a nod and a sinister laugh.

The Salome was moored at the landing near Fort Massac. General Wilkinson, whose barge lay in port, was stopping temporarily at this station before proceeding to his headquarters in St. Louis. Burr must win Wilkinson, and to the winning of an ally so influential he must bring to bear all the arts of address and insinuation, for he had to deal with a wily character. Yet he did not doubt that, by discreet appeals to the vanity and cupidity of the general, he could induce that blandest of politicians to embark in an enterprise which promised evergreen laurels and rich returns of gold.

Arrayed in his best cloth, with boots freshly polished and face smoothly shaven, with queue and ruffles in perfect condition, a Beau Brummel of exterior proprieties and a Machiavelli in finesse, Aaron Burr presented himself at the barracks, and was welcomed with effusive cordiality by his friend and comrade. The two shook hands with the hearty familiarity of veterans glad to renew old associations.

"Colonel Burr, I am delighted to see you here. Your letter, written in Philadelphia, reached me at the capital. Pray, take this big chair; it is rather comfortable."

"Very elegant, I should say, general, especially for a remote outpost like this. The Government, I imagine, does not furnish you with such costly articles."

"Oh, no, no, certainly not; the chair is part of the furniture of my barge. I must provide myself with these necessaries from my private purse. Necessaries, I say; for use breeds wants; I was habituated from my birth to social refinements, ease and the luxuries of the table.—You must take a cup of kindness with me. What will you drink? I have here sherry, whiskey, peach-brandy and applejack."

The general, as he enumerated the liquors, stepped to the sideboard, which, with its array of bottles, looked like a bar.

Wilkinson was a handsome man, about forty-eight years old. Slightly under the average height, he was of symmetrical figure, and his countenance was agreeable, despite a deeply florid complexion. He held his head well, his walk was firm and dignified, and his bearing was graceful. The well-fitting suit of blue and yellow uniform which he wore with an air of pomp and authority was very becoming to his noble form.

Burr, out of courtesy, drank a glass of light wine, but his entertainer, apologizing for his own robuster taste, poured out a stiff tumbler of brandy, which he swallowed with relish.

"I congratulate you, general," began Burr, "on your appointment to the governorship. The President showed wisdom in his selection."

"I appreciate your confidence, colonel. My good name is my pearl of price. In the many stations I have filled I have always tried to do my duty, and shall try in this. I owe it to you, my dear sir, to say so much, for I believe I am indebted to the late Vice-President for my new position. Mr. Jefferson is understood to have appointed Wilkinson as a mark of favor to Colonel Burr."

"Possibly so; I claim no credit. But I am sincerely glad you are the man. The office is no sinecure. The state of feeling in regard to the Spanish boundary is ominous. Shall you be able to adjust the matter amicably or will the dispute result in war?"

"That is a question events must answer. I am devoted to my country and her interests, and whether as a leader of her armies or as governor of part of her wide domain I shall proceed with an eye single to those interests."

"I know, general, that whatever is right and just you will do, and I assume that when you speak of devotion to your country and her interests, you mean the people and their interests. Under a properly constituted government there should be no conflict between the welfare of the nation and the welfare of the individuals comprising the nation. If the authority of an arbitrary government prove oppressive, or if the liberties of those dwelling in a section be disregarded, I hold to the good old democratic rule that the injured have a right to protest and to resist. The principles for which you and I fought were the principles of individual liberty and of State sovereignty. We were revolutionists."

"Yes," said Wilkinson, playing with one of his brass buttons, "I fully agree with your fundamental propositions."

"But you don't see how they are going to help you in adjusting the boundary line between our country and the Spanish possessions. I have a suggestion to make. There ought to be no boundary line at all between the two countries. This republic, or perhaps I should say, the Western people, should wash out that line with Spanish blood, and make Louisiana and Mexico one domain. I go in for war."

"There is prospect of war, Colonel Burr, but Congress and the President seem timid about making an open declaration. In case hostilities should be precipitated by the Spaniards——"

"What in that case?"

"Why, then an invasion of Mexico might be a military necessity."

"Invasion? Would not the conquest of Mexico be easy? A sufficient force can be raised."

Wilkinson left off toying with his button and looked far away—far as Mexico, far as the Pacific Ocean.

"You are aware, governor—no man living has ampler knowledge of the facts than you have—that only five or six years ago Washington and Hamilton planned and were about to execute a project to seize the Spanish provinces, with British aid. The pretext was war with France, the real object was to take New Orleans, probably Mexico. You were the person whom they wisely entrusted with the management of the business."

"Yes, but not with the command of the troops."

"No; you were to organize the Legion of the West, not to lead it to victory, as you surely would have done had opportunity offered. Hamilton secured the leadership as his perquisite and was careful to see that I was not advanced. He dissuaded Washington from choosing me quartermaster. But they could not obscure my name nor dim your reputation. The people know what is what and who is who. They know 'little Burr' and they know the 'Washington of the West.'"

Wilkinson sat up straighter in his chair.

"The epoch in which it has been my lot to live has been eventful. I little dreamed, when a lad on a Maryland farm, what fortunes lay before me. Who could have prophesied, when you and I began our military career, that my humble services would ever be likened to those of the Father of our Country?"

"You are a better general than ever George Washington was," declared Burr, employing a tone and look so candid and emphatic that his sincerity was not doubted. "What he and Hamilton failed to accomplish, owing to the action of Jefferson in purchasing Louisiana, and so ending the French quasi war, why may not you and I bring to a successful issue? If there was no irregularity in that, there can be none in a renewal of essentially the same plans. Let the Legion of the West be organized once more, and the Washington of the West direct it as he will."

Wilkinson went to the sideboard and moistened his lips.

"There is much that I might tell you, colonel, concerning that proposed expedition of Hamilton's. Men are but men, and the philanthropist weeps over their frailties. For myself, I am open and above board; I abhor deceit and intrigue; I am a man whose head may err, but whose heart cannot be misled. That all are not so I have learned to my cost. You have no idea, sir, what whisperings, what suppression of motives, what secret understandings, marked the proceedings of eminent persons whose public or private interests were involved in the scheme of 1799."

"All men's consciences are not so sensitive as yours, general, nor do all men proceed so boldly. You have courage. But there is some excuse for the secret methods which your nature condemns. Prudence is a prime virtue. There are questions of method and of policy, which are best discussed confidentially, by sagacious men."

"Oh, yes, yes, yes, of course."

"For instance, we two, Wilkinson, here in private, may properly compare opinions on such subjects as this of the Spanish dispute. You and I are in substantial agreement on theories of government. I presume you have no more faith than I have in the permanency of the present

Constitution. It is on its trial, and I am of the opinion that it cannot last long."

"Colonel Burr, you are right. The Union is held together by a thread. Yet the salutary restraints of religion and morality are none the less binding. The hallowed bonds which connect the citizens and the State are not made of paper. There is a stronger law than the letter of the Constitution."

"Law, as the world goes," said Burr, "is whatever is boldly asserted and plausibly maintained. But I wish to speak to you of the prospect opening before us in the Mississippi Valley. Here are you, commander-in-chief of the Western troops and governor of Upper Louisiana. Immense power rests in your hands. Now, if it be the will of the people of Kentucky and the Southern States that Mexico should become a part of our common country, or should the sovereign citizens of this section prefer that Mexico shall become part of an independent republic or empire, formed by uniting all the States and Territories of the Southwest, including Mexico—I say if 'we, the people,' demand this, and volunteer to devote lives and fortunes and sacred honor to establish such a new nationality, could not you, would not you, must you not, as a patriot, as a friend of liberty, as a servant of the people, seize an opportunity of making yourself greater than Washington, by fathering a richer, freer and more glorious country than that now held together by a Constitution which, as you truly say, is no stronger than a thread?"

Is it possible that Burr when he uttered these words could have been aware that he was repeating arguments very similar to those which Baron Carondelet had addressed to Wilkinson nine years before, to induce him to deliver Kentucky to his Catholic Majesty, the King of Spain? Burr's proposal had so many points of coincidence with that made by the Spanish governor, that Wilkinson felt a momentary sense of being detected. There was also a confusion of impressions in his brain; the very service he had tendered to Spain, for gold and for glory, was now solicited against Spain for glory and for gold.

Burr saw that his words were striking home and resumed interrogatively:

"Were you not instrumental in the good work of separating Kentucky from Virginia? You made eloquent speeches, you managed everything."

"Yes, I pleased everybody."

"You will please more by abetting a grateful constituency in their efforts to form a better government than the East can pledge them. If it was a good thing to separate Kentucky from Virginia, how much better to sever the Southwest from—"

"This much I will say," interrupted Wilkinson: "I am in favor of State sovereignty and the rights of secession. I am a consistent man. The principles I advocated in 1785 I still hold. My dear colonel," he continued, coming up to Burr and placing both hands on his shoulders, "I must reflect on all this; you broach momentous matter and you take me by surprise. No doubt you have considered the subject in all its phases. I have not. Tell me what you have learned, so far, in regard to the drift of popular feeling."

"I have learned much and am learning more every day. I have conversed with men of every rank, in the East and in the South and in the West, and I am sure of the ground I walk on. These people of Kentucky and Tennessee are ripe for war with the abhorred Spaniard. They have a thousand grievances. They hate New England and mistrust the Federal Government. They are ready for any new combination which can be shown conducive to their prosperity locally. They only wait a leader or leaders. The destiny of the West is manifestly independence. What I intend is this: I shall go to New Orleans, the very heart of the disturbed region, and shall ascertain the wishes, temper and resources of the people upon whom we have to depend. On my return I will report to you the results of my inquiry and observation, and then, if you desire, we may hold further conference."

"I must take time to reflect. Prudence, to recall your own words, is a prime virtue. I am a public servant, an officer of the Government, entrusted with sacred obligations. Your advice, however, cannot be other than wise and statesmanlike."

"General Wilkinson, we are old friends—comrades in arms once; now associates in a magnificent enterprise, if you so will—an enterprise harmful to no American citizen, vastly beneficial to Louisiana, Mexico, and the West in general, and fraught with sure and superb fortunes for the men who have the ability, the courage and the fortitude to carry it to a successful issue."

The general, again stepping to the sideboard and filling two glasses from the brandy bottle, passed one of them to his guest.

"This to the memory of past successes and the hope of future prosperity for us both."

"I drink to the hope more than to the memory, for the past is an empty chest, the future a full coffer," said Burr, and drained his glass.

"You take your liquor like a hero!" joked Wilkinson. "It will do you good, colonel."

The men shook hands and Burr departed, after promising to renew the conversation next day. Slowly he walked along the river bank, saying to himself, "If I could only rely on him. He is slippery as an eel, but a net of golden promise will hold him if anything will. I fancy I have caught James Wilkinson, and if so, half the battle is won."

Wilkinson sat in his big easy-chair, pondering. "Aaron Burr is a shrewd manipulator of men. Naturally he is looking out for his own elevation. He is a falling angel. But his plans are good and hold out strong inducements to the course he proposes. If he will undertake to fit out an expedition and provide recruits, I see no reason why I should not avail myself of the results of his energy. I am in power already—I combine the authority of general and governor—and I cannot see how Burr's co-operation can lessen my dignity or prevent my aggrandizement. Precaution is the word. We shall see how events develop. Perhaps this scheme will open my way to attain the height of my ambition. So long as the signs are propitious I will be safe in trusting them; but should disaster threaten, I can at any time change my policy. Precaution! No precipitancy, no ill-considered pledges."

Thus reflected General Wilkinson. Then, left alone, he gradually yielded to the sedative effect of dinner and drink and fell into a drowse. The dusk of evening had stolen over the river and darkened the woods around the fort. The sound of footsteps at the door startled the sleeper.

"Who's that?"

A swarthy boatman with a leathern coat slouched in.

"Palafox. You back again?"

"Don't call me Palafox, general. I've changed my name for reasons you might guess. Palafox ha'n't been a safe name to carry since that business at the mouth of the Ohio."

"You need not worry yourself about that 'business,' as you call it, of ten or eleven years ago. I got you out of a bad scrape; your associates, who were arrested, and tried were discharged; the accusations are forgotten. What do you want, Palafox?"

"I tell you I'm not Palafox—I'm Captain Burke Pierce—that's the name I've been going by at Pittsburg and all along the Ohio. I left the other name in New Orleans. Folks don't forget names or deeds so soon as I wish they would. I know the court cleared the men, but they don't forget the trick played on them. Pepillo, who was the helmsman of the piroque, isn't dead, and he would shoot or stab me on sight. Vexeranno is alive yet, too, and he is one of the three who planned to do it."

"Speak no more of the horrible affair, my friend. We were none of us gainers by it. You know how much I lost. But I saved you from arrest, and you ought to be grateful. Why are you here?"

"General Wilkinson, I don't know whether I am thankful or not. You call me your friend, and I have been your friend. It wasn't so much for my sake that you got me off as to keep evidence from leaking out that might have made somebody else uncomfortable. Yes, I've done things for you that you ought to be grateful for, governor! Why am I here? I'm here for back pay. You owe me six hundred dollars."

"Man, you are mad. You presume on my generosity and my past indulgence toward you. I have already paid you more than I should have done, and you owe to me your life and your safety. You overestimate the value of your past services, and I am tired of your importunity. Remember that I am the commander-in-chief of the army and the governor of Louisiana. Do you think it safe to trifle with me? How did you get by the guard to-night?"

"Walked; same as I got by Aaron Burr."

Wilkinson looked up anxiously.

"Palafox—I won't be harsh with you. Take a dram. You were faithful to me and to your duty in former years, and I hope to find profitable employment for you again. Here are five dollars; now leave the premises."

Palafox took the money and disappeared in the gathering gloom. General Wilkinson closed the door and locked it. Then he sat back in his big chair, bowed his brow, and with arms folded sat meditating the past. At length he rose, shook his head, as if sadly answering in the negative some question of conscience, and—took another glass of brandy.

IX.: DON'T FORGET THE BITTERS.

Monsieur Deville, having consulted Dr. Goforth, on vaccination, milk-sickness and miasma, took the mail-packet for Gallipolis. Arlington, after transacting the business which brought him to Cincinnati, started for his distant Virginia home, not by water nor by the direct route through Kentucky to the Old Wilderness Road, but across southern Ohio, over the highway which led to Marietta. The young man told landlord Yeatman that his object in choosing this roundabout course was to see the country; and he told the truth, but not the whole truth. Arlington cared not so much about going to Marietta as about getting there. He had not escaped the consequences of his recent perilous exposure to the rays of bewitching eyes. As he rode along through the woods he saw flocks of paroquets fluttering their emerald wings and making love as they flew. The red birds were singing bridal songs in the sugar-trees, and the shy hermit thrush betrayed his domestic secrets by husbandly notes piped from the spice-brush thicket. The wild flowers, too, anemone, puccoon and addertongue, nodding in the light breeze, seemed conscious of the joy of life in spring.

The pilgrimage to the Muskingum was one long meditation on Evaleen Hale. Arlington was powerless to break the rosy mesh which entangled him. The bright image of the golden-haired New England girl waylaid him again and again. He reached Marietta on a fine, bright morning, and having consigned his horse to the care of the ostler of the Travellers' Rest, he presently started out in search of the dwelling-place of Evaleen, trusting, like Shelley's Indian lover, to the Spirit in his feet.

It did not take long to make the rounds of the prim, Puritan village, and though he caught sight of more than one pretty maid peeping with coy curiosity from cottage window or garden plot, he saw no face comparable with that which he had cherished in memory since seeing the original in Blennerhassett's parlor. A lame soldier of the Revolutionary War pointed out to him the squares named Campus Martius and Capitolium, and directed him to follow the Sacra Via, through a covert way, to the wonderful ancient earthworks hard by—vast enclosures, terraces and tumuli, resembling natural hills, but, in fact, the piled-up monuments of the Mound Builders. The greatest and most impressive of these mysterious remains, a huge mound in the form of a sugar-loaf, appealed so strongly to Arlington's imagination, that, contemplating it, he for a time forgot everything else, losing himself in admiration and conjecture. Intending a closer inspection of the steep, artificial hill, he crossed a dry fosse which ran around it in a perfect circle, and was clambering up the mound when a voice from above startled him.

"Come up, come right up! There's a good path starts t'other side of that wild gooseberry bush."

Looking aloft, Arlington beheld, seated on the summit of the mound, the grotesque figure of Plutarch Byle.

"It blows a body, don't it?" said Byle, recognizing the Southerner with a familiar nod. "Give us your hand; I'll haul you safe to the peak of Aryrat. I'm right glad to see you, and I'm not sorry he isn't along with you. Have you got rid of him for good?"

"Do you mean Colonel Burr?"

"Exactly; he's a sort of burr I hope to God will never stick to me or to any friend of mine. I like you, Burlington, and I congratulate you, as the saying is, that you pulled him off. Folks oughtn't to be too familiar with strangers, ought they? You or I might be taken in by appearances. I confess I was deceived in—I won't say that man, but that hoop-snake. He was as fine looking a man as I am. But let's not mention him. Which way do you hail from now? When did you strike Marietta?"

"To-day, Mr. Byle."

"Call me Plutarch. I don't like European forms. How long do you calculate to stay, Burlingham?"

"Not long. I am on my return to Virginia, and stop in Marietta to see these earthworks. You are acquainted here. Do you know—do you know of a family by the name of Hale?"

"Well, yes; that is, I know old Squire George Hale by sight, and I met his daughter once in a sort of social way like, at Mrs. Blennerhassett's. The Hales is a fine family, regular high posts with a silk tester; they're upper-crust Boston quality. George hasn't lived here long, only about a year, and I've been away up on Yok River, at brother Virgil's, most of the time for the last five year. The Hales are blue blood, and no mistake. The young woman is a seek-no-farther. She is about to marry a feller from Massachusetts, who is here now a-sparking like fox-fire. I don't know the particulars, but I put this and that together, and I'm satisfied it's a match, and though I'm always danged sorry for any girl who gets married, I reckon this feller is about as decent as any of us. His names is Danvers—Captain Danvers; a right peert young chap, in the reg'lar army. I saw them yesterday, Evaleen and him—her name's Evaleen—walking, spooney-like, down by Muskingum, and I says to myself, 'By the holy artichokes, I'd like to be in the captain's military boots.'"

"Are you sure they are engaged?" queried Arlington.

"Yes, sure as coffin-nails; why? Do you know the Spring Beauty?"

"I have met her."

"I'll bet you took a fancy to her the minute you sot eyes on her. So did I; but I nipped it in the bud. You look as if you might be hugely in love, Burlington. I know adzactly how you feel. Everything is prodigious out here in the West—big trees, big fish, big mammoth bones, and big hearts. I'll swan! the kind of love that you are liable to in these tremendous woods is like the rest of the works of Nature, immense. Howsomever, a man can stand a terrible sight of love and get over it. I know what I'm talking about. Love's a queer complaint! By ginger, I realize from experience how it takes hold of the system. You mightn't guess it, but I pulled through the toughest case of woman-stroke that ever a young feller was took with.

'Cheeks of my youth,

Bathed in tears have you been.'

It's facts I'm stating. Still, a good constitution does mend fast when the flightiness and distress in the imagination leaves him and he cools down to his right mind. And there's medicine for every ailment, balm in Gilead, by gum, even for love sickness. The seed-pods of the cucumber tree soaked in raw whiskey makes a first-rate bitters for all such like fevers. I'm sorry for you, but—hold up, what did I tell you? Look yonder! Do you see that couple walking this way from Campus Martius? That's them!"

Looking in the direction indicated by Plutarch's long forefinger, Arlington saw a man and a woman, side by side, slowly approaching the mound, so absorbed in each other's companionship that they seemed oblivious to the landscape and the sky. Neither glanced upward, though they came so near the base of the hill that the envious spy on the summit, peering down, identified the person and the voice of the lady as belonging unmistakably to Miss Hale. The pair paused under a dog-wood from which Captain Danvers plucked a flowery bough; then they resumed their stroll, walking toward the village, arm in arm.

"Shall I holler to them?" asked Byle with the friendliest intentions.

"By no means!" said Arlington hastily. "I have not the slightest interest in either of them. What have you here in your basket—botanical specimens?"

The inquiry set Plutarch's tongue running on his favorite theme. "I'm a sort of self-made doctor, Mr. —— won't you please write your name out just as you spell it yourself, and let me have it? I ain't sure of the accent. I've been digging roots and so on, for brother Blennerhassett. He's an odd fish—he fancies he knows yarbs. Well, now, he does; that is, he can learn and is learning faster than you would believe a near-sighted United Irishman could learn anything outside of books. He knows ginseng from pleuresy-root, anyhow. This plant—I'm taking the whole thing, root and stem, to show him how it grows—is the genuine Indian physic; I got it right by a big rotten log in Putnam's woods. What do you say to taking a tour to Blennerhassett's with me in my piroque? I've got as snug a piroque as ever oversot."

There was no reason why Arlington should not seize this offered opportunity of once more visiting the island, and pay his respects to the proprietor, whom he had some curiosity to meet. Besides, might he not chance to learn the true condition of affairs regarding Evaleen Hale and the objectionable captain?

Rocking on lazy eddies of a sheltered cove lay the piroque. It was a dugout or canoe, made by hollowing with axe and adz a section of a cucumber tree. One-fourth of its length was covered with canvas stretched on hoops, forming a canopy to shed rain and to screen the passenger from the sun's rays. The cosy shelter was made use of by Plutarch as a receptacle for "specimens" of all varieties, animal, vegetable and mineral. The boat was propelled by a paddle, and, as the owner had warned Arlington, was liable to be toppled over by any heedless movement of its occupants. In this craft, the distance from Marietta to the island was measured without accident. Landed on the gravelly beach, Plutarch bent his steps toward the dazzling white house, Arlington at his side. Peter Taylor, puttering in the front yard, greeted the visitors in his saturnine style.

"Which way is the Highcockolorum?" inquired Plutarch, thrusting out his hand.

The gardener was perplexed.

"I mean your boss. Ah, there he is, with a gun! What's the fraction now? When I first came to this place his little boy offered to stick a tin sword through me, and I wonder now if pap means to shoot me!"

"'E couldn't 'it you at ten paces," grumbled the Englishman, manifesting grim enjoyment. Byle winked in response. Blennerhassett, leading Dominick by the hand, came to meet them, and Arlington was courteously received.

"I regret my absence at the time you did us the honor to call. I have since had a delightful letter from Colonel Burr, who promises to favor us again. Mrs. Blennerhassett told me every particular of your brief sojourn here. She was charmed with her guests. I am sorry she happens to be from home. She has gone to spend the day with friends in Marietta."

"That's where she was, by gum, the first time I called here," broke in Byle, whose unconscious temerity Blennerhassett, not being able to rebuke, had concluded to tolerate. "I have fetched you a lot more plants and roots, and the spines of that big cat-fish I told you about. Here's another curiosity—the wing of a queer bird that I don't know—maybe you will—I shot the fowl flying. I see you own a rifle!"

"Yes," answered the recluse, placing the piece in Plutarch's hands. "You are familiar with American guns. What is your opinion of this one? It was recommended to me as an excellent article, and I bought it at an enormous price, so my neighbors tell me. But from my indifferent success in bringing down game with it, I am forced to the conclusion that the barrel must be defective. Peter thinks not, but he is more of an adept in horticulture than in shooting."

The gardener was miffed by this left-handed compliment, but he did not venture to resent the impeachment. Plutarch handled the gun with the confident facility of an expert, poised it to ascertain the weight, noticed the calibre and the maker's name, admired the beauty of the stock, and tested the action of the trigger, lightly lifting the maple breech to his shoulder. The spectators marvelled at the delicate touch of his seemingly coarse fingers.

"This is a good rifle," said he. "Do you see that red head on the top of that tree t'other side of the house?" No one did perceive the bird which the hunter professed to discover on the top of a tall sycamore distinctly visible at a distance of many rods beyond the roof. Byle drew up the rifle and fired.

"Run, bub, and pick him up," said Plutarch, dropping the butt of the rifle and resting it carelessly on the toe of his shoe. Dominick hesitated, but the black man, Scipio, who had drawn near to witness the shooting, trudged away to the foot of the tree, where he found a dead woodpecker lying on the ground. He picked up the bird, still warm and bleeding, and brought it to Blennerhassett, who expressed enthusiastic admiration for the marksman's skill. Plutarch received the praise without showing the pleased vanity he inwardly felt, and having reloaded the gun with neat celerity, he passed it to the owner, saying in his unceremonious way, "Now, boss, it's your turn."

Blennerhassett at first declined to make an exhibition of his skill, but on persuasion consented to fire at a mark under the direction of his faithful servant, Peter Taylor, who was accustomed to attend him on hunting excursions. Mr. Byle, with accommodating alacrity, offered his hat as a suitable target, having stuck a maple leaf on the centre of the crown to answer as the bull's eye. The party shifted ground to the rear premises, and the hat was fixed to the side of the barn. Blennerhassett took his place directly in front of the mark, at a distance from it of twenty steps deliberately paced off by Plutarch. When their chief cocked the rifle there was a general commotion among the servants, black and white, for by this time the whole retinue of the establishment, including ostler, footman, butler, field hands and housemaids, had collected to see the sport. The principal actor, being self-absorbed as well as near-sighted, was scarcely aware of the tittering assemblage. Abstracted from every other thought, he fixed his attention on the great business in hand, not without misgiving and nervous agitation. When he lifted the rifle to his shoulder, and, trembling with excitement, pointed it in the manner he conceived to be proper, Peter Taylor, stationed at his master's back as prompter and artillerist, gave directions: "Now, sir, cool and steady! 'Old her level! Not so 'igh, Mr. Blennerhassett. There! So! 'Old on! 'Old on! A leetle more up! Ready! Fire!"

In agitation, the gentleman drew the trigger, and the next instant a pane of window-glass, fully six feet from the outmost rim of Mr. Byle's straw hat, was shivered to pieces, and the fragments were heard to tinkle as they fell within the barn. The chagrin of the mortified rifleman was cunningly abated by Peter's declaring that he himself was at fault in confining his master's attention to vertical rather than to horizontal considerations; but while he thus explained away the failure, he winked at the other servants and whispered aside to Plutarch that, though horticulture was his profession, he was a better shot than his distinguished employer.

"That's claiming a good deal, isn't it?" replied Byle, following with his eye the humiliated subject of their comment, who, conscious that he had made himself ridiculous, withdrew from the scene and tried to recover lost dignity by retiring with his guest to the privacy of his library. There, rallying his spirits, he dilated upon law, science and belles-lettres, oblivious of the fact that his commonplace remarks were tedious to a lively mind. He was opinionated, though not egotistical; revered authority, took himself seriously, and was a hero worshipper lacking humor and imagination. Pedantically conscious of imparting his stored wisdom to the attentive listener, whom he desired to entertain, he glowed with ingenuous enthusiasm while he commented, in mildly magisterial fashion, on books and authors. He read aloud extracts from "Shaftsbury's Characteristics," nodding approval of the dullest sentences. Then he opened a large new folio, illustrated with allegorical plates and profusely annotated.

"This is my latest literary treasure, Erasmus Darwin's wonderful poem, 'The Temple of Nature,' recently published, and superior, I think, to the 'Botanic Garden.' Let me read from the first canto, on the Production of Life."

Arlington in "wise passivity" submitted to the infliction, and with feigned pleasure followed the torturer's voice, delivering page after page of solemn science in polished heroic couplets. At length, in a lull between the lines on Imitation and those on Appetency, the young man mustered courage to broach the subject nearest his heart, by asking the irrelevant question, "You are acquainted, I dare say, with the prominent families of Marietta; do you happen to know a gentleman by the name of Hale? George Hale?"

Blennerhassett, keeping one eye on the Temple of Nature, answered mechanically:

"Yes; George Hale is one of our best citizens. He is held in high esteem, a man of some wealth and of great probity, but not college bred. I am sure, Mr. Arlington, you will discern high poetical qualities in this passage from the second canto, entitled Reproduction of Life. Shall I read it aloud?"

"By all means, sir. I should be delighted to hear you read the entire volume, but I regret that I have engagements up the river."

"I will detain you only a moment, Mr. Arlington. Perhaps you would like to carry the book with you to read on your way back. This is the passage I referred to:

'Now, young Desires, on purple pinions borne,
Mount the warm gale of Manhood's rising morn;
With softer fires through Virgin bosoms dart,
Flush the pale cheek, and goad the tender heart!'

Those are well-constructed verses, my dear sir—equal to Dryden. 'On purple pinions borne,' sounds well. The alliteration is pleasing. Note the effect, also, in the phrase 'Manhood's morn,' and the last line is poetical,

'Flush the pale cheek, and goad the tender heart.'

Or this, suggesting how love and sympathy causes affinities which—

'Melt into Lymph or kindle into gas.'

There are those who contend that scientific truths cannot be stated poetically; but here, I am sure, science and sentiment are at one. Am I not right?"

"Doubtless your judgment is correct," assented Chester, uncertain whether Blennerhassett was speaking in earnest or in irony. "I confess I am not a literary student. Pardon the interruption and my inquisitiveness, but am I correctly informed that the young lady to whom I was introduced, a few weeks ago, when I called here, is related to Mr. Hale of whom we were speaking?"

"Quite right; she is his daughter, Miss Evaleen, an amiable girl. Margaret and the boys think the world of her."

Arlington made another effort to satisfy his jealous curiosity. "I was told by a gentleman in Marietta that Miss Hale is about to be married. Am I correctly informed? The lucky man is to be envied."

Blennerhassett, whose eyes were still picking poetic gems from Darwin, answered vaguely.

"Oh, to be sure. A fortunate man. She will make an excellent wife. Did you hear such a report? Not surprising; I remember now that Margaret mentioned something of Evaleen's prospects in that way—to the effect, I believe, that she, that is, Miss Hale, had received gallant attentions from an eligible young man—a suitor. Women take more interest than we men do in affairs of this nature. I can give no particulars."

"This Captain Danvers—?" faltered Chester.

"Danvers? Danvers?" repeated the absent-minded philosopher amiably. "Ah, yes. Captain Danvers is at present stopping at the Hale residence. My wife tells me that Evaleen and he are exceedingly devoted to each other. Naturally. You would be welcome, I assure you, if you should call. They are very hospitable."

Without further inquiries, Arlington presently took leave to join Byle, with whom he voyaged back to Marietta. Wrapped in meditation he sat, taciturn, ballasting the unstable piroque which his stalwart comrade propelled with astonishing speed against the current. Chester spoke not a dozen sentences during the tedious passage from the island to the village. Byle, strange to say, also held his tongue, but he watched his melancholy companion with varying facial expressions, eloquent of fellow-feeling. The piroque was brought to shore on the east bank of the Muskingum, a short distance above the mouth of the river.

"You can tell your grandchildren that you sot your foot just where Rufus Putnam did when he jumped off the Mayflower in 1788. This is the spot where the first settlers of Ohio landed."

"You make me feel quite like a historical character," said Arlington, and thanked his obliging guide.

"I don't reckon history is all over yet, Arlington. Good-night, and take keer of yourself. I'm goshamighty sorry your goose is cooked in regards to Evaleen. Still, this Danvers is a perfect gentleman—you'd say so yourself if you knowed him as she does. By dad, we can't all have the same girl, or others would suffer. Don't forget the bitters. Speaking of bitters and how to cure trouble in this vale of tears, as the saying is, I reckon you have heard of a man by the name of Jonathan Edwards? He's dead now, but he made his living by preaching, and he wrote books. The only one of his works that I ever read was his Rules, and they are elegant. One of Jonathan's rules I learned by heart: 'When you feel pain, think of the pains of martyrdom and of hell.' You might try that. But whatever you try, don't forget the bitters—fruit of the cucumber tree in raw whiskey."

"Don't forget the bitters." These words kept repeating themselves in Chester's mind long after he had gone to bed in the small room assigned to him by the host of the Travellers' Rest. He slept wretchedly, rose late the next morning, breakfasted, and after ordering his horse to be saddled at nine o'clock, walked to the wharf where lay the mail-boat ready to start down the Ohio. Among the few taking passage on the vessel was Captain Danvers, who had been ordered to report for service in St. Louis, and was on his way thither. Arlington observed the fine-looking young officer with the petulant dislike of foiled envy. So spiteful was his mood that he wished a pretext for saying or doing something offensive to his handsome rival. Such a pretext was afforded. A veteran major who had accompanied Danvers to the boat, to bid him good-bye, called out:

"Captain, don't let the Indians scalp you or the Spaniards take you prisoner. If you had been three weeks sooner you might have had Aaron Burr for a fellow-traveller. He stopped here on his way down the river."

"I would not travel on the same boat with Aaron Burr. I consider him guilty of murder."

Arlington's wrath broke forth. "Any man who says that speaks calumny."

"Do you mean to insult me, sir? I never saw you before, and did not address you."

"I do not stand on ceremony with those who traduce my friends," retorted the Southerner sneeringly. "Colonel Burr is my friend—you have maligned him."

Danvers contemptuously replied: "You seem proud of your alleged intimacy with a notorious criminal. Perhaps you are the Vice-President's brother, or are you his man-servant?"

The taunt raised a laugh at Arlington, who roared out:

"Burr did right in calling Hamilton to the field; he vindicated his own honor."

"Push off! Loosen that line!" shouted the captain from the deck. "Hurry up! blast you! we're a year behind time!"

The boat-hands made a show of haste without making speed, reluctant to miss the chance of witnessing a fight.

"Captain Danvers, perhaps, like other Yankees, you preach against duelling, but do not scruple to traduce men who are not present to resent your words."

"You know my name!" cried Danvers, "but are wrong in supposing that I will stand an affront. If you are a gentleman—"

"If? Couldn't you waive ifs and buts long enough to try the Weehauken experiment and then investigate my pedigree? The question is, are you a man or a dastard?"

"Swaller your fire, young salamander," broke in the captain of the boat. "We hain't got no time to fuss nor fight duels. Push off, there, boys! Get your poles in hand and give her a reverend set! If the feller on shore is hankering for gore let him swim after us. Let go that cordelle, you cussed, lazy, flat-bellied, Hockhocking idiot! Can't you learn that a vessel won't navigate while she's tied to a tree and stuck fast in the mud?"

Soon in midstream, the boat moved away rapidly, impelled by the triple force of current, wind and oars, and the Virginian was jeered at from deck and shore. It completed his mortification to observe Danvers waving him a disdainful farewell. He returned to the tavern, paid his reckoning, mounted his horse, and rode away dejected and miserable. Self-disgust wrought in him a revulsion against Ohio, Marietta and the Blennerhassetts, and caused him, for the moment, to wish he had never met Evaleen. He rode along the village street, his mind's ear ringing with Byle's parting advice: "Don't forget the bitters." While his horse was trotting past a house that stood back from the street, in the midst of shrubbery, he thought he heard his own name spoken. On turning his head, he saw two ladies observing him from a leaf-screened veranda. His impulse was to halt; he drew bridle, but, recalling the scene on the wharf, he spurred on.

"My dear girl," exclaimed the elder of the two ladies, watching the unheeding horseman, "that gentleman is Mr. Arlington or Mr. Arlington's twin brother."

Evaleen's lips trembled as she replied hesitatingly, "It cannot be he; he would have called. He knows we live in Marietta."

"I am sure it is Mr. Arlington, and I cannot account for his failing to pay you his respects. He showed a decided interest in you that day on the island. To my eye it looked very like love at first sight; and I cannot help believing that his sole errand in Marietta is to see you again."

Evaleen, reddening, plucked leaflets from the honeysuckle which covered the porch.

"What am I to Mr. Arlington?"

"Perhaps more than he is to you. I wish he could have met Captain Danvers."

Evaleen's blush faded.

"I may never see Warren again," she sighed; "he is reckless and will not shun Spanish bullets or yellow fever. I can't bear to think of what he must endure in the army."

"Be proud that he has gone to the war as a brave man should. I admire men who are fearless."

"Oh, Margaret, you don't know how dear he is to me!"

"My darling, I understand. But Natchez is not out of the world, even if the soldiers should be sent there. After all, there may be no fighting. But I can't solve the mystery of our Virginia friend's ungallant conduct."

Midday came and went, the afternoon wasted away, the sun set, but the disappointing cavalier came not back to the village. Madam Blennerhassett said no more about him, though she noticed that at intervals Evaleen furtively glanced through an open window eastward down the long perspective of the shaded road.

X.: "NOW TO MY CHARMS AND TO MY WILY TRAINS."

Burr tarried at Massac, spinning subtle webs to entangle human flies. He "lived along the line" of correspondence, keeping in touch with former associates and recent acquaintances. In his ark, seated at a rough table, he wrote to those he hoped to gain or feared to lose. He did not neglect the Blennerhassetts, nor Arlington, nor the confiding young law-students of Pittsburg. A lengthy letter was penned to the Hon. John Smith, and, at the same sitting, a model billet-doux to Mrs. Rosemary. Other business was combined with this epistolary industry, for, even before the stamp of the writer's seal was lifted from the soft, red wafer on the widow's letter, a backwoods settler came, by appointment, to close a bargain by which the flatboat "Salome" was sold.

The somewhat damaged vessel was knocked to pieces by its new owner, who used the timber to construct a shanty, a stable, and a pig-pen, for his family and other live-stock. Before this degrading transmutation was begun, the original proprietor of the now abandoned craft removed to the commodious cabin of an elegant barge, provided by the courtesy of Wilkinson. In this convenient vessel, navigated by a select crew under command of a faithful sergeant, the sole passenger embarked for New Orleans. In frequent conference with Wilkinson he had amplified and enforced the arguments broached at the first interview. On the day set for the statesman's departure, the two men spoke together, very confidentially.

"Good-bye, Aaron; I augur well of your undertaking. The auspices are favorable. We are engaged in a scheme full of danger, requiring enterprise; but, if successful, fraught with fortune and glory."

"General, we are engaged, not in a scheme, but in a sublime exploit. We are to create an ideal commonwealth. The materials are ready. I go to take seizin of the grandest dominion on the curve of the globe. Military force will be requisite to sustain civil polity. The names Burr and Wilkinson are linked together in the chain of destiny. Farewell, and God bless you. When I return, I will hasten to join you at St. Louis, and give a full report of my stewardship."

With rhetoric like this, the parting guest closed his valedictory. His barge was soon under way. Down the calm Ohio, down the solemn Mississippi fared Aaron Burr, bound for the prodigal South. Swept along by the urgent stream, his boat seemed the plaything of fate, and the unstable element upon which it rode and rocked and trembled, he likened to human life, fleeting, turbulent, treacherous, yet grandly beautiful. Yielding to that mood in which the judgment and the will are suspended, and the passive brain is played upon by every sight and sound, he sat in an easy chair smoking, lost in sensuous languor, like an Asian prince. He was, for the time, possessed by the sensation of being royal. He enjoyed by anticipation the prerogatives of sovereignty, the power, the luxury, the voluptuous pleasure. The objects of his ambition appeared then how easy of attainment! To accomplish seemed no more difficult than to desire. The stream was running his way, and the wind was blowing his way. As surely as the Mississippi goes to the Mexican Gulf, would destiny waft Burr to the ocean of his desire. Imaginations so extravagant, courted in solitude and fed by indolence, served to beguile the days of the long voyage from Fort Massac to New Orleans.

At last the barge rounded into port, late in the afternoon of a perfect summer day. Aaron the First, standing upon deck, was coming unto his own; or rather, the city came floating out to meet her king. The bending shore which gives the name Crescent City to the emporium of the South, was lined with ships from every sea, and with innumerable river craft. New Orleans was one of the richest marts on the hemisphere. Burr stepped ashore and quickly ascended the levee. Hundreds of pleasure-seekers swarmed the footpaths or rested on the benches under the rows of orange trees which shaded the broad causeway.

On turning his eyes towards the city, Burr experienced a thrill of surprise. The prospect surpassed his pre-conceptions. In the subdued glow of the setting sun, he saw all things touched with a visionary splendour. Streets, roofs, belfries, the cathedral spire, and the flag of the Union streaming far away above the fort, appeared objects in an enchanted scene. Were the seven cities of Cibola clustered in one golden capital?

The spell was broken by the practical promptings of common sense. Not in possession, but only in pursuit of a treasury and a scepter, the would-be monarch addressed himself to the solution of his complicated problem. It was necessary to learn how the Louisianians regarded the Federal government, how much prejudice they felt against the Atlantic States, and whether they could be influenced to break away from the Union and to organize a separate autonomy. Burr wished further to know who and how many were disposed to wage war against the Spaniards with the ulterior design of conquering Mexico. In order to learn the inside facts he must gain the confidence of all, must make himself popular, must fathom hearts and steal away brains. The final success of his plans would depend on the good-will of the people. The good-will of the people must be won by address—by social tact. Social tact was Aaron Burr's art of arts. He deliberately set about the delicate business of captivating a city that he might eventually capture it.

Wilkinson had pressed upon him letters of introduction to the magnates of the town. Neither letters nor formal receptions were needed to introduce Aaron Burr to society. His manner was passport, entitling him to cross all borders; his sympathy was cosmopolitan, his toleration unlimited, his pleasure, to please others, his study urbanity. Jews thought him a Hebrew, and Christians voted him orthodox. The amiable but capricious creoles, easy to take offense, yet blind in their devotion to those they confide in, swarmed to his standard. The Roman Catholic bishop countenanced him, endorsed his aims, and signalized an official friendliness by accompanying him on a visit to the Ursuline Convent, and there the son of a Protestant preacher chatted pleasantly with my lady prioress and her demure nuns. Burr went everywhere, and wherever he went, he made discreet use of his opportunity to inquire, to observe, to listen, to make friends and proselytes. He felt the pulse of public sentiment. Never to any person did he fully disclose his designs. Without argument or appeal, he convinced, persuaded, and inflamed the victims of his corrupting influence. To the avaricious his intimations promised riches; to the luxurious, pleasure; to those disaffected towards the East, revolt and secession.

Affairs in the Southwest were unsettled. Only a year and a half had elapsed since Louisiana had passed into American hands. Jefferson's land purchase was a current topic of conversation.

Opinions differed, and men hotly discussed the question whether, even if the President had a constitutional right, he had a moral warrant for saddling upon the young republic a wild domain, of doubtful value, sparsely inhabited by Indians and already dedicated, by tradition, to the rule of an alien, white population. The Spaniard and the Frenchman, sold and transferred, by one power to another, could not be expected to submit. The citizens had long yielded willing allegiance to his Spanish majesty, the emblem of whose sovereignty had been hauled down, to give place to the tri-color of France; and now that second banner had disappeared. Though an American governor ruled the district, there prevailed among the populace a hope and belief, that, after a brief meteoric display, the red, white and blue, emblazoned with stars, would fade and vanish from its proud height over the old fort, new garrisoned by American soldiers. Spanish officers in disguise lingered in the haunts of their former dignity and sway. They stirred up secret dissension. They deemed themselves not extinguished, though eclipsed. Discontent and resistance were in the air. War-clouds hung dark along the Mexican and Floridan border, rumbling with ominous thunder.

Into this chaos of troubled politics, and conflicting interests, Aaron Burr came exploring, vigilant to note and sedulous to question. The sum of the impressions which he received confirmed him in the belief that the people of the West and Southwest were ready and anxious to separate their section from the Atlantic States; and he felt convinced that it would be no trouble "to enlist recruits and make arrangements for a private expedition against Mexico," especially in case of war with Spain.

It was the middle of September when, true to his promise, Burr appeared at St. Louis, in Wilkinson's quarters, to unfold the tale of his triumph in New Orleans. In the course of his animated narrative, he said:

"There is an infinite difference between floating down to New Orleans in your delightful barge, and jogging homeward a thousand miles on horseback. That interminable stretch of dreary wilderness from Natchez to Nashville, along the Indian trail, over sandy wastes, through pine woods, was intolerable. I was glad enough to reach Tennessee and old Kentucky. The people of Frankfort treated me very handsomely, as did those of Lexington. I paid my respects to the local idol, the young Virginia orator and rising lawyer, Henry Clay. That man is a prodigy—he will make his mark. I wish he were hand in hand with us, like Jackson, and ready to embark his fortune at our prompting."

"So do I. Clay is a rising power, notwithstanding his conceit. He will make a stir in Congress some of these days."

"That he will," said Burr, and proceeded with his story, at the close of which he exclaimed,

"I wish you could attend one of the meetings of the Mexican Society in New Orleans. Its object is to discuss means of emancipating Mexico. You should hear, as I have heard, the outspoken discontents of the creole population. They adore the institution of African slavery. They hate New England. They will not buy even a Yankee clock if it is adorned with an image of the Yankee Goddess of Liberty. But they are mine, every mother's son of them, and what is more important, every father's daughter of them. I took the city by storm, and the outlying provinces belong to us. We have a people and, virtually, an army. The moral conquest is complete. When the hour strikes for extending the borders of our conceded realm, you are the chosen Cæsar."

"Can we depend on David Clarke's co-operation?"

"Why not? His interests are bound up in ours. We have a host of stanch adherents, in all parts of the country and on the high sea, and in Europe, soldiers, statesmen, capitalists. I need not name them to you. All these are to be kept in mind and treated with due consideration. Our enterprise is in its preliminary stage. The shrewd work of enlisting recruits must be intrusted to carefully selected captains. I have the ways and means clearly in my head. Every detail must be worked out in practice."

"Burr, you are more circumspect than I gave you credit for being. There is always danger in the dark. Have you entertained the possibility of defection?"

"I have measured my ground, and calculated the curve of my leap. I shall not fall into an abyss, or dash myself upon a rock. If we fail to sever the Union, and do not succeed in the conquest of Mexico, I have so masked our designs as to make them appear in the guise of innocent land-speculations on the Wachita river."

XI.: PALAFOX GROWS INSOLENT.

Early in October Wilkinson's duties required him to visit the town of Genevive, some fifty miles south of St. Louis. The best cabin in a keelboat had been furnished in sumptuous style for the accommodation of the self-indulgent chief. Such was the attractiveness of this cosy retreat that the general preferred it to his official quarters on the shore and he occasionally spent a whole afternoon reading, writing or dozing there in undisturbed privacy.

On the day before that fixed for his departure he prolonged his stay in the cabin to a late hour, for reasons partly physical, partly mental. His robust health and ebullient spirits were suffering an unwonted depression. Even his strong constitution could not withstand the "miasmatic" vapor of the lowlands near the Western watercourses. The malarial poison had entered his blood, causing low fever, dull headache and general hypochondria. Copious doses of Peruvian bark bitters aggravated the unpleasant symptoms. Moreover, the weather had turned unseasonably raw and gusty. The characteristic mildness of October gave way to gloomy inclemency. The month was not like its usual self, and Wilkinson partook of its exceptional harsh melancholy. Appropriate for a season so dreary was the sad name of Fall—Fall, the period of decline, decay and death. For the first time in his life Wilkinson "heard the voice which tells men they are old," though he was not old.

The general sat holding in his hand a short letter, in cipher. The last sentence did not please him. "God bless you and grant you a safe deliverance from factions and factious men." These words Wilkinson read over and over. To him, in his dejected mood, with nerves unstrung and head swimming in quinine bitters, the blessing sounded ironical; a mocking face seemed concealed behind the mask of considerate friendliness. The tone of the communication struck him as patronizing, perhaps unconsciously made so, but the more offensive on that account. One suspicious fancy engenders another; it now occurred to the general that his former comrade and late guest, in more than one unguarded speech, had arrogated superiority, and that he had presumed, without sufficient warrant, on the subserviency of men greater than himself.

"Does he think I am committed to him, body and soul? Does he take it for granted that I am a tool and a fool? Burr should consider his own position and mine. I have had too much experience in the world to be caught by this shrewd contriver, or by any man."

Wilkinson put the letter away, and taking a book, threw himself on his bed. The volume he had chosen was a fine copy of the Sentimental Journey, his favorite reading. The italicised wit and glossy licentiousness of Yorick did not fix attention. Neither the "Dead Ass," nor the "Starling," nor the fair "Fille de chambre," had now a charm to steal the reader from his petty miseries of head and heart. Casting the book aside, he again arose, paced nervously up and down the cramped cabin, and once more sought comfort in the cushioned seat. Prudence bade him seek home before nightfall, but the inertia of despondency kept him from going. The gathering darkness, the whining wind, the sound of restless water lapping and sucking around the keel, suggested superstitious forebodings and called up dismal images. To every mood there is a season; this was Wilkinson's hour of self-examination. He looked backward on his deeds and inward on his motives. He mistrusted the future. If he were sure that Burr's rainbow dipped its gorgeous ends in gold, no accusing ghost of the past would deter him from chasing the yellow temptation over mountains or through bogs. He was not given to brooding over bygone failures, nor was he much afraid that his buried sins would arise to find him out. He began to think better of his friend's message. Burr was certainly a deep man and bold; he had genius, he had perseverance, enthusiasm, resource, resolution. Taking him all in all, he was a masterful spirit, a fit partner, nay, even a leader for James Wilkinson.

To dispel mental gloom, the general summoned his familiar, the nimble spirit of alcohol. One dram proved so enlivening, by going "straight to the spot," that another was tossed off, from a sense of gratitude. Evidently the best ingredient in the bitters was the solvent, not the Peruvian bark. Wilkinson placed the bottle in a cupboard, and was preparing to leave the cabin, when the door opened and in walked Palafox. The commander-in-chief, whom fever and quinine had rendered hot-headed, stared angrily.

"What does this mean? Didn't I warn you never again to come to me unless sent for? You sneak in without so much as knocking! Your effrontery deserves a horsewhip! Begone!"

Instead of going, the intruding boatman pulled off his slouch hat and made a humble bow: "I beg your pardon, general, but I used to come and go, you recollect, by your order, informally, like a kind of private secretary, and I can't get rid of the familiar habit."

"Familiar! I should say so! You are brazen! I doubt you are drunk or you would not have the audacity to invade my privacy and speak as you do."

"Well, governor, what if I am drunk? You don't see anything disgraceful in that, do you?"

The insolence of this personal thrust enraged Wilkinson beyond endurance. In his indignation he snatched a sheathed sword from the wall and struck Palafox a rash blow. The ruffian recoiled, staggering, and clutched at the hilt of a dirk in his belt.

"Is that enough for you?" cried the furious general.

The Spaniard, livid and trembling, checked the impulse to draw his dirk, and slowly raising his hand to the bleeding welt on his forehead, said with sullen irony:

"It's now more'n three months since I invaded your privacy, as you call it. I came all the way from Natchez for money, not for abuse. You owe me, and if you are a man of your word you'll pay me. I want to leave this part of the country, and won't bother you any more after you've paid what's coming to me, unless you want to hear some facts concerning your own good that I've picked up for you."

The unabashed, persistent importunity of Palafox, astounded Wilkinson. There was an accent of admiration in his exclamation, "You dare-devil!"

"I'm not daring you, general, and if I was, you are not a devil, only a debtor."

The dignity of Wilkinson could not suffer further saucy retort or question.

"This farce must end. I cannot bandy words with such as you. Not another dollar shall you receive from me—not a penny. You had my final word at Massac, last Spring. Quit this boat instantly, and leave St. Louis. If I see you again, or hear of your hanging around the garrison, I'll settle your account in short order."

"I don't belong to the army."

"No!" answered the chief, sternly, "but I do; and I have civil authority also. If you had justice, Palafox, you would hang. I am ashamed of myself to speak to you further. Now, go."

"Yes, I'll go; I'll go in a minute; but I've got a scrap of paper I want to read to you. Will you hear it?"

Not unwilling to learn what might be the purport of the writing so dramatically introduced, and in order to get rid of Palafox without further violence, Wilkinson consented to listen.

With his back to the door, the lowering Spaniard read the following: "It is not necessary to suggest to a gentleman of your experience and knowledge of the world, that man, throughout the world, is governed by private interest, however variously modified it may be. Some men are avaricious, some are vain, others are ambitious. To detect the prevailing passion, to lay hold of and to make most of it is the profoundest secret of political science."

Pausing, he asked sarcastically:

"Are those your sentiments? Folks say you wrote this to Gardoqui, in January, 1789. That was before your plot with the Spanish Minister, Carondelet. Liars say, and say in print, that you hatched up a plan to split the West from the East, and to put the West under Spanish control. They say, these malicious liars do, that Tom Power brought ten thousand dollars bribe money, packed in barrels of sugar and bags of coffee, from New Madrid to Louisville, and that Philip Nolan conveyed the sweetened lucre to Fort Washington."

Wilkinson laughed. "You do not believe such absurdities, do you Palafox?"

"Why should I disbelieve? Carondelet's plan seems excellent to me, a Spaniard. We have been talking about events that happened ten years since. I was in your service nearly twenty years ago; you sent correspondence down the river when I was a boy, but I was a good, careful boy, and always tried to act with intelligence. I've saved lots of nice letters. I'm fond of good reading."

Whether it was owing to illness or quinine or conscience, a slight dizziness came over Wilkinson; his head swam; he leaned far back in his chair, and endeavored to steady his thoughts. Palafox cast on him a sidelong malicious glance and continued his monologue:

"Yes, I've got lots of fine sentiments in my archives. Here's an original. It's tolerable old, you see, stained and worn." This he said displaying a soiled paper, which he drew carefully from a large leathern pocket-book. "Let's see. Yes, this is the original of a fine letter, a copy of which I delivered to Governor Miro."

"Miro!" exclaimed Wilkinson.

"Yes; Miro, that's the name—Don Estevan Miro, Spanish governor of Louisiana, before Carondelet's day."

Wilkinson rose menacingly. Palafox did not flinch, but leering significantly, read these words:

"My situation is mortally painful because, whilst I abhor all duplicity, I am obliged to dissemble. This makes me extremely desirous of resorting to some contrivance that will put me in a position in which I flatter myself to be able to profess myself publicly the vassal of his Catholic majesty, and, therefore, claim his protection, in whatever public or private measures I may devise to promote the interests of the crown."

"There, general, I should say this might be valuable property for you to possess, and damaging to you if it falls under the eye of the public," remarked Palafox, thrusting the letters into his pocket. "It bears your signature. I deciphered every secret letter that touched my hand from you to Miro and Carondelet, and from them to you. Now, hadn't you better buy the whole damned correspondence?"

"Buy?" sneered Wilkinson, trembling with passion. "So this is all the desperate attempt of a felon to levy blackmail upon his benefactor!"

The boatman turned to lift the latch.

"You won't buy, then?"

No reply was vouchsafed the desperado.

"I'll tell you what I'll do. I'll throw in a spice of Aaron Burr pepper that he happened to spill in my sight. You and Aaron appear to be thick. He and I are chums, too. He is one of us. The colonel is a lovely mole, very smooth and shiny, but he don't always tunnel deep enough to hide his track."

"Begone!"

"O, I'm going. If you won't buy, I'll keep. Good-bye, general."

He deliberately put on his slouch hat and backed out through the narrow doorway. As a parting salute he touched with his finger the red contusion on his forehead. Wilkinson stood a few seconds, in rigid silence, then stepped to the open door and called aloud:

"Palafox! Comeback!"

No answer was returned to the cry, nor did the vanished figure reappear. Not even the sound of his retreating footfalls could be heard. A dense fog had risen, shrouding the river and crawling over cottage and chapel and fort. Alone, in the boat's cabin, by the dim light of a flickering lamp, the general waited and waited, anxious to soothe and conciliate the malignant underling, once his minion, now an unscrupulous enemy, too dangerous to be despised. The proud officer listened for a returning step or a relenting voice, but heard no other noise than that made by the whining winds, and by the waters of the Mississippi fretting and swirling around the keel of his solitary boat.

XII.: SNARING A PHILOSOPHER.

After his tour in the West, Burr, homeward bound, pursued his way from St. Louis to Vincennes, thence to Cincinnati, and up the Ohio to the beautiful island he had visited in the month of May. Change of season had transformed a paradise of soft verdure and tender bloom into an Eden of gorgeous foliage and gaudy flowers. The house of Blennerhassett he saw embowered in trees magnificently colored by the wonder-working frosts of October. The place was Færie Land, but had not Gloriana been there, it may be doubted whether other attractions of the lovely isle would have detained the restless conspirer. Once more the American statesman stood in the presence of the fairest dame west of the Alleghanies, and she received him with cordial words and kind eyes.

"We have been expecting this visit. Your letters to my husband kept us both in hope you would not fail to honor us before your return to Philadelphia."

"The boat which brought me up-stream, madam, rounded into your wharf of its own motion, attracted by some lodestone or guiding star. I am here again, after many days."

"You have wandered far since you happened to discover our hiding-place last May."

"Wandered is the word. Like a pilgrim, I went in Spring to come back in Autumn."

"Bringing the palm?"

"Palm, olive, laurel, myrtle—the whole botany of lucky leaves. How are my boys, Dominick and—what's the younger one's name?—Yes, Harman, how are they? I am due in Philadelphia, but I delay business to indulge inclination."

"You did not quite forget the lonely island and its solitary family?"

"He would be an insane palmer who could forget the most attractive shrine in the round of his long pilgrimage——"

As Burr was saying these words, a soft shuffling step was heard in the adjoining room, and a grave gentleman in spectacles made his appearance in the doorway.

"Colonel Burr, my husband."

"A happiness and an honor to meet you, Colonel Burr."

Bow followed bow, urbane word echoed word, awkwardly protracting the salutatory ceremony until Burr felt like a Chinese mandarin at a court reception. According to his wife's judgment, Mr. Blennerhassett acquitted himself admirably; she felt that Burr must recognize sterling manhood and aristocratic breeding. This he did, and more, for at a glance he read the book and volume of her husband's character, interpreting more accurately than it was in her nature to do. The woman's partial eye discovered the sound qualities it wished to see, while the calculating insight of the man of the world detected the flaws he was too willing to find.

The solemnities of introduction being safely over, Blennerhassett monopolized the guest, and led the way to his study, eager to set forth a feast of information. Among his books he could talk like a book; out of the library he lost energy. There was one source from which he took a current of mental force more vitalizing than any stream of ideas from books, and that source was the superior intellect of his wife. Hardly could he make up his mind on any practical matter, unassisted by her thinking and advice. Doubly dependent, he was not the man to cope with the daring, self-reliant, versatile Aaron Burr. But once in his stronghold, bulwarked by standard editions, and, as it were, in the arsenal of established science, the philosopher rose to his best. He fairly glowed with learning's soft fire, while exhibiting his telescope, microscope, electrical machine, et cetera, and stating to the last shilling what each piece of apparatus cost and how it was to be used. Burr, himself a victim of mild bibliomania, took most interest in the loaded shelves, along which his eyes travelled with rapid discrimination.

"I see familiars here. Your Voltaire is a match for mine. Ah!—Rousseau, Bentley, Gibbon, Hume—I fancy myself in my study on Richmond Hill. You must be a free-thinker. Where is the Holy Bible? I hope you are not past that?"

"The Sacred Scripture? I have two copies. I believe they are both in Margaret's room—I mean Mrs. Blennerhassett's. She reads the Bible frequently, especially the poetical parts. The Hebrew mind is poetical. I have searched the Scripture in vain for scientific data. There is little or no exact science in the work. Nothing on physic, though they claim that St. Luke was a doctor. Let me show you a remarkable volume—centuries old—this folio copy of Hippocrates, translated from the original Greek into Arabic and from Arabic into Latin. My favorite reading, however, is purely literary—the book of books—the incomparable Homer. Alexander the Great kept his Homer in a golden box; I keep mine in my head, sir, or perhaps I should say, in my heart. I have committed to memory the greater part of the epic."

"Is it possible?"

To Burr's consternation, the host seemed desirous of proving that it was possible, by reciting the Iliad.

Blennerhassett kept hexameters flowing several minutes, marking quantity with tongue and moving finger.

"What a pity we lack spondees, in English, colonel. Do you write verse, sir?"

"Not I. I suppose you do?"

"No; not since leaving college. I admire poetry, but I could never master the meters. It is different with Margaret—I mean my wife. She writes correctly. She is a born poet. You recall Horace, 'poeta nascitur.' I confine my pen to the composition of music and political essays."

"I have heard of your political writings, but not of your musical compositions," said Burr; the last half of the speech being true. "Nor have I had the good fortune to read the poems of Madam Blennerhassett. Are they in print?"

"Some have been published, fugitively; the most of them remain in manuscript."

"Sir, you could not give me a greater pleasure than the perusal of those poems would afford."

The near-sighted sage unlocked a rosewood cabinet and took out three leaves of tinted paper which he gave to Burr. On the pages were written, in fine hand, several stanzas under the title, "Indian Summer."

"Read this at your leisure and give me your opinion." Burr, bowing, took the manuscript, and the complaisant husband, pointing to a pile of sheet music, spoke on. "This is of my own composition. Do you play the violoncello?"

Burr shook his head.

"Perhaps you prefer the violin or the flute?"

"No, I cannot play any instrument—not even a jewsharp."

"Not even that?" murmured the other, with a sigh of infinite regret. "I am fond of the violincello, the viola da gamba of medieval times. Properly it is not a viol—not a base viol as some suppose, but a violin of extra large size. That is what it is."

While imparting this knowledge, the speaker drew from a baize bag the instrument, and tuned it. He placed an open music book upon a rest, and proceeded to entertain his audience of one. He played and played and played. The best way to please such an artist is to humor the illusion that his exertions give pleasure. No human performance can last forever—not even a concert. A string broke, and the musician, putting his 'cello aside with a sigh, suffered the conversation to run in a new channel opened by Burr.

"Bravo! You play delightfully. There is magic in your fingers. Beware of such skill; it may charm yourself to your injury. You have read everything; you remember Bunyan's episode of the Enchanted Ground. This island reminds me of that valley of rest. Is it possible you have forgotten the world since abandoning public affairs?"

"No, sir; no. I sought retirement for many reasons, but I am a cosmopolitan. I care for the welfare of the race. I may describe myself as a philanthropist, a humanitarian. I know Europe, I am learning America. My local attachments are not strong, though my principles are like iron. I left my native country to seek a larger freedom in the United States."

"Then why do you confine your liberty? This is a pent-up field for a man of broad views."

"I beg your pardon. Solitude is the best school in which to study society. In this seclusion I read, and reading makes a full man. Though a newcomer, I try to keep myself informed concerning this country's history and institutions. I do not understand all the complications of your politics; I am no partisan. No one is better prepared than yourself to expound public matters. This dispute in regard to the boundary line between Louisiana and Mexico threatens war, does it not?"

"I fear not," replied Burr, remarking an opportunity to inform and bias an unwary savant. The lump had invited the leaven.

"I fear not."

"Then you desire war?"

"This Government should take care of its own, at all hazards. The Spaniards wish to provoke hostilities. My friend and fellow-officer, General Wilkinson, commander-in-chief of the Western troops, holds the army in readiness to advance into Mexico at a moment's warning."

"At a moment's warning?" repeated Blennerhassett, dubiously. "General Wilkinson told you so? Is he—a reliable officer?"

"He and I are most intimate friends. We consult on public and on private concerns. I have just returned from his headquarters in St. Louis, where we were considering a business enterprise—the purchase of a large tract on the Wachita river, between the Red and the Sabine."

"Do you purpose returning South to remain?"

"My intention is to buy those fertile lands, establish a colony, and develop the resources of the region, as a sure and easy means of making my own fortune, and the fortunes of my associates."

"You are confident that the prospect of increasing your capital is good?"

"I am absolutely certain. I speak positively, but not rashly."

Blennerhassett nodded slowly, three or four times, and Burr spoke on.

"That the investment will prove enormously profitable I have not the shadow of a shade of doubt. General Wilkinson knows the property, and so do I. There are more than a million acres to be had for fifty thousand dollars. The present value is ten times that amount."

"If the inquiry is not impertinent, sir, have you organized a joint stock company? Have you completed your plans?"

"Practically, everything is arranged. Negotiations are afoot. The necessary capital will be forthcoming. We take no risk. To you I will say, in confidence, that the number of shareholders will be severely limited. You know how desirable it is, in partnerships of this kind, to admit only men of unimpeachable honor."

Again Blennerhassett nodded three or four times, like an automaton. Burr, affecting to dismiss the topic, turned again to the book-shelves and fell to reading the gilded titles. A copy of "The Prince" arrested his eye. Taking this down, he opened it at random, and read aloud: "Men will always prove bad, unless by necessity they are compelled to be good."

"What do you think of that as an estimate of human nature?"

"Abominable!"

Burr fluttered the leaves of the famous treatise and came upon this sentence, marked by a pen: "It is of great consequence to disguise your inclination and to play the hypocrite well; and men are so simple in their temper and so submissive, that he that is neat and cleanly in his collusions shall never want people to practice upon."

"Why did you mark that passage?"

"To condemn the doctrine. The hypocrite can never thrive; the plain, honest man always sees through the disguise. Virtue is all-seeing, but fraud is blind."

"You mint apothegms, sir. It is an intellectual feast to hear you talk."

Burr replaced Machiavelli on its shelf, confronted his host, and, in a tone deferential and almost apologetic, said, "You must not accuse me of flattery, sir, when I bluntly charge you with defrauding the world and robbing that humanity which you profess to love."

"I can't find any flattery in such accusation. Kindly explain what you mean. Whom do I defraud? and how is it flattery to charge a man with insincerity?"

"Well, you seem to me to be evading your duty to the world, by hiding from its great public interests, enterprises and conflicts. You linger here, a magnificent hermit. If ever a philanthropist hid his light under a bushel, thou art the man. If ever brilliant talents rusted in a napkin, yours do. Your noble wife is cut off from the splendid career appropriate to her, and is compelled to devote her days to rural walks and the direction of a few negro slaves. Not to dwell on the sacrifice of mother and sons, your own learning, fortune, and extraordinary mental powers—your genius for dealing with men—are here employed, not in the service of mankind, but in——" Burr was tempted to say "fiddling," but he substituted the words—"gazing at the stars through a telescope. Pardon me for speaking strongly. It is only a few hours since we first met, but I am drawn to you. I admire and esteem you, and my motive in this perhaps impertinent appeal, is the wish to serve you."

Blennerhassett felt much gratified by the insidious censure. His portrait, amiably regarding its original from the wall, listened approvingly to Burr, and smiled acquiescence. "Does the mild-eyed thing recollect me?" mused Burr. The picture betrayed no sign of recognition and the original spoke.

"Such candor is rare, and I appreciate it. I am honored by the outspoken confidence of the man I know you to be, not only from what I have read of your political course, which I wholly approve, but from Mrs. Blennerhassett's reports of your conversation. Her judgment is unerring. I defer to it. You will confer a great favor on me by explaining, in detail, your Southern plans."

Thus solicited, Burr adroitly availed himself of the opportunity to divulge, not only his project of settling the Bastrop lands, but such part of his other plans as he deemed it prudent to reveal at the time. He learned to his satisfaction that Blennerhassett had no repugnance to the idea of separating the Western States from the Eastern and of invading Mexico. Burr's angling had gone on for an hour, with lures so tempting that the gudgeon seemed about to swallow bait, hook and all, when the conversation was disturbed by an unusual clamor of excited voices coming from the negro quarters. Blennerhassett, in a flurry, excused himself, and hastened to inquire what was the matter. He found his servants, black and white, huddled together around Scipio, who had just told the grinning crowd that Honest Moses was missing from the plantation, having been enticed by an Ohio farmer to cross the river and run away to the free North.

This was Scipio's story, but Peter Taylor, who stood smoking a small pipe, with looks of austere indifference to all human interests, had another theory to account for the leave-taking of Moses.

"I've no hidea 'e ran away to Ohio. That lazy nigger 'ated work too much to run away to Ohio. I suspicion that the rascal drifted away on a flatboat."

"What makes you think so, Peter?"

"I can't say that I altogether think anything sure about the nigger. It isn't my business to think about other people's business. I only say I suspicion. If I knew what was hid in the future, I would have told. But it's my firm suspicion that a boatman by the name of Sheldrake lured Honest Moses away on a flatboat."

"No; Mars Taylor," reiterated Scipio, "Moses done tole Ransom he was gwine to run off, up Muskingum."

"When did he tell you?"

"Las' Crismus."

"For de Lawd sake!" cried out Juno, the kitchen maid, whose rolling eyes were the first to see the master approaching. "I never 'spected Honest Moses of sneaking fum his good home and kind Mars and Missus like a brack thief in de night. Whar's Daniel? I hy'ard him prayin' for Moses yesterday."

"No prayin' is gwine to keep Honest Moses fum de debil. Dat nigger's not got no religion to his name—not a speck. Didn't I tell Missus when she thought she cotched me and Ransom sellin' watermillions and sweet 'tatoes to de boys from Marietta, dat it was Moses done it?"

Exasperated, perplexed, not knowing how to act, Blennerhassett sought his wife, with whom he held a closet conference, lamenting his troubles and soliciting counsel. The lady advised him to summon Peter Taylor, and suggested that the two should go across the river to Belpre, there consult the squire, and set in motion every available agency to insure the recapture of the fugitive. The much-worried philosopher begged Burr to excuse him for a couple of hours, and hurriedly started on his vexatious quest, accompanied by the phlegmatic gardener. Complying good-naturedly with a proposal of Dominick and little Harman, and convoyed by those devoted children, Burr explored orchards, fields and stockyard, and won the extravagant praises of the black people by visiting their quarters and greeting every one, from Scipio to the youngest pickaninny, with a cheerful word and a smile. Every slave on the plantation was in voluntary bonds to "Mars Burr, de fine gen'leman wi' de coal brack eyes."

XIII.: THE ENCHANTED GROUND.

While Blennerhassett tramped about Belpre, his wife assumed the government at home, and Burr studied fresh means of invading her heart. The lady neither saw nor wished any escape from the pleasant task of entertaining the affable "pilgrim." Considering how seldom a person of extraordinary mental gifts brought to her isolated home the sparkle of wit, the hostess made the most of a golden opportunity. She waited with eagerness for Burr's return from his ramble with the boys, whose adhesiveness she knew by experience might prove too constant, like the clinging of Sindbad's Old Man of the Sea.

Burr, despite his professed fondness for the company of boys, longed to exchange the society of Dominick and Harman for that of their winsome mother. Therefore, he managed to engage the lads in the construction of a mimic fort in a cornfield. Promising to inspect the grand earthwork when it was completed, the colonel slipped away to reconnoiter another field.

Retreating in good order, he arrived at the long portico, and, under its cover, passed to the hall, through which he reached the cosy room where he and Arlington had been entertained. The French sofa, the ebony stand, the clavier, looked familiar. The gilded harp stood invitingly in a place of honor. He drew near the instrument, and, smiling to himself, thrummed a few notes on the lower strings. As if summoned by the sound, from the routine of household tasks, the mistress of the mansion entered in her regal manner and begged pardon for having neglected her guest.

Burr was in his element as the bird in air; his winged words now skimmed the surface of common levels, now soared, then circled round subjects grave or gay, often fluttering, but never failing. The range of discussion was wide and free. They talked society, arts, countries, travels, the pleasure of life and its pain. He told of his sojourn in New Orleans, describing a city not celestial, but abounding in the delights of this world. She gave reminiscences of her birthplace, the Isle of Wight, spoke of her marriage and subsequent journeyings in Europe and America.

Burr recalled the incidents of his previous visit, and besought madam to sing again the songs which had delighted him that evening after the ramble in the woods. She cheerfully complied; for singing was her prime accomplishment. The lady felt keen enjoyment in the consciousness of being understood and sympathized with, by a man of brains and character.

The hour for lunch having arrived, Burr was conducted to the dining-room, and the pair sat down to a dainty repast, served by a black damsel, who cast furtive glances upon the stranger, and observed that the "Missus" wore her finest jewels and seemed refreshed by the cares of hospitality. Never before had such enlivening gossip been heard by a servant in that sober house. The table-talk played familiarly with names and individuals.

"What became of the handsome young Arlington?"

"You think him handsome? He is in Virginia. I expect him to join me in a business enterprise. A fine fellow, thorough-bred. His name calls to mind your protégée, the golden-haired Yankee beauty. Arlington was smitten by her demure eyes—pierced to the heart. Those wild violets worked him woe."

"Are you sure? Did he own it?"

"He did not confess in words, but I divined the secret, which was no secret, for he revealed it by every sign known to the Court of Love. He was struck as by lightning—stunned by a love bolt."

"The stroke was harmless. On his return from Cincinnati he passed through Marietta, where he knows Evaleen lives, and made no effort to meet her, but rode by her house; I was with her on the porch, and we both saw him trot past on a black horse. He stared our way and must have identified us, yet he turned his face forward and spurred on."

"Incredible! Your eyes deceived you."

"No; it was Mr. Arlington; he made a flying trip to the island in company with a peculiar person, one Plutarch Byle."

"Byle? I shall never forget Plutarch!" interjected Burr, laughingly. "Dominick christened our fort, 'Fort Byle.'"

"Have you seen our gaunt Hercules? Isn't he an odd Grecian? In his 'piroque' he brought Mr. Arlington here. I was from home, as I said. My husband suggested to your Virginian friend that he ought to call on the Hales, but the faithless cavalier slighted us. I much doubt his interest in Evaleen."

"I am certain he was smitten."

"Then he is inconstant, or else belongs to the tribe of faint hearts. How ridiculous the idea of folks falling in love at first sight! Yet they often do. The girl was pleased with him, and she still likes him."

"Likes him, does she?" drawled Burr, sarcastically, and lifted a gherkin to his teeth.

"Yes, don't you like him?"

"Very much."

He bit the pickle quite savagely.

"What do you think of her?"

"It cannot be the fault of the male sex that she remains single."

"Some women are not inclined to marry."

"Is Miss Hale one of those foolish virgins?"

"She is wise in taking time to select. She has many suitors."

"And you think she likes Arlington?"

"I know she does."

"Humph! she might do better."

"She might fare worse."

"Does he write to her?"

"No, not that I know of."

"He is an idiot."

"You show a jealous interest in the young man." Here madam halted abruptly. "Pardon me; I hear the boys; their father must have returned."

She rose expecting to receive her husband at the dining-room door, but the footsteps she heard were not his. The vociferous boys came rushing in. "Fort Byle" was finished. Wouldn't "General" Burr come and see?

"You should not storm in, rudely, children; you disturb us. Harman, you have ruined your clothes; you are covered from head to foot with—I don't know what!"

"Spanish needles and sticktights; they won't hurt. Juno will scrape them off. We're hungry."

"Won't he come to the fort after luncheon?" importuned Dominick.

"Yes, I will come."

"Listen," said the mother. "My son, you must first go with me to the ferry. I am uneasy about papa. He did not intend to be gone longer than a couple of hours. We must try to meet him. Perhaps the colonel will go along, down to the landing."

"Certainly," replied the colonel, studying how to get rid of the "sticktights."

After luncheon, all set out on the proposed walk to the river-side. The island and the vistas it commanded naturally drew folks out of doors. Finer weather could not be imagined. The distance from the lawn to the wharf, by way of the winding road, measured not less than a quarter of a mile. The boys raced ahead in the frolic fashion of human colts, yelling, leaping and throwing stones. Slowly the matron and her escort followed, far in the wake of the obstreperous juveniles.

"They are growing up like savages," said the mother, deprecatingly. "What shall I do with them? To teach them properly seems impossible. I am the parent of a brace of barbarians. Yet they are dear sweet boys—loving and brave. They despise meanness and never tell lies."

"Then you are the mother of nobles. They will be men—to-morrow. Plato truly says the boy is the most unmanageable of animals. Boys have an element of the cruel and ferocious. But we need not take this much to heart. They will outgrow the savage. We must not look for ripe fruit on green sprouts, nor for elaborate reason or virtue in children."

"Yet I cannot bear to have them grow up in wild ignorance."

"No; youth must be guided. No greater evil can befall a lad than to be left to do as he pleases. Yet in well-born children, such as yours, much may be trusted to nature. I rely on human essence. Freedom is the best school. I don't believe we are born with evil passions and base propensities. God made our faculties. The doctrine of total depravity slanders the Creator. The perfect man uses all, abuses none of his organs or energies. To educate a man is to give his hands, brain, and heart their maximum power. This can be done outside of academies. The free schooling out of school, which your sons now enjoy, is a discipline towards success in life. Those fellows will be of some account, depend upon it. The ancient Eastern wisdom said, 'Know thyself'; the new Western oracle says, 'Do something worth doing.'"

"How true and how encouraging," exclaimed the enthusiast at his side. "I wish Mr. Blennerhassett could hear your broad views. But I am not sure you are right in relying entirely on weak human nature. I was taught to mistrust the natural man. Is not conversion necessary?"

"In case the soul begins with a pure inheritance, I see no necessity for regeneration. We come into the world potentially complete. The thorough development of body and mind will furnish the world with a perfect man. The best education gives man's natural powers the right direction and the greatest efficiency. We must trust in what we are,—in our own selfhood. Give man elbow room, give him breathing space, liberty to think, feel and do. This is true living."

Mrs. Blennerhassett stooped to pick up a blood-red leaf. They were nearing the boat-landing. The way was overarched by spreading branches of gigantic maple-trees. The boys had wandered to the head of the island, two furlongs away.

"What of woman's education? Should it differ from man's?"

"No; I train my daughter as I might train a son."

"Are her thoughts like yours?"

"I put slight restraint on her thoughts or emotions. There is no sex in soul. Woman should be free as the free breeze singing in the leaves over our head, and ruffling the waves out yonder on the river."

"You grow eloquent. Is it the singing breeze or the rippling water that causes you to put your principles in language so poetical?"

"Do I speak poetically? That grand oak tree may shed Dodonian influence. It looks the king of trees—the emperor. These magnificent maples, robed and crowned in emerald, gold, and royal crimson, are the queens."

"I am glad you love the forest, and are susceptible to nature's subtile appeals. I don't like people who have no feeling for scenery, and are not affected by the sublime and beautiful in nature. Mr. Blennerhassett does not agree with me in applying such a test to judge one's friends by. He thinks I might be deceived, and says that very wicked folks may delight in very lovely scenes. In my opinion the good and the beautiful are in harmony, and a wicked heart seldom goes with an æsthetic taste. I may be wrong, but I like to think that souls which are thrilled by the stars and the mountains and the sea, and by such forms and colors as we now contemplate, must be the nobler and purer for the experience."

Burr listened attentively to this rhapsody. The melodious voice spoke on: "I never grow tired gazing on this landscape. Splendid!"

"Splendid!" echoed Burr.

A subdued rapture animated the lady's features and imparted fresh vitality of beauty to her breathing form. She advanced to the edge of the water, stepped upon the ferryboat, an uncouth scow, like a floating wharf, with stout railing upon the sides. From this platform she could take in a fuller prospect. The joy of admiration possessed her. She stood, self-forgetful, looking upon the gleaming river and the distant, gorgeous Ohio hills. Burr, lingering on the bank, a few yards behind, certainly took an intense human interest in the landscape, seeing in the foreground that symmetrical figure, with plump arm outstretched. To be the sole spectator of that unstudied pose was worth more than the Vatican and all the galleries in the world.

"See the bright sunshine, the soft shadow, the dim gold of the water, and the misty blue of the sky! Those magnificent hills seem not solid substance but piled clouds, yellow, and green, and scarlet. Can any other valley in the world show a more satisfactory picture, outlines as lovely, tints so delicate!"

"Nowhere else, in all my travels," murmured Burr, speaking from his point of view. "Nowhere have I seen so much beauty at a single glance. The picture is unrivalled."

"Do you say this in earnest or only to please me?" queried the frank gentlewoman, turning her face shoreward in time to see a pair of dark eyes regarding her with unaccountable ardor. Burr courteously proffered his hand to assist her from the pedestal, the deck of the scow. She accepted his aid, and lightly sprang to the damp sand of the beach, into which her foot sank deep enough to print a pretty track.

"Look out, you will soil your shoes; shall I remove the mud?" said Burr, taking out his handkerchief.

"No, thanks; it is only clean sand." A tuft of soft green grass furnished a ready mat, on which she wiped her small foot, not invisible to Burr while he modestly inspected the mussel shells and polished pebbles washed ashore by the plashing ripples. From the beach he picked a bone-like fragment resembling milky quartz. This he brought to the lady, who had chosen a mossy seat on the trunk of a fallen sycamore.

"It is a lucky-stone," she remarked. "It brings fortune."

"I will send it to Theodosia," said the finder, pocketing the treasure.

A pensive mood had succeeded the anxious wife's elation. She gazed across the river expectantly. Not a rowboat in sight, excepting a skiff lying alongside the scow.

"I fear he is having needless bother. How miserable! Our slaves are a burden, not worth the trifles they pilfer. I wish they would all run away, then we might have an excuse for flying."

"And could you leave your earthly paradise?"

"Yes; though I am attached to the island. I should regret to lose the trees, the river, the sky."

"Earth and sky stretch far. I sympathize with your feeling for the place. I told your husband it was like Bunyan's Enchanted Ground. Beulah, however, and the Delectable Mountains lie beyond the Enchanted Ground."

"More poetry!"

"Could I make verse, I would sing of October in the Ohio Valley, or of Indian Summer, which comes in November, don't it?"

She glanced up inquiringly. He held some leaves of pink paper covered with writing, recognizing which, she flushed.

"How did you come by that? Did he——?"

She made a motion as if to take the paper. Burr, pretending not to see the gesture, began to read in a low voice, infusing into the verse more thought and sentiment than it contained. His perfect reading gave the commonplace stanzas æsthetic effect. The authoress confessed their merit to her secret soul.

"I am vexed that Harman gave you that. It is silly stuff."

"On the contrary, it is literature. You don't know, madam, how good it is. I have a favor to beg; allow this poem to be printed in the Port Folio. I know the editor, Jo Dennie, and shall call and give him this copy when I reach Philadelphia. You will not deny me this pleasure?"

Confident that she would not take offense he slid the lines on Indian Summer into his breast pocket, to keep company with the lucky-stone. The situation had become riskily sentimental and intensely stimulating to Burr's disposition as a social trifler. He was reckless of consequences, vain of conquest over any woman, and scrupulous only to avoid failure in his amours. The more innocent and virtuous the victim, the keener and more careful was he in pursuit. To entrap unsuspecting game without exciting alarm he considered the most exquisite art of gallantry. What sport it was to entangle this superb creature in a web of invisible gossamer threads!

"Tell me more about your Theodosia. Have you a picture of her?"

The question and request smote the father's conscience with a momentary compunction.

"I will tell you all about Theodosia. I like to think and speak of her. She is my life, my soul, my ambition, my joy. Theodosia has no fault that I can see, no trait which I do not admire and love. She is——"

The sentence was stopped short by a startling cry—a scream. Madam Blennerhassett sprang to her feet, trembling, and saw Dominick running towards her. He fell at her feet exhausted, caught at her gown and gasped:

"Harman! Harman will drown!"

She took the boy's hand and made him stand up.

"Be a man. Keep calm. Speak plain. What is the matter?"

"O mother! He wouldn't mind me! He pushed a rotten, old leaky dugout from the sandbar and climbed in, with a piece of paddle, and got out so far that the current caught him."

"What sandbar? Which channel?"

"This side. The Ohio side."

The mother suddenly grew faint. Speech forsook her tongue. The trees vanished and the air was a blur, through which she saw a moving shape that looked the shadow of a human figure. All this in an instant. The swoon passed, the trees reappeared, the shadow took the form of Aaron Burr, tugging at a chain which fastened a skiff to a timber of the scow. A violent jerk wrenched out the strong staple that held the chain padlocked to the ferryboat, and the mother saw the colonel leap into the skiff, seize the oars, and launch out into midstream. This natural act, heroic in her esteem, she saw and her heart grew big with gratitude. She beheld another sight which caused at once a shock of hope and a shudder of despair. She had hurried to the deck of the scow to get an unobstructed view of the river both up stream and down. Dominick at her side uttered a wild cry. "There he comes now!"

"There he comes!" But where she could not at first make out. Dominick pointed to an object like a drifting log in the middle of the swift-flowing stream. The object—a wooden trough, not three yards long—carried one mariner, the venturesome baby, Harman. The tiny craft and its helpless passenger came into plain view nearly opposite the landing. Burr's boat was rapidly nearing the crazy dugout when the terror-stricken castaway, catching a glimpse of his mother, rashly stood up and called "Mamma! Mamma!"

"Sit down! Sit down!" shouted Burr.

"Keep still! Sit down!" screamed Dominick.

The distracted mother, to enforce obedience, added gestures to cries. The scared child, further agitated by these demonstrations, entirely lost self-control. His posture caused the unstable trough to topple over and the lad was plunged into the flood. The frothing mouth of a wave swallowed him. No; his doom was not sealed; taught by instinct or by pluck, the little fellow had the presence of mind to save himself by clinging to the capsized canoe. He held on tenaciously, drifting like a part of the treacherous log. Burr's skiff was in full chase a few rods in the wake. The mother watched the race, breathless, numb, with all-seeing eye. Her hands gripped the oaken bar fastened across that end of the ferryboat which was farthest out in the river and she stretched forward head and body, heedless of the down-tumbling mass of her loosened hair, reckless of everything but the fate of her boy. Her strained gaze kept focussed on the precious drift. Dominick wept aloud.

"What shall we do? What shall we do? Oh, if papa were only here!"

"Hush! Don't cry. Don't speak. What could your father do? Pray with all your soul; pray to Heaven that Colonel Burr may save your brother."

The aching eyes measured the diminishing distance between the two boats. It seemed to the mother possible, for nothing is impossible to faith, that by the sheer force of her projected will she might hold the child back from death. Even while she solaced her dread with this fancy the gliding log slipped free from the lad's tired fingers, and again the woman watching from the ferry gave up hope. She shuddered, closed her eyes, and pressed her forehead hard against the oak railing.

"O my God, my God! our darling is gone!"

At this crisis Dominick believed he saw what his mother, bowed and blinded, did not see—a miracle working. Pantingly he cried out "Mamma!" The only response to his call was a moan and the despairing words, "Drowned! My baby is drowned!"

"No! No! Look, mother! See there! Colonel Burr won't let Harman sink! Look! He has him by the arm, he has pulled him into the skiff. It did good to pray."

Burr, acting as any man would have done under the circumstances, having rescued the child without danger to himself and with little difficulty, was a demi-god in the estimation of the Blennerhassett family. Little Harman's misadventure, the enforced long swimming in rough water, the two duckings and their disagreeable effects on throat and lungs, left him in a wretched condition, but by no means in need of a coffin. His teeth chattered, his hands were blue, he whimpered, but when Burr landed him high, if not dry, on a bed of gravel at the river's margin, the drenched youngster mustered heroism enough to comfort his mother by piping out the assurance, "I'm all right."

"Thank God you are, my sweet pet, and thank Colonel Burr for saving you," sobbed Madam Blennerhassett, while she gathered the shivering young one into her bosom, and almost extinguished the life that was left in him with tears and fondlings.

Burr took off his coat, and wrapped it about the protesting infant, and carried him home, a feat as glorious, in the mother's mind, as his historic exploit of bearing Montgomery's body from the battlefield. Dry clothing, doses of cordial, vigorous chafing of body and limbs, by many loving hands, soon brought the patient "round." By the time his father came home, soon after the rescue, the urchin declared he was "well" and would rather upset again in the river than be rubbed and hugged any more.

The endeavors of Blennerhassett to trace Honest Moses proved futile. That the slave had escaped by water, the balance of testimony rendered probable. Abe Sheldrake, in all likelihood, had coaxed the negro away.

When night came, Blennerhassett, holding curtain council, as usual, with his wife, dutifully repeated to her what Burr had revealed of the Wachita speculation, and asked advice. She made up his mind promptly. "Share the enterprise, if you think he really wishes your co-operation. Do whatever he desires. We can never cancel our debt of obligation. We owe him everything. He saved your namesake's life."

Convinced by this womanly reasoning, Harman, senior, could scarcely sleep nor wait till morning, so eager was he to lay his influence, his purse and his property at Burr's disposal. Before the clock struck five he was out of bed, and the quavering of his flute disturbed the colonel's slumber. No sooner was breakfast over than the conference on the land-purchase project was resumed, Madam Blennerhassett participating.

"You propose," said Blennerhassett, "to buy forty thousand acres for forty thousand dollars, and you have the pledge of Mr. Clarke, of New Orleans, and of your son-in-law, Governor Alston, that they will stand surety for you. I will gladly make a third with these gentlemen."

The offer was graciously accepted as a trust betokening future transactions of mutual profit. Further confidential discourse ensued, and it was agreed that Mr. Blennerhassett should assist the cause by writing, under a pseudonym, a series of essays for the Ohio Gazette, on the commercial interests of the West, indirectly favoring disunion.

Burr congratulated himself on the successful issue of his second campaign in the Enchanted Ground. He had won the islanders. Promising to keep the Blennerhassetts apprised of the progress of his plans, he bade old and young good-bye, and departed for Philadelphia, the lucky-stone in his breast pocket.

XIV.: A LARGESS OF CORONETS.

   The story leaps over a period of nine months. The winter of 1805-6 disrobed the trees on Blennerhassett's Island and spring again reclothed them. Wild violets once more sprinkled the glades and a new flowering of rosebushes in the garden fronting the house increased the fame and complacency of Peter Taylor. Another July plumed the maize, where the plough had obliterated Fort Byle. At last came imperial August, and with the glowing month returned Aaron Burr, his designs ripened, his enthusiasm culminant. The silent wheelwork of conspiracy had now been in operation for upward of a year. The arch complotter was of buoyant heart and happy tongue, for he came accompanied by Theodosia, the loved associate in whom he reposed absolute trust, the good familiar whom he invoked when all other spirits failed him.

   Theodosia made no enemies. Her beauty attracted and her amiability retained the devotion of men, the friendship of women. Nature had lavished upon her those rare, delicate, elusive qualities which go to make up that top flower of evolution, the woman of fascination, a creature indefinable, like poetry. In New York, city and State, she was a reigning belle, caressed by society; she had been named the social queen of South Carolina, under the title of la Sainte Madam Alston. To Theodosia, his only child, whose education he directed, whose opinions he had shaped, whose sympathies were always with him, right or wrong, who after her marriage scarce less than before, looked to him for guidance, as he to her for implicit approval—to her Burr confided every detail of his plan of conquest, every vaulting anticipation of sovereignty. "Be what my heart desires and it will console me for all the evils of life. With a little more determination you will obtain all that my ambition or vanity fondly imagines." In this strain was the father wont to appeal to the daughter, by letter. His thoughts, like carrier pigeons, were always homing to her. Hounded by obloquy, accused of murder, when he fled from Richmond Hill after the duel at Weehauken, he sought security and absolution in the sanctuary of la Sainte Alston's house in Charleston. "You and your boy will control my fate," he had exclaimed. And now, when the seek-no-further hung ruddy on the orchard bough, and the wild bigonia swang in air ten thousand trumpets of red gold, Burr reappeared at the White House of Blennerhassett, according to his promise, bringing with him Theodosia Alston and her little son.

   "Behold," said Burr to Madam Blennerhassett, in the ornate style he had learned to use when addressing her, "this is my Sheba, to whom I have not told the half of your bounty or the king's wisdom. She has not come to prove him with hard questions, but to repose under his almug trees. My daughter, Mrs. Alston."

   "She is no stranger to my thoughts," said the hostess, embracing and kissing Theodosia. "Our minds have met in our correspondence. How very young you look, and how like your father. And the baby resembles you both."

   "No baby," chimed in Burr, cheerily. "He has grown a big boy, have you not, Gamp? Harman must take charge of him and teach him to build forts, play Indian, and go buccaneering in a dugout."

   "What a funny name!" returned Harman, partly in self-defense.

"Gamp is his short, everyday name," explained the colonel. "It means grandpa. But on great public occasions, when Gamp is on his dignity, we must address him by his full title, Don Gampillo."

Theodosia valued the lightest foam-bell on the wayward surface of fashion, yet had escaped what Burr condemned as "the cursed effects of fashionable education," and it is needless to say that conventional ceremonies were waived between herself and the lady of the isle.

"You came from Marietta; were you agreeably entertained there?"

"They lionized father."

"No; they 'snaked' me. I was dragged into service by main force."

"Father means that they insisted on his drilling the militia. We arrived on a muster day, and nothing would do but he must prove the right to his rank by explaining the manual of arms. There are ever so many old soldiers in Marietta."

"Yes, I drilled the men as soldiers, in the afternoon, and she drilled them as captives, in the evening, at the ball; a modified fan-drill made them march to her orders. Theodosia danced with at least a dozen distinguished citizens."

"How many wives, widows, spinsters and school-girls did you lead up and down?" retorted Theodosia.

"I don't know; I didn't count; I dance for politeness, not for victory. My daughter has a drop of coquette's blood in her veins; though where it came from I can't imagine. Do you recollect, Theodosia, the remark of the Mayor of New York, when he invited you to go on board a war vessel? 'Don't bring any of your sparks on board, for they have a magazine and we should all be blown up.'"

To the ponderous mind of Mr. Blennerhassett, the feather-light badinage flying back and forth between Mrs. Alston and her sire, smacked of unbecoming levity. He had looked up a topic for weightier talk.

"Did you name your daughter, may I ask, Colonel Burr, anticipating extraordinary rank for her? Had you in mind Theodosius the First, called the Great, or the second and more famous emperor of the name? Eudosia was a Roman empress, wife of the second Theodosius. She was a poetess."

The man of facts glanced significantly toward his own wife, and resumed:

"Perhaps you had the name Eudosia vaguely in your memory when you chose the name Theodosia. History informs us that Theodosius was controlled by his wife and by his sister Pulcheria."

"My Theodosia was so christened," answered Burr, "because I like the name. It sounds well. I like it the better now that you tell us it suggests a possibility of imperial sway. Who knows what may come to pass?"

In anticipation of the third advent of Burr to the island, many letters had been exchanged, and it was arranged that, for some months at least, "the close contriver" of the vast enterprise in hand should remain with Theodosia and Don Gampillo in the mansion, the island being an eligible point for headquarters. Around this nucleus the hitherto mobile elements of his design should crystallize into definite shape.

What had Burr been doing in the three-quarters of a year which had elapsed since he bade good-bye to the Blennerhassetts in October? He had employed most of this time in Washington and Philadelphia, writing hundreds of letters, sounding the President, tampering with civil and military officials, intrigueing with the British Minister, in a word, organizing a conspiracy, which he believed would eventually give him a dictator's unlimited command over a magnificent realm. To Wilkinson he had written in cipher many letters, one of which ran thus: "The execution of our project is postponed until December; want of water in the Ohio rendered movement impracticable; other reasons rendered delay expedient. The association is enlarged and comprises all that Wilkinson could wish. Confidence limited to few. Though this delay was irksome, it will enable us to move with more certainty and dignity. Burr will be through the United States this summer. Administration damned, which Randolph aids. Nothing has been heard from the brigadier since October. Address Burr at Washington."

The "brigadier" remained in St. Louis until late in August, when he was ordered to collect his force at Fort Adams, now Vicksburg, and in September he transferred the troops to Natchitoches on the Red River, to defend the western frontier against threatened invasion by Spaniards beyond the Sabine.

Arlington, ignorant of the treasonable designs of Burr, but zealous against Spain and ambitious to share in the conquest of Mexico, had volunteered to make a tour through Kentucky and Tennessee, to Natchez and New Orleans, on business relating to the Wachita lands, which Burr had purchased. The Virginian started on his long journey early in autumn.

To Blennerhassett, Burr dilated in confidential privacy:

"All is planned and ready to be put into execution. The iron is red on the anvil. At least five hundred men are pledged to me, and I have on my memorandum books, the names of as many thousands who will join us when wanted. Every man is to receive one hundred acres of the Bastrop land, besides his regular pay. All are to present themselves armed and equipped, when boats are provided for their transportation and the signal is given. I have told none of the volunteers exactly what will be expected of them, but all are devoted to us. Of prominent persons now in our confidence and ready to act at a word from me, I could name scores, besides yourself and Governor Alston. Among our confederates are Commodore Truxton, the British Minister at Washington, and the Catholic Bishop of New Orleans."

"Have you considered," asked Blennerhassett, "what might be the condition of our venture, in case General Wilkinson fails to second your designs against Mexico?"

"Even that contingency, I have taken into account, though we do Wilkinson injustice to suppose it possible that he will fail us. Our plans are excellent. If the Mexican string should break—as it will not—the Wachita string, which you helped to twist, will send a sure arrow to the mark of our high calling. Failure, my dear sir, is not possible. The gods invite to glory and to fortune."

In collocutions of this tenor, Burr, adapting himself to the moods of his sedate ally, unfolded his purposes. The philosopher heard, acquiesced, and accepted the part assigned to him in the execution of the great business. Blennerhassett's temperament, however, was such as to check, in some degree, the full flow of Burr's exuberant speech. It was always with constraint and reservation that the latter communicated himself to the head of the house. Not so when in familiar converse with Madam Blennerhassett and Theodosia; uninfluenced by the dampening presence of the husband, he poured out his innermost cogitations, assurances, optimistic surmises. The three were in perfect accord. One evening they were seated in the seclusion of the library. The children had gone to sleep, upstairs, Harman and Gampy under the same chintz canopy. Mr. Blennerhassett, detained in Marietta on an errand relating to the affairs of the Wachita company, probably would not reach home before morning. Theodosia asked for a sentimental ballad.

"Not a love-song," said Burr, "but something heroic—a battle hymn or a stirring march."

"Will you both agree to a compromise and accept some half-romantic, half-pious verses which I composed and set to music? The colonel will remember the incident which suggested the lines."

The harp was brought in from the adjoining room and Mrs. Blennerhassett sang her original lay with the following chorus:

"No longer in Enchanted Ground
Thy lingering feet delay;
Beulah's borders lie beyond,
Rise, pilgrim, and away!"

"Bravo! Well sung and well said!" Burr emphasized this verdict by clapping his hands, and Theodosia joined in the applause.

"Your allegory is no enigma to me," said she. "There is this difference between us and Bunyan's pilgrim—he left the Enchanted Ground forever—you can return when you please, and as often as you please. Our promised land takes in and retains all the desirable property on the road to the Shining Gates, and we shall possess the Happy City without crossing that awful river."

"Ah, yes," quoth Burr, in low, earnest tones, as if uttering the authentic revelations of an oracle. "This life we are sure of. The part of wisdom is to live as if to-day were our only day, and yet provide for an infinite series of to-morrows. Dum vivimus vivamus. When we are established in Eldorado, in my new Spain, my Mexican Cathay, in our Woman's Paradise, where the tree of knowledge is not forbidden—then will you think the Golden Age is come again. Ours will be no feeble Republic, no Union of States loosely tied together by a filament; we will have a firmer government, a strong, liberal, enlightened Empire. That grand old Roman word, Imperium, pleases my ear. I will extirpate the Spanish power from the continent, and establish a throne at the old capital of the Montezumas."

"Father!" asked Theodosia, catching fresh enthusiasm. "The Western States will hasten to cast off their allegiance to the East, whose rulers have traduced and persecuted you, and they will claim the protection of your banner?"

"That, my daughter, is for the future to decide. If the States west of the Alleghanies, exercising the sacred right to secede, renounce the Union, and seek to join our Empire, we shall welcome them."

"New Orleans would be your capital city, at first, would it not?—and our home would be there and not in Mexico?"

"As you choose, Theodosia," replied Burr, caressing his daughter's hand.

"And you know, my dear Mrs. Blennerhassett," chimed the radiant favorite, "you will be a duchess and your husband Minister to the Court of St. James; Mr. Alston is Chief Grandee and Secretary of State."

In such airy nothings did the credulous women put their trust, entranced by the voice of the sanguine charmer. Their faith in him was absolute. For was not this daring leader wise and powerful and popular? Had he not been Vice President and had he not come within one vote of being President of the United States? He was cheated out of that one vote. Why should he not establish an independent government in that great West, through which his tour had been as the triumphal progress of a beloved monarch?

In the course of the talk, Madam Blennerhassett chanced to mention the name of Miss Hale.

"Ah! Miss Hale!" said Burr, his eyes brightening, "I have often thought of that splendid woman in connection with our court. She must be approached on the subject, madam, and by you."

Theodosia glanced at her beautiful friend with a look of jealous surprise.

"There are difficulties in the way, Colonel Burr," answered the lady of the island, coloring deeply. "Her father, one of the most influential citizens of Marietta, entertains a violent prejudice against you."

"We want nothing to do with him, then," said Theodosia, sharply.

"Ah, my dear child, there are many good men who do not know Aaron Burr as you know him, and whose political antipathies we must tolerate. But his antagonism need not prevent his peerless daughter from accepting the coronet of a countess."

"Countess!" exclaimed Theodosia. "Is this young woman a sorceress? Has she bewitched you?"

Mrs. Blennerhassett glimpsed her own image in the mirror. "Perhaps Colonel Burr anticipates raising the countess to the throne of an empire."

"I will have a voice in that, and so will Gampy," declared Theodosia, with a merry laugh. "The succession is fixed."

"You should become acquainted with Miss Evaleen Hale, Mrs. Alston. Evaleen is my most intimate friend. She is now in much anxiety on account of an uncle in New Orleans, a wealthy merchant, who was stabbed in the back by a drunken Spaniard. The wound caused partial paralysis, and Richard Hale desires his niece, who has always been a favorite, to come and attend him in his helpless condition. Several urgent letters have decided her to make the tedious and not altogether safe journey down the river on a barge, which is to start from Marietta within six weeks."

"Did I not say the gods are propitious?" broke in Burr; "Miss Hale is going our way at an opportune time. Her rich uncle will bequeath her his fortune and go to Heaven; she will take the money and go to Mexico."

XV.: THERE BE LAND RATS AND WATER RATS.

At some distance north of Natchez, and below the third Chickasaw bluff, near the bank of one of the bayous, which seem to run from rather than toward the Mississippi, a band of desperadoes had established a temporary abode, sometime in the year 1805. They were an organized league of robbers, bandits of stream and shore, preying on the solitary traveller who rode through the pines on the way between Natchez and the North, and more frequently surprising the unwary farmer or trader, transporting goods to market by water. A number of flatboats laden with the plunder of the freebooters lay moored close to the north shore, under the shelter of the overhanging bushes, at the distance of a mile or two up this narrow but deep creek. Farther up the bayou, and a few rods from it, in an obscure hollow and almost hidden by cypress trees, from which depended curtains and streamers of gray Spanish moss, stood a log building, the rendezvous of the outlaws. The structure was low and long, consisting of three huts so joined as to look like one.

If a wandering stranger chanced upon this out-of-the-way and forbidding lodge, he might read, painted on a board over the entrance of the cabin, the words, "Cacosotte's Tavern." Within the dingy front cell or bar-room of the prison-like shanty, one evening in the early part of September, five or six persons had assembled. They were rough characters, engaged in drinking and coarse talk. One of the company was a negro. The only woman there was a big-bosomed, brown-visaged, black-eyed, savage looking creature not destitute of wild charm. If long hair be a glory to woman, then was this dark female covered with glory—her glossy mane fell far down over her shoulders and back. Whether she was English, French, Spanish or Indian, or a mixture of these, neither her looks nor her speech determined. She spoke little, and took small interest in what others said, yet seemed to regard herself as the responsible mistress of the premises. She had charge of the housekeeping, such as it was, and dealt out tobacco and liquor. It appeared, however, that she was not the sole manager of Cacosotte's Tavern. Cacosotte himself claimed superior authority, as proprietor.

Cacosotte was a most ill-favored knave, of a purplish yellow complexion and mumbling speech. His comrades called him "Sott" for brevity, or "Nine Eyes," not because he had nine eyes, as he had only one, but because he boasted he had "gouged" nine enemies—that is, dug out their organs of sight with thumb and fingers.

Two of the select party were Burke Pierce and Abe Sheldrake. The least conspicuous individual in the room was a sullen, suspicious, cat-footed man, who kept his slouch hat pulled over his face, and sat apart, smoking a pipe. He was a fresh recruit, and had given his name as Turlipe. Only one day had he been sworn to the service of the brigands, promising to do the bidding of their chief, Burke Pierce.

Expurgated of much grossness and profanity, the discursive talk, in this hiding place of criminals, may be partially reproduced as follows. The chief is first to speak:

"There was a French hunter, who hid a lot of skins in a clearing close by Red River, at a place called 'Cache la Turlipe.' Are you akin to that Turlipe?"

The sullen man shook his head.

"Have you been in the business before this?"

"More or less. I have run on the river all my life; was patron on a Kentucky boat."

"'Tain't a business, it's a profession," put in Nine Eyes. "But the profits ain't wot they used to be, and the risks is greater. I mind the time, cap, when Cave in the Rock, up the Ohio, jest below Massac, was the headquarters of the biggest men in our line. Wilson's boys done their wreck'n along by Hurricane, and stored their stuff in the cave. They carried on the Last Night-Cap game when they could get hold of a good customer."

"What's that?" asked Sheldrake. Cacosotte grinned and winked at Pierce.

"Your pard's too green to plug, cap."

"Don't you Pittsburgers drink a las' snort before goin' to bed? Well, can't you see the pint? They played the game this-a-way. Lodgers at the House of Natur often oversleep themselves—couldn't wake up. There was a sign down on the river bank, jest under the cave—'Wilson's Liquor Vault and House for Entertainment.' The durn fool farmers comin' down the river with their produce had a cur'osity to see what the plague a vault was like and how Wilson's liquor tasted. They clim up, got drunk, were put to bed, and——" Here Nine Eyes went through a pantomime suggestive of throat-cutting. The black man, who stuck close by Sheldrake's side, twisted in his seat, and showed the white of his eyes. Sott, delighted to note these signs of trepidation, went on with his reminiscences.

"Cap'n, you ric'lect Colonel Plug, that carried on at Hurricane Island and the mouth of Cash, after Wilson was nabbed? Plug was a Yankee, and a hell of a smart un. He was from Pensylvany. His real name was Fluger, but we called him Plug and his woming Pluggie. I got into a misunderstanding with the colonel about that lady; colonel allowed her and me was too thick, so me and him, begad, had a rough-and-tumble, and that's how I come by this here." He pointed to his empty eye-socket. "Pluggie was one of your furriners—jest like Mex, but not so pooty."

"If she was half as handsome as Mex," said Pierce, "I don't wonder that you gave your right eye for her."

To this compliment Mex responded by resentfully casting the contents of a whiskey glass into Pierce's face and breast, whereupon the men all laughed loud.

"You dasn't smoke the senorita, cap," mumbled Nine Eyes, aside to Pierce.

"The purtiest wench I ever seen," babbled Sheldrake, "was the one me and you spied through the winder at Blennerhassett's, that night Aaron Burr and his pard from Virginy stopped over. I'll never forgit how we snuck up and seen them two sparkin' on the sofy."

"Right you are, Abe; and I was a damned fool not to nab her that day, when she was pullin' posies in the woods——"

"She'd of been a screechin' armful for you, Burke, with them shiny yaller curls of hern flyin' over your shoulder!"

This side colloquy, Mex heard, and her countenance glowered. Noiselessly she came to the bench upon which Palafox sat, and pressed close to his side. The captain, without looking at her, mechanically stroked her long mane.

"Fine wimming," remarked Sott, sagely, "is like pizen vine, pooty and clingin,' but pesky dangerous; I hadn't better teched Pluggie. A woming of your own is worse yet. She spiles on you, and you can't sell her as you do a hoss or a nigger."

Pierce looked at the darky, who grinned self-consciously.

"How many times over has Abe sold you since you ran away from the island?"

"Seben times," answered Honest Moses, and chuckled. "Mistah Sheldrake done sell me fo' cash, plunk down; I fugitives back to him, and he done sell me agin fo' mo' cash. I gits mo' money out o' speculatin' in dis heah darky, dan Scipio and Dan'l can git ahookin' watermillions fo' a hundred yeahs."

Nine Eyes took up his dropped theme.

"The hoss trade," said he, "the hoss trade don't pay here as it did with Wilson's boys. There's more risk in gettin' rid of a hoss than in sellin' the same nigger ten times over. Say, cap, is your new man onto the pass words and signs?" The speaker flung out three fingers of his left hand, to which signal Pierce responded by an answering gesture. But the captain had grown tired of Cacosotte's conversation. He ordered Mex to bring him another drink. Then, turning to Sheldrake, he said in undertones:

"Abe, you mind that trip from Pittsburg to Massac. Recollect what I told you that night? Before many weeks there's going to be a chance for men like us to make our fortunes as easy as floating down the Mississip."

The jealous eye of Mex was constantly dartling, and her ear was alert to catch every syllable Pierce uttered. She paid no attention to Sheldrake, who responded guardedly to his chief's overtures.

"Captain, if you know a safer way, I'd like to learn it. Now that the army is at Fort Adams, and soldiers is comin' and goin' from St. Louis to Orleans, we can't do nothin' widout bein' found out by Gen'l Wilkinson."

"Wilkinson," growled Pierce, with an oath. "Do you suppose I am afraid of his big names, 'General' and 'Governor'? Jimmy Wilkinson owes me money, and he owes me an apology, and he's got to come down from his high horse, or I'm a liar. Eh? Sheldrake, did you ever hear anybody call me a liar? Did you, Mex? Did you, Sott? ever hear any one say Burke Pierce was a liar or a foot-licker?"

"I'd hate to be in the place of the man that 'u'd dare," swore Cacosotte, hastily. He had noticed the excessive drinking, with dread of the probable consequence.

"I guess you would hate to rile me up even if you was a great general, dressed in uniform, and with gold epaulettes and buttons all over. I want to say to you, Abe, and you, Sott, and you over there smoking your pipe, you raw recruit—I've got in my pocket, what will bring the brigadier to terms. Bet your souls on it! Bet your black hair, Mex! Say, you raw recruit, where's your pal? Where's the feller you said wanted to join us? Open you jaws!"

"He is down on the boat," said the sullen man, rising and emptying his pipe. "I'll go hunt him."

"You'll be back and bunk here, or will you sleep on one of the boats?" asked Cacosotte.

"If it's all the same to you, I'll come back and bunk here."

The night was advancing, and the great white owls were beginning a dismal hooting in the cypress trees. Upon reaching the place where the boats were moored to the bushy shore of the bayou, Turlipe called:

"Hello, are you there?"

A man scrambled up the bank in response to the call. The two Spaniards sat upon the bank of the bayou, and held a long consultation in their native language. It was eleven o'clock when Pepillo, alias Turlipe, arose to go back to the tavern.

"You needn't come along, Vexeranno; I can do the job without help. Only stay here and wait. Have the skiff ready to carry us down stream as fast as we can row. I may come back any time in the night."

While Pepillo, squatting on the ground beside the sluggish estuary, imparted to his accomplice the details of a bloody design, Palafox in the tavern waxed more and more violent. He menaced an imaginary foe with clinched fist. Mex tried to soothe him. He sat for a while in sulky quiet. Rousing again, he ordered a candle, opened a leathern wallet, and took from it a number of soiled papers. His hand shook.

"Look here, Abe, these old letters are worth more money than all our plunder will fetch."

No response came from Sheldrake, who had prudently retired to the second compartment of the row of huts opening into one another. The whimsical Cacosotte had named the several rooms "Hell," "Purgatory," and "Heaven." Sheldrake sought a sleeping couch in "Purgatory," whither Honest Moses had preceded him to "flop" in a corner.

Mex stood behind the captain while he sat fumbling over a timeworn manuscript, peering at its hieroglyphics in the dim light of the candle. Cacosotte, yawning, rubbed his one eye, and groped his way to a slumber-rug in "Heaven." Then Mex put her brown hand timidly on the shoulder of Palafox.

"One in woods—not nab—no! no!" she said, shaking her head violently and frowning.

"What you jabbering about now? Don't you see I'm busy?"

"Woman through window—not big Mex—look so!"

She wrinkled her features, and shrank down mimicking a dwarf. The robber now understanding her speech and pantomime, slapped his thigh, guffawed exasperatingly, and, roughly pushing the jealous barbarian aside, "No, Mex, she don't look like that. Tall, white as your teeth, smooth and purty as an antelope——"

"Mex purtier. Mex not Choctaw—Castiliano. Look blood." She nipped her forearm with sharp teeth, and crimson drops oozed.

Palafox laughed.

The mane shook, and the wild eyes glared behind the half-drunken man, who continued to fumble his papers. Before long his hand fell heavily, his eyes closed, and he slept. Mex shook him by the shoulders. Partially aroused, he looked up, thrust the papers and the wallet deep within a breast pocket, quitted the bench, and lay down on a pallet in the corner of the room. Mechanically he deposited a primed pistol under his blanket, ready to hand. Soon he was snoring.

An hour went by. The new recruit had not returned. Mex scarcely kept her eyes open where she crouched, Indian fashion, on a buffalo robe, behind the bar. Nine Eyes had bolted the outer door before retiring. Eleven o'clock; the white owls were at their boldest, hooting lugubrious serenades to the answering wolves. Pepillo was at the cabin door, trying the latch. Mex heard the sound, got up, and unfastened the bolts.

"Sh!" said she, and giving him the candle, pointed to the back room; then drowsily resumed her nest on the buffalo robe. Pepillo took the feeble light; nodded, but did not immediately follow directions. He set the candle down upon the floor in front of the bar, so that its faint flicker, unobserved by the woman, made objects barely visible in the room. This done, he shuffled his feet slightly to apprise the half-conscious guardian of the ominous house that he was obeying her orders, and vanished in the rear darkness. The dead hush of sleep now reigned over the place. So it seemed, but the stealthy Pepillo was wide awake. He remained motionless, breathless, hidden in the gloom of the second cabin. At length he reappeared, took up the candle, stood awhile listening, then moved cautiously to the edge of the counter, behind which the woman slept in her lair. He peeped over to assure himself of her complete somnolence. Satisfied that Mex would not likely be roused by any slight disturbance, he stole to the front door and undid the fastenings so softly that not a creak of the bolt sliding from its staple was heard even by his own quick ear. But when he swung the door open, providing for his ready escape, the hinges gave out a complaining sigh. The sound was faint, but it startled Mex. She raised her drowsy head, and through the mass of sable hair tangling over her half-open eyes, peered out from behind the shelter of the bar. Pepillo had drawn a poignard and was tip-toeing toward the sleeping captain. Mex gave a catamount cry. Palafox started up, pistol in hand, none too soon to avoid the deadly blade of the assassin. "Palafox!" This one word was all Pepillo uttered. In the act of springing to stab, he leaped to his own death, shot through the head. As he fell, the poignard, escaping his relaxed grasp, rang on the floor. Mex, who tiger-like had sprung from her covert, snatched up the shiny weapon, and fiercely stabbed it into Pepillo's lifeless breast.

Cacosotte and Sheldrake, roused by the report of a pistol, hurried in, staring amazedly at Palafox, Mex and the fallen Spaniard.

"Carry that out," ordered Palafox, nodding toward the body. "Tie a stone to its neck and chuck it into the bayou." The two men obeyed. "Get something, Mex, and wipe up that puddle," pointing to the blood on the floor. "You must keep Hell clean."

The wild creature, quivering with ferocious passions, put a fondling arm around the manslayer.

"Mex wake captain. Help kill. Mex Castiliano. Nigger wench—no!—Injun squaw—no!—Your woman."

XVI.: A PATRIOT NOT TO BE TAMPERED WITH.

Four men on horseback were nearing the country house of Colonel George Morgan, a veteran of the Revolutionary War, living near Cannonsburg, Pennsylvania. Two of the riders were Colonel Morgan's stalwart sons, and they were escorting Aaron Burr and Colonel Dupeister, one of Burr's confederates. The ex-Vice-President rode beside the elder brother, who was an officer of high rank in the militia.

"Speaking of Washington County, General Morgan,—are the people of your neighborhood prosperous and contented?"

"We are a community of farmers, very prosperous and hopeful. Our population is increasing rapidly. We have no cause for discontent."

"What is the condition of the new college at the county seat? I am told there is an educational awakening among your young men."

"Yes; we are proud of Jefferson College; the institution is now in its fourth year, and is flourishing beyond expectation."

"You call it Jefferson College; it was named for Washington and Jefferson, was it not? The lesser star is in the ascendant, and twinkles amazingly now that the greater has set. Don't you think we are too much be-Jeffersoned?"

"Thomas Jefferson is an able man," was the commonplace reply, spoken bluntly, and accompanied by a look of irritation at the sarcastic question. Burr, conscious of the disapproval implied in the officer's curt answer, managed to change partners so as to ride abreast of the younger brother, Thomas, while Dupeister spurred forward and engaged John in discourse on stock-raising and the prospect of crops. With Thomas, an aspiring soul, in the flush of those discursive hopes and speculations which make ambitious youth restless, Burr employed his usual suasive arts, hopeful of winning a recruit.

"Your brother and I were speaking about the outlook here, for enterprising citizens. What are your pursuits? Are you a Knight of the Plow?"

"No, sir; not permanently; I am trying to make a lawyer of myself."

"That's good in a way, as a stepping-stone. The study of the law disciplines the mind, but is not profitable otherwise. The practice is a species of servitude, often a servitude to inferiors, for doubtful reward. Politics is better, but not the best."

"What is the best?"

"That depends upon the man. Some are easily contented. But I am not sure that contentment is a trait of a noble mind. I used to own negro slaves in New York. They were contented. To rest satisfied is the virtue of slaves."

"Yes, the niggers are contented, generally speaking. You were about to say what you think the best profession."

"The best for an ignorant African may be bondage to a good master; the best for you would be something more aspiring. I regard military life—the profession of arms, as the highest and most independent."

"Not in times of peace."

"This is not a time of peace, Mr. Morgan. We are on the eve of war and stupendous conquests. I speak advisedly. I am a soldier myself. You have heard rumors of war on the Sabine?"

"Yes; rumors. The Morgans are a military family, also; and I feel fighting blood stir in me when I read about the Spaniards."

"Does the red stuff boil? Your blood is right. You can't help it. If you, or your younger brother—I believe you have a brother besides the general?"

"Yes, George. My name is Thomas. They call me Tom."

"Tom, eh? Well, then, Tom, I was about to say if you and your brother George——"

"Spur up, gentlemen, we are leaving you behind," shouted General Morgan, looking back. "We are within half a mile of father's residence."

"More talk another time," said Burr, not finishing his sentence, and the pair, urging their horses to a faster gait came up with the others. Just then the party met a robust countryman who saluted the Morgans, as he trotted by on a skittish colt.

"What a fine-looking fellow! I wish I had ten thousand just such vigorous young giants!"

"What would you do with them?" the general asked. "Ten thousand would form a large colony. That is one of the farm hands. Those are our barns and the house is just beyond."

On their arrival, Colonel George Morgan stood on the porch to receive his guests. A well-preserved old gentleman, he might have said:

"My age is as a lusty winter,

Frosty, but kindly."

His career had been eventful, aggressive, venturesome, and romantic. At the close of the Revolutionary War he felt aggrieved because of the non-payment of claims he held against the Government. Odium attached to his name on account of his procuring from Spain a grant of lands west of the Mississippi, on which he founded the village of New Madrid. He had expressed sympathy for Aaron Burr, whom he regarded as a much-abused statesman. The prevailing sentiment among army men justified the duel with Hamilton.

After dinner, the visitors repaired to the parlor, where was held a conversation in which Burr was the principal talker. More virulent and less discreet than usual, he indulged in witty flings at public men and roundly censured the administration, not aware that most of his auditors heard him with impatience. Colonel Morgan attempted to introduce another theme, by referring to the rapid spread of population westward.

"When I first went out West on my New Madrid scheme, there was scarcely a family between the Alleghanies and the Ohio. Now we have three great States. We shall have to remove the National capital to Pittsburg."

"No, never," said Burr, positively. "In less than five years you will be totally divided from the Eastern States."

"God forbid! I hope no such disaster will come in my time."

"Disaster or no disaster, the Union will split, or I am a false prophet. How can it be otherwise? What is to hold us together? Congress is a shadow, the executive a phantom too thin to cast a shadow. With two hundred armed men I could drive Congress, the President and Cabinet into the Potomac; with five hundred I could take New York City. Ask Colonel Dupeister!"

Dupeister nodded an emphatic yes; but not so did bluff John Morgan.

"By God, sir, you couldn't take our little village of Cannonsburg with five hundred men!"

"That, then, is because you are at the head of the militia. I should want your Cannonsburgers in my five hundred. But I talk too loud. Pardon; let us get out of doors; I would like to go the round of your plantation and look through the mill. Tom, won't you oblige us?"

While Tom piloted the visitors about the place, the eldest son took occasion to speak a word of warning to the father. "You may depend upon it, Colonel Burr is here on a secret errand to you. He will open himself to you this night. He is engaged in some suspicious enterprise in which he wants Tom to join."

"What foolishness you talk, my son; Aaron Burr is a soldier, a loyal man who fought for his country's flag; he would never do a dishonorable thing; certainly he would not approach me with improper suggestions."

"Then my precaution is needless. Yet have your mind prepared. Tom revealed to mother some of Burr's words, which, if seriously meant, are not such as you will approve."

The subject was dropped, nor was any more said in the course of the afternoon on political topics. About nine o'clock the guests were shown to their bedrooms and the members of the family also retired, except Colonel and Mrs. Morgan. They were in the habit of sitting up late, the wife reading aloud to her husband in the quiet hours, after the rest of the family had retired. The book which engaged their attention was "Modern Chivalry," the first novel written and published west of the Alleghanies. They had reached that part of the story which describes how Teague O'Regan was treated to a coat of tar and feathers. The passage amused the grizzled colonel, and he listened eagerly to the words:

"By this time they had sunk the butt end of the sapling in the hole dug for it, and it stood erect with a flag displayed in the air, and was called a liberty pole. The bed and pillow-cases had been cut open, and were brought forward. The committee seized Teague and conveyed him to a cart, in which the keg of tar had been placed."

"That's correct," interrupted the veteran. "That's the way to do it. Read on."

Mrs. Morgan proceeded: "They stripped him to the waist, and, pouring the tar upon his naked body, emptied at the same time a bed of feathers on his head, which, adhering to the viscous fluid, gave him the appearance of a wild fowl of the forest."

"Ha! ha! I've seen that done more than once; the author describes it well. What next?"

The tall Dutch clock in the next room, after a grumble and whirr, struck eleven, as if reproving the old couple for sitting up so late to read a novel. Before the ringing of the last stroke died away, footsteps were heard descending the stairs. Mrs. Morgan gave her husband a significant glance, saying in a low tone, "John was right; you have it now," and hurriedly left the parlor by a back door. She had scarcely made her exit when Burr entered, with a lighted candle in his hand.

"What, Colonel Burr, are you still up?"

"You yourself are not yet abed. Do I intrude?"

"Oh, no, no, no! Take a chair. We have a practice of sitting up to read after the children have gone to bed. John, Tom, and George are the children. Mrs. Morgan has been reading aloud from 'Modern Chivalry.'"

"A clever book," said Burr, "very lively and ingenious."

"I agree with you. The story gives a true picture of scenes which the author must have witnessed in Pittsburg. We were laughing over the account of Teague's adventure with the tar-and-feather committee. Poor Teague! He should have been spared. His persecutors were guilty, and not he."

"That's the way of the world, Colonel Morgan. Often the wrong man is blackened with the tar of calumny. You and I have not escaped. Pardon me for claiming a few moments' conference. You have had much experience, know many public men, and are a judge of human nature. I wish to ask your counsel."

Morgan blinked hard at the candle, nodding his willingness to listen, and tapping nervously on the table with his middle finger. Burr drew from an inside pocket a long, narrow memorandum book, written full of names.

"This is what I call my Roster of the Faithful," he said, and looked searchingly into the face of the patriarch, whose glum reticence puzzled him.

"Umph! Faithful to what?"

"To their principles and their friends. I assume that we know each other's history and political views. Colonel Morgan has not always had justice from those clothed in brief authority; you have freely exercised your individual right to better your worldly condition; you were not acting inconsistently as a citizen when you entered into perfectly proper contracts with a foreign 'power.'" The speaker paused, for he was aware of a bristling antagonism on Morgan's part.

"Yes," grunted the old gentleman, "perfectly proper."

Burr hesitated, more and more doubtful of his ground; but his was an audacious nature. Turning over the leaves of his memorandum book, he asked,

"Do you know Mr. Vigo, at Fort Vincent, a Spaniard?"

"I ought to know him! I have every reason to believe he was deeply involved in the British Conspiracy of '88, the object of which was to separate the States. The design which Vigo abetted was nefarious, yes, sir, nefarious! yes, damnable! The same disloyal and turbulent spirit caused the Whiskey Rebellion here in Pennsylvania, which General Dave Morgan, General Neville, and I crushed out. The diabolic sentiment of disunion survives yet; Pittsburg tolerates a set of seditious young men, a nest of vipers of the Vigo species."

The general checked his tirade, noticing that Colonel Burr put the list of names into his pocket with an air of hurt dignity.

"You must excuse me; I would not be rude, but soldiers use plain terms. You asked me about Vigo, and you have my opinion."

"Your feeling in regard to Colonel Vigo certainly is not flattering to the gentleman. I regard him as a deserving patriot. May you not be in error? Give the devil his due. You must not tar-and-feather the wrong man."

"Yes, yes, yes! I mean to be just. The devil should have his due. As for Vigo, I want no dealings with him, or with any of his stripe. I shouldn't hesitate to recommend a coat of tar-and-feathers and a ride upon a fence-rail for him. And if I should ever detect Tom, or any of my boys, even sympathizing in any attempt to dissolve the Union, I would warm the pitch for them myself, as sure as there is a God Almighty."

"Good-night," said Burr, stiffly, and went upstairs to bed. The next morning he and Dupeister rose early, and were on the way to Pittsburg before their host was well awake. The sons arose betimes, however, and bade the parting guests good speed.

After breakfast, Colonel Morgan summoned his family and told what had passed between himself and guest.

"He has insulted us by assuming us to be traitors at heart. Aaron Burr is meditating dangerous designs. I will write to the President."

Tom and George, impressed by their father's stern seriousness, and now realizing the presumably infamous nature of the service to which temptation might have lured them, hung their heads. The mother held hers high. Her jealous patriotism was alarmed and quickened. No taint of disloyalty should infect her sons, nor should word or look of hers hint weak misgiving of their rectitude. She assumed the Morgan stock incorruptible, and spoke proudly as befits an American matron. There was no tremor in her voice, no indecision in her steady eye, which flashed the sentiments uttered by the tongue.

"The brightest name in the world's history is that of George Washington—the blackest that of——" She paused, and her youngest son pronounced the detested name, "Benedict Arnold."

"Benedict Arnold—yes; his sword was recreant, his heart false. In all our annals only this one officer's record is polluted, God forbid the rise of a second traitor. But, my sons, if treason should again threaten liberty, I know on which side the Morgans will be found."

So speaking, this true "Daughter of the Revolution" unlocked a colonial chest containing relics cherished as credentials of family honor, and took from it a banner, tattered and rent in battles of the Revolutionary War. Dark stains consecrated its stripes and stars.

"This is my only brother's blood. My boys are patriots by inheritance from two lines of ancestors; you will always stand faithful to your Mother Land as to me, your mother."

"Have no fear for us, mother," said Tom. "The Morgans and the American flag stand or fall together."

"Amen!" added the deep voice of the husband and father.

XVII.: THE BUSY NOTE OF PREPARATION.

"Peggin' away, all hands, eh? I never heard such a swishing of handsaws and banging of hammers; you make more noise than ten navy yards. How you getting along?"

"Not so briskly as I could wish; we are under contract to finish fifteen of these large batteaux, besides a sixty-foot keelboat by December."

"Sassyfax! Fifteen? What for?"

"To carry colonists down the Mississippi to the Wachita lands. The big keelboat is to transport provisions."

"You don't say! Now, how many men will them fifteen boats accommodate, when they're done? 'Bout thirty to a boat?"

"Yes; thirty or forty; we calculate the whole fleet will carry five hundred men."

"Five hundred! I'll swan! Do you think they'll ever drum up five hundred lunatics for such an expedition?"

"You'll have to ask Mr. Blennerhassett about that. My business is to build the boats, not to man them."

"Right you are, mister; every man ought to mind his own business, and I'll bet a pewter toothpick you understand flatboats, even if you don't know anything else. I will speak to my friend Mr. B. in regard to his end of the business, for I see him coming. That's him walking this way along the shore; you can know Harman a mile off by his stoop. 'Fore I go, I'll take a squint at the extra-fine ark they tell me you are fixing up for the family—I mean Blennerhassett's own folks. Blame my buttons, if I don't always hate to pronounce that larruping long name Blennerhassett! Byle is a heap shorter and better name. I s'pose you reco'nize me, don't you? I'm pretty well known in these parts. Plutarch is my Christian name. Did you ever read Plutarch's Lives? I didn't write 'em, but I'm living one of 'em. I ought to know you, you're dadblamed face is familiar, but bejiggered if I haven't let your last name slip my mind."

The ship-carpenter, to whom these questions and comments were addressed, had resumed his work, not paying any attention to Mr. Byle, who, finding his words unheeded, gave no sign of discomfiture, and went on talking to himself in the friendliest manner.

"Here we are, five miles above the mouth of Muskingum, making batteaux to go five million miles south of the jumping-off place of creation! Will I go with you, friends and fellow-citizens? No, not by a jugful. Do you think Byle is a plumb fool? I wouldn't mind going on a voyage with the madam and the young ones, but not with such an addle-pate as the near-sighted. Nor with Colonel Hoop Snake! No, there's no use arguing; I tell you once for all, I won't go. I'd no more trust in him than I'd trust you, old Muskingum, not to undermine your banks at Spring flood. A felon who would murder Alexander Hamilton—what crime wouldn't he commit? I'm consarned sorry for the family over on the island; ain't you, neighbor? Yes, you; I ask you, Mr. Jay Bird, singing and chattering to yourself on the willows. How are you?"

"Pretty well, I thank you," replied a stoop-shouldered pedestrian, who, drawing near, had recognized the voice without distinctly seeing the person of Byle. "How are you?"

"I was talking to that other jay, Mr. B. But I'd ruther talk to you. I'm hearty. How's all your kith an' kin? I thought of coming down to the island, to see you, but now you're here, I'll put off the trip a week or so. Jist say to the boys I'm making a crossgun for 'em. Give my regards to your better half, and I wish you'd tell Scipio that the melon he sent me was luscious. I'm here on a kind o' important business; came clear up from town to inquire about this expedition. You're managing the colony matters, and you're the codger to give me the real facts."

Blennerhassett, who had undertaken to use every means in his power to induce men to join the proposed colony, suffered Byle's fraternal confidences with as good a grace as possible, hoping to enlist a useful factotum.

"I will gladly give any information you desire in regard to the Wachita settlement, and our plans for the winter."

"I knowed you would. I told what-ye-call-him—the boss carpenter so. He allowed I'd best ask you for the particulars, and it's fair to you that I should. You pay for all this lumber and hammering and sawing, out of your own pocket; you have a right to answer questions. How much is the whole caboodle going to cost you?"

"Perhaps that question is not pertinent to our present interview. I presume you wish to learn the conditions of our agreement with volunteers?"

"That's so; you don't presume a speck; I wish to learn all about everything. What are the conditions?"

"We pledge ourselves to pay every man who goes with us fair wages, and to give every one a hundred acres of the Bastrop land. Each man is to provide himself with a blanket, a good rifle and a supply of ammunition."

"What do you want with rifles? Do you expect to have to fight?"

"Not necessarily; all pioneers need guns. Did not the forty men who settled Marietta bring rifles and ammunition?"

"I swow you've got me, Mr. B. No man can keep house without a gun, I admit that. I'd as soon go without my head. I've got a gun, all right, and a blanket. What else?"

"That is all. Be ready on the first of December with your blanket and rifle, and we'll provide for your other wants."

"Well, that looks fair. But let me give you a bit of advice before you start. Don't you go at all. As sure as my name is Byle, you'll be sorry for yourself and Maggy, as you call her, if you do go. You mustn't git mad at me, Harman, for speaking out plain. I'm friendly to you and your folks; don't like to see you put upon; and I consider it my goshdurned duty to tell you that this here Colonel Beelzebub is making a cussed fool of you. I'd have no hobnobbing with a hoop snake. Don't trust ary shape of a sarpent in your apple-tree. You know your eyes are not as long-ranged as some. This is God's truth with the bark off. He don't talk to Adam in the Garden in our days, but I sh'd think you'd hear what mortal men are saying. You're a readin' man—haven't you come across what the press wrote about that scorpion in your bozom?

'Oh, Aaron Burr, what have you done?

You've shot our General Hamilton!

You stood behind a bunch of thistles,
And murdered him with two horse-pistols!'
Excuse my interest in you; a full kittle will bile over. I've lots and slithers of United States information that ain't to be found in your green emerald Erin, no more than snakes is."

Blennerhassett was in doubt whether to consider himself insulted or befriended. He had misgivings concerning Burr and the colony. Common sense told him that Byle might be more than half right.

"Do you know anything of the far West?" he asked. "Report gives out that it is a marvellous region."

Byle had a spice of mischief in his composition. He could not resist a humorous impulse to gull a credulous foreigner.

"Maybe I can give you some curious facts not generally known. I'm a sort of bookworm myself. I've nosed the Coon Skin Library. Did anybody ever tell you of the Missouri salt mountain? a mountain of real salt one hundred and eighty miles long, and forty-five broad, white as snow, and glittering in the sun? No vegetation grows near it, but a river of brine runs from its base. I have a chunk of the salt."

"Wonderful, wonderful!" ejaculated Blennerhassett.

"Isn't it wonderful? But not so contrary to nature as the shoe-and-stocking trees that grow at the headwaters of this Muskingum River."

"That seems impossible—shoe-and-stocking trees, did you say?"

"It does sound improbable, I admit, but seeing is believing. I've pulled half-grown shoes off one of those trees with these hands. I don't expect you to take my word. I didn't believe the story myself at first, and can't bring my mind to believe what my own brother Virgil told me he had seen and tasted—the Whiskey Lake in Southern Kentucky."

Gullible as he was, Blennerhassett looked incredulous. Byle's expression was serious to solemnity. His big blue eyes vouched for his perfect sanity.

"Now, I must go," said he, turning away; "I've a heap of things to do and folks to see before sunset. Good-bye."

Genuine kindness had prompted Plutarch to blurt out unsought counsel, and he hurried away, congratulating himself on having discharged an obligation to his conscience. His long, swinging strides propelled him to Marietta in half an hour. Near the court-house he met a gentleman, whom he accosted, taking him cordially by the hand and inquiring, "Isn't this Squire George Hale?"

"George Hale is my name," returned the gentleman, reservedly, and disengaging his fingers from the strong grip of the tall man.

"Yes, you are the individual I took you to be, and no mistake. I seldom forget faces, though I get names crooked now and then. Your name and your corporosity go together; you look hale and hearty! I never was picked up but once, in shaking hands with a stranger, but that once was enough. Before I knew what I was about I shook hands, last May was a year ago, with—I vow I'm ashamed to tell you who with. Are you going home, Mr. Hale? Is Miss Evaleen in town now?

The first time I met your daughter she was down at Blennerhassett's! The last time was here in Marietta, out by the big mound. Is she as well as usual?"

Mr. Hale stared in blank bewilderment. He first surmised that an escaped lunatic was face to face with him. Yet there was coherence in the strange man's speech, and nothing wild in his looks. In fact, Mr. Hale had frequently seen the gaunt, gigantic figure of Plutarch dodging about the town, and had heard his name spoken as that of a very eccentric person. Like everybody else who was brought within speaking distance of the oddity, the sedate New Englander was at a loss how to behave toward him. Plutarch was never at a loss. Detecting a hair lodged on the squire's shoulder, he picked it off, and winked.

"A pretty long hair, old man, to be found on your collar. I hope it came from one of your own women-folks. What's the last word from Captain Danvers? When is that knot to be tied, anyhow? If you'll give me an invite, I'll be there, sure. I told young Burlington—no, I mean Arlington—all the facts just as they are."

"You did? What facts? Who is Arlington?"

"Don't you know Arlington, Squire Hale? Is it possible? Well, well, well! Now that explains a good deal. These young folks are as sly as a gallinipper. You have to keep your eye skinned to see all that goes on, by land and river, and especially on islands. There's not a bit of criticism to be made on Evaleen's conduct, nor on Arlington's. He couldn't help himself, no more than a fly in a honey-pot. The minute he saw your gal, he fell slap dab in love with her. The poor feller was nigh about dead for love the day we sot on the summit."

"What rigmarole is this? You sot on the summit? Arlington? My daughter? Tell me simply and briefly what you mean."

"I mean briefly and simply, Mr. Chester Arlington, of Virginia, came here to spark Evaleen; he as good as told me so; that is, I am satisfied he did; it stands to reason and the nature of a gentleman! Secondly, I told him it was no go. I said to Chester, 'You must hunt up another sweetheart, for Leeny Hale is engaged. She is going to be married,' says I, 'to Captain Warren P. Danvers.'"

"You told this Mr. Arlington that my daughter was engaged to marry Captain Danvers?"

"Yes; that's what I told him. Isn't that so? Of course, she couldn't marry 'em both at once, and I wanted to put Chester out of misery. That's why I broke it to him. You may tell the betrothed, as you call it, I mean your daughter, as much or as little as you please; but if that young woman had saw how that young man looked when I told him he couldn't have her, I do believe she might have shook Danvers and took Arlington. That's what I had to say to you, Squire Hale, and now I've said it, I feel easier. I must be going. Mighty fine weather, this! Good-bye! Gals will fool their daddies."

Away went Byle, about everybody's business, and home hastened George Hale, not so much to tell Evaleen what he had heard concerning herself, as to learn from her the solution of the mystery of Arlington, Danvers and "the summit."

Day after day, and week after week, the shipwrights plied their tasks with saw and hammer, with adz and mallet, constructing the vessels to convey men and goods down the river in the

Winter. A large purchase of provisions, ham, bacon, flour, whiskey, was made in advance, and various accoutrements were secretly collected in anticipation of Burr's enterprise.

New gods had been set up in the sequestered home of the Blennerhassetts. The Lares and Penates there honored were not now the images of Emmett and Agnew, not the names of dead ancestors, but the living spirit and example of Napoleon and the magic word Empire. No longer could the harpsichord charm or the strings of the viol allure. The music-books gathered dust in the alcove, and the "Iliad" stood unopened on the shelf. Instead of rambling in the woods, or strolling on the banks of the Ohio, or galloping to Marietta clad in a crimson cloak, or giving banquets or balls to entertain the admiring gentry of Belpre, Madam Blennerhassett spent busy days and anxious nights working and planning for a potential greatness, a prospective high emprise. A change had come over the spirit of her dream. She had ceased to feel an interest in domestic duties and pleasures; she neglected the simple cares of the plantation, took no satisfaction in binding up the bruises of her slaves, or curing their ailments with medicine and kindness; the talk of Peter Taylor about flowers and fruit, or of Thomas Neal, concerning pet heifers, and new milk and butter and cheese, became tedious; the jokes and laughter of the farm-hands and dairymaids she heard with irritation; nor could the prattle and play of her romping boys divert her mind from the one absorbing theme—the descent of the Mississippi, the conquest of Mexico, the creation of a New World. In close daily communion with Theodosia, she dwelt not in a white frame house on a woody island of the Ohio River, not in the present; but in the future, and in a marble palace in the splendid domain of Aaron I. The two enthusiastic women, allied in a common cause, inspired alike by the experience of wifehood and maternity, similarly ambitious, passionate and imaginative, reciprocated each other's sentiments and strengthened each other's resolution.

The summer flew away. In October, Governor Alston visited the island. Many consultations were held in the gilded parlor and in the hushed library; more plans were divulged, more pledges given—and Burr departed never again to cross the threshold of the house on the island. Theodosia and her husband and child went to Lexington, Kentucky, whither they were accompanied by Blennerhassett.

Left alone in the great ghost-white house, its mistress wandered from room to room, restless and melancholy. The boys were at play on the lawn; she could hear their mirthful shouts. She felt a vague longing, like homesickness, and yet she was at home. Wearily she sat down in her husband's study chair in the quiet library. She glanced round at the books, the apparatus, the musical instruments. Everything presented an unnatural aspect. Startled by the snapping of a string on the untouched violincello, she uttered an involuntary exclamation, rose, and went up close to the portrait of her husband. But owing to the dimness of the light or the sadness of her mood, the features, instead of smiling, seemed to regard her with a mournful gaze. A sense of desolation overwhelmed her. Endeavoring once more to fly from herself, she called her children. They came, and she kissed them, putting an arm around each.

"Dominick, do you want to go away, away to Mexico, and become rich and great?"

"No, no, mamma; I want to live here forever with you and papa."

"We both do," iterated Harman. "We both do."

"Colonel Burr will be there to take care of us all. He saved your life, Harman, and he loves you, I am sure."

"Mamma, he loves you, but he don't love papa."

The mother blushed, and a big tear rolled down her cheek.

XVIII.: THE VOYAGE OF THE BUCKEYE.

George Hale, yielding to the importuning letters of his brother Richard, consented that Evaleen should risk the peril of a voyage to New Orleans. Luckily the young lady was to have travelling companions. One of her uncle's letters contained this passage: "Ask your father to hunt up my old-time friend, Dr. Eloy Deville, to whose care and medical skill I owe my life. He still lives, I believe, in Gallipolis. Tell dear old Frenchy and little Lucrèce—I suppose she is now almost grown—that I have unearthed family facts much to their worldly advantage. They must come to this city, to the French quarter. My discoveries are astounding, but credible. Eloy may inherit a fortune. I will see that he loses nothing. My advice is, come at once. The doctor and his daughter will be good company for you on your voyage."

Eloy was easily induced to do as his friend and former patient advised.

"Oui, monsieur, certainment shall we depart most glad from ze log hut. Lucrèce, ma chère fille, dance for ze delight! We shall, on ze to-morrow, us depart, on ze joli bateau with ze mademoiselle; quick shall run ze stream, row ze oar, fly ze sail—we come right away to ze excellent long friend of your father. Ze honor and ze felicity shall be to me to serve mademoiselle for ze sake of her divine uncle, for ze own beautiful sake of ze fair angel."

The Buckeye, on which Evaleen and her friends took passage, carried a cargo for the Southern market. The crew numbered eight picked men, commanded by Eli Winslow, a talkative Vermonter, with none too much experience on the Mississippi, but overstocked with self-confidence.

Such clothing and household goods as he thought essential to take along for himself and daughter, Doctor Deville packed in old trunks, or tied up in bundles, all of which were deposited on the river bank, six hours ahead of time. The luggage included a basket of Bordeaux, a surgeon's case, a chest of medicine, and a violin in a green bag. At last the barge hove in sight, announced by the echoing of the boat horn. The fidgety Frenchman gave Lucrèce a kiss and almost dislocated her arm by pulling her after him to the landing. A long half hour he had yet to wait before The Buckeye was made fast to the posts on the bank and Eloy was helped on board, still holding fast to his chère fille. It would require a volume to report the conversation which enlivened the many days' journey down the Ohio and the Mississippi. The doctor chirruped constantly. He knew a little of everything, and talked much of nothing, very amusingly. Often he sang French songs, often played dance tunes on the violin, now and then took an enlivening taste of wine.

Past Cincinnati, past Louisville and the Falls of the Ohio, past Shawnee Town, past Fort Massac, and Diamond Island and Battery Rock, the vessel moved slowly and steadily along. The voyagers were told that the lower river was infested still by wreckers, one scene of whose frequent depredations was Wolf Island. Captain Winslow discoursed much on the state of Western commerce, and the dangers which menaced travel.

"A great part," said he, "of the Territory of Mississippi, stretching from Tennessee to Natchez, is unbroken forest, inhabited by Indians, and infested with wolves and panthers. We shall see no sign of civilization on the eastern shore until after we have skirted six hundred miles of waste, howling wilderness."

At length they came to where the Ohio is merged and lost in the Mississippi. The turbid onhurrying volume of mighty waters heaved and foamed, as if troubled by furious, disturbing forces working below. The boat shuddered and its strong joints groaned in the strenuous hug of the river.

"Hereafter we can proceed only by daylight," said Winslow. "We shall have many dangers to contend with—a succession of chutes, races, chains, and cypress bends. You will see no end of this gloomy forest. There are plenty of rattlesnakes, bears, and catamounts in those jungles, doctor."

"Par bleu! Ze catamount shall stay in ze jungle and delight heself with her family amiable. We not shall invite heem to tea. Are no inhabitants in this wilderness?"

"A few whites and some Indians. See those squaws digging wild potatoes for food."

"Do many boats go to New Orleans?" asked Miss Hale.

"Yes, ma'am; all sorts from a birch canoe to a full-rigged ship. Hundreds are lost. We are now coming to a wreck-heap."

The passengers saw an immense huddle of drifted logs, and the broken timbers of shattered boats, and entire scows, rotting, half-submerged, or warping high and dry on top of the hill of confused ruin. The sight of these hulks, abandoned to the grinding eddies, added a sense of dread to the weary anxiety already felt by the girls. The progress down the Ohio had been tedious; how much more so the interminable windings on the Mississippi, and the long, lonesome nights, made sleepless by the cries of birds that flit in darkness, and by the howls of wild beasts. Evaleen's nocturnal fears, when the barge lay moored, were not so well founded as were the apprehensions which daylight renewed, of disaster on the treacherous flood. The more she learned of the river, the more she realized the risks of each day's navigation.

"Young ladies, see! That is a sawyer; an ugly one, sticking its sharp horn up to hook us. I don't mind a danger which shows above water; but your sleeping sawyer is the mischief to be dreaded."

"What's a sleeping sawyer?"

"If I could point out the nasty thing, I wouldn't dread it; a sleeping sawyer does its sawing under the surface. We are liable to run on to the point of one any second."

"Mercy! Do you think we are coming on a sleeping sawyer now?" asked Evaleen.

The captain hoped not, and directed attention to another phenomenon not of a nature to induce feelings of security.

"What do you see away down the river?"

"Do you mean that low island?"

"Yes, an island and not an island. Wait until we drift nearer. You will see river moss and rank water plants growing over the surface, but it is not part of the firm land; it is a wooden island."

"How? A wooden island?"

"Just so. We shall see many such. Logs and all kinds of drift lodge against the upper part of a stable island or peninsula, and the accumulated mass grows into a great raft matted together by roots and vines. The whole thing, driven by winds or currents, sometimes swings free from its anchorage and drifts away. Then it is called a floating, or wandering island."

Lucrèce, who had been sweeping the circle of the horizon with the seaman's glass, caught far to the northward, the glimpse of a sail.

"I see away up the river what looks like a leetle black house, with a white thing on the roof."

"That boat," said Winslow, "is miles and miles behind us; it is above the second bend. Let me look.—She carries a square sail, amidships, as we do, but she is not a barge. Stop, I know what she is—there's a flag at the top of the mast—she must be a government transport, coming with troops for Fort Adams or the Natchitoches country."

Lucrèce caught a quick breath and asked eagerly:

"Troops from St. Louis, think you?"

"Most likely, miss."

Evaleen's interest was also excited, but she kept silent, and soon slipped away alone into her cabin. The French maiden remained on deck a long time, watching the transport, whenever she could bring it within the field of vision.

"The soldiers, will they perhaps overtake us?" she inquired, turning her brilliant big eyes to Winslow.

"Like enough; but you needn't be afraid of the reg'lars; they won't molest us."

"I haf no fear; I haf curiositee."

At last Lucrèce returned the glass to the captain, thanked him, and slowly sought her companion, keeping a small, brown hand just over her heart to make sure that a precious letter which she carried there was still safe and in its right place.

Lucrèce and Evaleen had readily fallen into sympathetic relations. Days of chattering on deck, and nights of prattle before falling asleep on the same couch, left few girlish secrets unexchanged. The scant experience of Lucrèce's isolated life had brought her only a small stock of personal doings or feelings to disclose. Yet, up to the hour of her coming into the private cabin, after seeing the government transport, she had not told the very thing which she knew would most surely enlist the sympathy of Evaleen or of any other woman.

Now, Lucrèce was moved to pour out her simple heart in maiden confidence to Miss Hale, her only female friend.

"Ah, ma sweet Evaleen, I no more shall be able to hide my feeling—I tell you, right as it happen, the beginning and the end of my story, that no person shall know.

"One day, at Gallipolis, a young soldier there stopped. He came in the mail-boat, and the reason he entered our cottage was one of the boatmen had been hurt by accident—his arm crushed, poor man—and as papa is known by all as a surgeon, the young officer—he was capitaine—he run up the hill to our log cabin. I tell him mon père, alas, was not at home—mon père had gone that day to Belpie. The very handsome face—how shall I say?—was upset by disappointment—teach me if I use the wrong word. I saw the sad regret and was grieved also. He looked in my eyes with a kind pity for the hurt boatman, and quickly I spoke. 'Monsieur, I, also, can use the instruments of mon père, and wrap the bandages. Always I assist. Mon père names me his aide. I will go and dress the hurt arm.' The young man did not say no, but his eyes were full of doubt, very much in doubt of me. I took the surgeon's case, and we made haste to the mail-boat. How they all did stare and stare! I had handled the sharp knives, and my father had taught me perfection. Instantly I did the operation nécessaire, the brave captain much helping. Then the gallant soldier brought me home, carrying the case, and, oh, my Evaleen, how shall I say, he kissed my lips, say 'Forgive,' and went away. I have see him no more."

As Evaleen listened to these naive sentences, her expression grew more and more troubled.

"Kissed you!"

Lucrèce nodded.

"At Gallipolis? A captain? Do you know his name?"

"His name—oh, yes, I know his name—Warren Danvers."

Evaleen's lip quivered. A shade of anxiety and pain saddened her countenance.

"I should resent the insult," she said coldly. "Have you told me all?"

"No, my sweetest sister; I confess to you now my great, precious secret. Alas, I give my heart that day. I love that only man."

"You love him? This is the silliest tale I ever heard. Let us go out and breathe the fresh air. Absurd! Do you fancy he loves you?"

"He has written me one letter of love—here it is."

Lucrèce drew a tiny note from her bosom and went with Evaleen near the prow of the barge to take the evening breeze. The first pale stars were barely visible in the clear sky.

Lucrèce unfolded the missive, and held it up in the dim light, but she did not know that tears were blinding Evaleen's eyes.

"Sometime, Lucrèce, but not now, I will tell you a story of foolish love to match your own. We are all alike, and we all hope against reason."

"No; there is no reason, no wisdom, no prudence—only love. Yes, yes, something more, as I see the only star that shines there above the dark trees, and seems to die and live again while we look at it. I see the hope that my soldier loves me and will be faithful."

On the sixth day after leaving the mouth of the Ohio, the boat had passed the third Chickasaw Bluff, and was within fifty miles of Natchez, when blue-black clouds suddenly overcast the sky, and a violent storm burst upon the river. Buffeted by opposing forces, the Mississippi soon began to fume and rage like a wrathful brute. The three passengers were on deck.

"How wicked the river looks under this indigo sky!" said Evaleen. "I wish we were ashore. There must be extreme danger in such a high wind."

"There is always danger on the Mississippi, but such gusts soon blow over. We are safer in midstream than near shore. I'll manage the boat, never fear. You and Miss Deville had best go into the cabin before the rain comes upon us."

The girls had scarcely found shelter when a volley of big drops swept, rattling, over the deck. Soon the waves rose so high as to bury the running board of the barge. The cotton-wood trees along the shore were twisted and torn up; blinding spray and rain filled the dark air. The captain saw his vessel in danger of drifting upon a wooden island, and could not decide whether to steer to the right or to the left of the obstruction. Voices from the eastern bank of the river were heard, shouting through the storm.

"Sheer clear of the island! This is the safe channel! Row in close to this side! There's a bayou here!"

Winslow could not see the men who gave this warning, but he was relieved. The halloo and answering shouts were heard by Lucrèce and Evaleen. Regardless of advice, and wind, and rain, they returned to deck. The men, unable to steady the barge, lost presence of mind; the captain knew not what orders to give, but finally commanded,

"Lower the yawl, we will try to make fast to a tree. Quick! Steady! Four of you jump in! John, take charge of the cordelle; can you row, doctor? We need help."

"Certainment. Do not fear, my two brave daughters; this good shower shall refresh ze atmosphere."

He sprang into the yawl with the others, and seized the oars. The barge was driven and sucked toward a revolving eddy. Evaleen, observing the consternation of the rivermen, felt a sudden shock of terror.

"Lucrèce!" she cried, grasping the French girl by the wrist. "We are lost! We shall drown! The men can do nothing! How the boat creaks and trembles!"

Lucrèce was preternaturally calm. She took Evaleen protectingly in her arms.

"Have no fear, my sister. Mon père shall not let us perish—he has the strong rope. And see! see, is there not somebody who could come to our aid?"

Evaleen gazed through the driving haze, and saw, tossing on the rough water, a skiff which seemed to be making toilsome progress toward the doomed craft. Farther up the stream she thought she could discern the party in the yawl, striving to reach shore with the cumbersome cordelle. Pole, nor oar, nor rudder could save the Buckeye from the fury of the eddy. The slender craft, sixty feet in length, was whirled round and round with dizzy rapidity. The violence of the down-pull at the vortex broke her in the middle. All on board fled aft, to the highest deck, an elevation peculiar to barges. There remained the forlorn hope that the men in the skiff might approach the sinking wreck. This they did. They pulled alongside the half-hull, and with great difficulty and risk succeeded in taking the girls aboard. Three of the four boat-hands on the barge at the time of the disaster perished in the funnel of the eddy. One swam ashore. Evaleen devoutly thanked the Divine Power for her deliverance. Lucrèce crossed herself. The French girl's anxiety was now all for her father. She did not see the yawl, though it had landed.

"Mon père! O mon père—mon pauvre père!"

"He'll turn up, mam'sel," said a voice she did not like. There were two men in the skiff. Lucrèce now observed their appearance closely. A look at the features of the man who had spoken confirmed a reviving impression that he and the ribald boatman who had insulted her from the deck of Burr's flatboat at Gallipolis were the same. He affected not to identify her, but kept gloating eyes on Evaleen.

"You needn't feel a bit afraid, young ladies; you are in trusty hands. Our business is to save property and to rescue folks. We will row you to a safe place, and then come back and help the men pick up what they can of their wrecked goods."

Evaleen saw floating barrels and boxes, part of the cargo of the Buckeye. She also noticed skiffs putting out from shore.

"Them is some of our organization coming to save goods. This here eddy is a dangerous place for boats."

"Why did you direct our captain to pass this way, if it is a dangerous place?" asked Lucrèce.

"Oh, the island over yonder is a damned sight more dangerous, ain't it, Abe?"

"You are not rowing direct for the shore. I shall be very grateful to you, gentlemen, if you land us at the nearest point and assist our friends who are out on the water in a yawl."

"Be easy, miss; we'll look after your friends by and by. I reckon they can take care of themselves, though."

"Ladies fust, and gents next," interjected Sheldrake, leering at Evaleen. "We know how to be perlite to women. Don't we, cap? Specially to purty women. The young lady is right when she calls me and you gents, eh, cap?"

"Shut your gab, and mind your oar," answered the chief.

What object had these unknown watermen in conveying their unwilling passengers away from communication with Captain Winslow and Doctor Deville? Evaleen could not hide her dismay. Lucrèce grew desperate.

"Will you stop the boat, sir? I beg it as a favor. I must go back to mon père. He will think us drowned. I must find him."

"Keep cool, miss. We will help you to a place where you will be taken good care of, by nice folks. You can stay there and rest yourselves, and get a bite to eat and a glass of cordial, while we go back to look after the salvage."

Five minutes more and the skiff was brought to rest beside a scow loaded with damaged merchandise. The abducted women were hustled to the shore.

"Come along, miss; this way."

Thus speaking, Palafox, going ahead, almost dragged Evaleen by an obscure path to Cacosotte's Tavern. Lucrèce followed perforce, convoyed by Sheldrake. When they reached the threshold, the chief outlaw kicked the door, which was soon opened from within. The frowning face and bold bosom of Mex fronted the captives. With one hand she flung back the tangled hank of her long black hair, while the light of her black eyes shone full on Evaleen. The side glare cast on Lucrèce was less vicious.

"Mex, here is two fine ladies that will stop in our house a while," said Palafox. "Treat 'em to the best you've got. Take mighty good care of 'em till I come back, Blackie, or you'll hear from me. Put 'em in number three, there's most light there, and it's safer. Tell Sott, when he comes back, to keep his nine eyes on the front door, to see that nobody that oughtn't to gets in or out."

"One apiece for us, eh, Mex?" added Sheldrake.

The kidnappers departed, after fastening the outer bolt of the door. Mex, sole custodian of the unwilling guests, scowled upon them, in silence. Evaleen came to her with appealing looks.

"Please unlock the door and let us go. Here, take my purse. I will give you more if you will set us free—all I have. You are a woman; have pity; let us go."

Mex grasped the silken purse, keeping her eyes steadily on the beautiful pleader.

"You window woman?"

Evaleen, nonplussed, ventured to nod acquiescence with these unintelligible words.

"White antelope?"

The captive nodded again, in dumb perplexity, eager to encourage any sign of human kindness on the part of the wild being into whose power she had fallen.

"White Mex teeth." She showed her sharp incisors, presenting an aspect of fierce scorn.

"Castiliano. My home. Come."

The laconic hostess accompanied these words with a gesture, beckoning the young ladies to follow her, and led the way through the second room, to the heavy wooden portal of the third.

"Mex let lady out."

With exulting hearts, the girls heard this promise. The dark woman opened the door and motioned them to enter, which they did. Mex then slammed the door, and bolted it upon her unlucky prisoners.

XIX.: ARLINGTON'S RIDE.

Chester Arlington set out from his Virginia home for the Southwest, carrying in his brain many anticipations, memories, and dreams, having slight connection with his nominal duties as Burr's business agent. He hoped to swell his own fortune by speculation in Wachita land; certainly he was eager to be among the first to march into Mexico when the signal for invasion should be given, openly or secretly. Moreover, sheer restlessness and love of adventure prompted him to ride over the hills and far away.

As he proceeded westward along the Old Wilderness Road, through Cumberland Gap, into the heart of Kentucky, he had plenty of time for meditation. The varied prospects continually appealing to his eye mixed their images with pictures in his memory, especially with recollections of his journey down the Ohio. The interesting route over which he was now passing had been marked out by Boone and the early pioneers. Of the eighty thousand or more inhabitants living in Kentucky at this time, nearly all had come West on horseback or on foot. The famed region—the hunting ground of the Indians before the "Long Knives" invaded it—retained the chief features of a primeval forest. The settlers' houses were cabins in the clearing.

The Virginian's meditations were broken in upon by various diverting sights and sounds. His attention was attracted by some picturesque hunter, dressed in buckskin pantaloons, fringed jacket, broad yellow belt, and wolfskin cap, and carrying a long rifle; or, perchance, he exchanged good-humored remarks with a wayfaring rustic who proposed to swap horses. He wended his way through the Blue Grass region, through Lexington and Frankfort, and southward into Tennessee. Arlington found keen enjoyment in what he saw and heard, though never quite losing from consciousness a haunting memory of the Lady of the Violets. He read with curiosity the tavern signs, wondering what relation such names as "The General Washington," "The Sign of the Wagon," "The Seven Stars," "The Golden Bull," "The Red Lion" bore to the character of the entertainment advertised by the several symbols, for Chester never failed to revive at meal times a hearty regard for victuals and drink. The table fare in Kentucky and Tennessee was much the same wherever the traveller stopped—consisting of bacon, eggs, and of corn bread in the form of dodgers, or of big loaves weighing eight or ten pounds, cooked in a portable iron Dutch oven. Coffee the landlord always served, tea never, and no meal was complete without toddy. Peaches abounded; and a drink called metheglin, made of their juice mixed with whiskey and sweetened water, the thirsty traveller thought a rival to mint julep.

One night Arlington put up at a locally celebrated tavern on the border of Tennessee. He found the genial host—an honest gossip called Chin—enjoying a hospitable carouse with half a dozen boon companions soaked full of flip and peach brandy. The jolly topers welcomed the newcomer to share their cups. They imparted much old news, and volunteered many encomiums on the landlord and his inn. They took special pride in Chin's tavern, owing to the undoubted historical fact that the guest-room had been occupied by Louis Philippe one night in the year 1802. On requesting to be shown to bed, the Virginian was conducted by the landlord, candle in hand, to a bare loft, on the floor of which lay a straw tick covered by a blue blanket.

"There's a bed a young gentleman ought to be proud to sleep on," affirmed the host, waving the candle over the couch. "If it's good enough for the son of the Duke of Orleans, it's good enough for me or you, eh? Wouldn't you like an applejack or a stiff metheglin to make you sleep sound? The boys downstairs respect you, sir, for the way you liquored. A young man travellin' can't be too sociable or treat too often. Well, good-night; you're lucky to strike that bed; you don't lay every night under a kiver and onto a tick slep between by the son of the Duke of Orleans."

Chester found the bed conducive to dreams, in which he was happy beyond the happiness of duke or king, dreams of Blennerhassett's island in May, and of wandering with a wingless Yankee angel in that earthly Paradise. Next morning, in payment for lodging and breakfast, he offered a silver dollar.

"That's too much," said Chin. "Here, Joel, chop this coin. I must give you the change in sharpshanks. Will you have it in quarters or eighths?"

"In whatever form you please."

"Then make it quarters, Joel," directed the landlord, tossing the dollar to a negro, who neatly cut the piece into four equal segments, one of which was handed back to the departing guest.

Arlington proceeded southward toward Natchez, following the road over which Burr had travelled toilsomely nearly two years before. Though warned not to undertake the journey alone, our hero, like James Fitz James, chose to trace a dangerous path only because it was "dangerous known." Road, properly so called, none had yet been opened through the wilderness stretching from Tennessee to lower Louisiana, and spreading eastward from the Mississippi. The route led the traveller along an old trail, over sandy spaces shadowed by melancholy pines, beside stagnant lagoons, across sluggish streams, and into cypress swamps, the lurking-place of reptiles, the dreary haunt of bats and vultures. The road, at best, was an indifferent bridle path, and at worst, a blind labyrinth of seldom trodden ways in the woods. Arlington carried in his saddle-bags a supply of bread and cheese, and he kept ready primed, in holster at his pommel, a brace of big pistols.

On the evening of the second day after entering the piny woods of Mississippi, he came upon a party of Creeks and Cherokees. They were friendly; their chief offered the hospitality of the camp, venison to eat and a buffalo hide to sleep on. These mild savages spoke a few English words, and they had partially adopted the customs of white people. The men wore an upper garment, like a shirt, and, about their loins a girdle of blue cloth a yard and a half long. Their legs were bare, their feet shod with moccasins of stag-skin. They were shorn of all hair except a grotesque tuft on top of the head. To enhance their masculine beauty, they sported nose-rings and painted their faces red, blue or black. The dress of the squaws consisted of a shirt, a short petticoat, and ornamental gaiters. Not one of them suffered a ring in her nose or paint on her cheeks, and all seemed proud of their hair. A dusky beauty, the chief's daughter, insisted on picketing and feeding Arlington's horse. On the next morning, before quitting the camp, the young man gallantly gave her a silk scarf, a present which all the other Indians, from the chief down, envied her.

No adventure of an unpleasant kind befell Chester Arlington until after he had crossed Black

River, well on the way to Natchez. One day, in the dusk of evening, he heard a voice from a distance shout after him, "Ho, there!" He looked in the direction from which the shout had been sent, and returned an answering "Hello!" but could see no person, nor could he elicit another cry from the solitude. This unaccountable voice, sounding in the wilderness, had a disagreeable effect on Arlington's nerves, though he was not in the least alarmed by it. His horse, however, tired as the brute was, pricked up its ears, gave a suspicious snort, and moved with quicker pace. Perhaps half an hour passed; the twilight deepened, and the weary traveller looked right and left for a suitable camping spot for the coming night. He checked the horse, rose in his stirrups, turning his head to prospect a green nook near the bridle path, when, crack! whiz! and a bullet grazed his left ear. This was more serious than a lone cry in the wilderness. Horse and rider instantly sought security in flight. The spurs were hardly needed to urge the black stallion forward. A brisk gallop along such ready avenues as Jetty could follow in the darkening woods, rapidly put a safe distance between the traveller and the random highwayman who had shot at him. At any rate, Arlington decided to dismount and take the chances. He tethered the animal, ate a dodger, and slept on his arms.

    On the following morning new cause for anxiety arose. The bridle path was not to be found. In galloping away to avoid bullets, Chester had swerved much to the westward, and far from the obscure and crooked "trace." For a whole day he wandered circuitously, in vain search for the beaten course. The more stubbornly he resolved to keep "calm, cool, and collected," the worse confused were his calculations. He experienced sensations unlike any he had ever before felt. It vexed him to confess to himself that his usually clear brain was a muddle. He seemed not only to have missed the way, but had also lost the faculty of self-direction.

    The night was again coming on. Now, Arlington regretted his obstinacy in refusing the service of a guide. Danger for danger's sake was playing ironically with him. He reflected that the wisest thing for him to do was to save his strength, recover his wandering wits, and start afresh the next morning. Luckily his saddle-bags were stored with a good stock of rations. He tied his jaded horse to a cypress-tree, and sat down on the ground to endure as patiently as he could the long dark hours. "A prince's bed in Chin's loft," thought he, "is luxury compared with this. All comfort is relative. I will sleep if I can. I shall need myself to-morrow."

    The croaking of frogs in the swamp and the shrill trumpeting of the mosquito army attacking his face and hands were not agreeable lullabies. As the darkness deepened, a medley of doleful noises pervaded the horrible wilderness. An unearthly gabble of strange water-fowl broke out suddenly, was kept up for a few seconds only, and then ceased. Only once in the night did Arlington hear that demoniac gabble; but he lay awake for hours expecting and dreading to hear it again. The owls were not so sparing of their vocal performances, scores of them joining in concert to serenade the lost man. Sometimes their prolonged notes sounded like the wail of a deserted babe, sometimes like mocking laughter, and again like a deep guttural snore. Nothing worse than mosquitos, dismal sounds, and the dank vapor of the swamp afflicted the weary man, who, falling asleep at midnight, slept so soundly that on waking late next morning he reproached himself for not having dreamed as usual of Evaleen Hale.

"How do you feel this morning, Jetty?" he said, patting his black horse. "Are you well rested? I will get you the best breakfast to be had in this God-forsaken region, and we must trot on or stay here and perish. Never say die, Jetty."

Real difficulties invigorate the brain of a brave man. Arlington awoke with a definite plan of procedure in his mind. After feeding Jetty and breakfasting with keen gusto, he renewed his search for the lost path, keeping the points of the compass ever in view. Natchez lay to the south and also to the west. By going due south one must certainly strike the road at some point.

"Are you ready to start, my lad?" said the man to the horse. The horse whinnied an equine response, and was soon bearing his master southward through the underbrush. Many an hour was wasted; the sun climbed to the meridian, and no indication of the anxiously looked-for trail was seen. At length, just as Arlington's pioneering eye lit upon the shining surface of a lazy brook, a dozen yards away, Jetty suddenly halted, put nose to the ground and began to paw. The animal had found a path, scarcely discernible, yet a practicable road marked by hoof-tracks. The course of it was along the edge of the small stream flowing westerly. "Manifestly the rational thing to do now is to follow the new-found trail, which, in all probability, is the right road to Natchez, or if not, it may lead to the Mississippi, where a boat can be hailed."

Progress was slow and painful. The oppressive afternoon was half spent when a breeze started up, the precursor of a thunder-gust. The breeze, strengthening to a brisk gale, made Arlington hold fast to his hat, and caused the long streamers of Spanish moss to wave like gray banners from the limbs of the cypress-trees. The air grew murky, clouds were flying in dark blotches. A hurricane was sweeping across the country; the loud rush of it came roaring up the stream; it lashed and twisted and tore trees; poured down torrents; thundered around and above Arlington and his terrified horse, without doing either man or beast the slightest hurt, save deluging them with rain, and pounding them as with mighty hammers of wind. The storm swept past, the rain ceased, the wind died away, and the traveller thanked his stars he had escaped death. On, on, farther and farther toiled the travellers, now both afoot, Arlington leading his panting beast. The water-way on their south, near the bank of which the road lay, widened abruptly, and became a broad, natural canal, with crumbling shores. Arlington paused to speculate on the strange aspect of things. Long had he journeyed among bushes and trees, over logs and across streams and oozy marshes; now he deemed he was nearing the Mississippi. "I am De Soto the Second; an explorer of new regions, a discoverer of strange watercourses. This Acheron at my left must flow into some larger body of water, if it flows at all. Courage, Jetty! We are on the way to the Father of Waters."

Climbing once more into the saddle, Arlington resumed his ride, patting his horse on the neck, and encouraging him with words.

"Patience, good boy; keep up a day or two more. Surely this widening stream on our left creeps to the big river. See! A boat! A vessel made by man's hands lies on the shore of this Dead Sea!"

Joyfully Chester sprang to the ground, and leaving the animal to browse, ran down to the edge of the bluff to learn if any living creature were aboard. He discovered three or four large boats, freighted with barrels and boxes. He called, but no answer came back. Turning to look after his horse, he noticed a foot-path leading into a thicket, and having pushed his way amid the wet bushes, he came into a broader path, which brought him to a supposititious tavern, the headquarters of Palafox's gang.

"A queer place for a public house," thought Arlington, reading the sign over the door. "Table set in the wilderness; I am out of danger of starvation, anyhow. Blessed be the name of Cacosotte."

Thus communing with himself, the young man pounded vigorously on the puncheon door. No one came to open to him. Loudly he called in the hearty manner of the backwoodsman:

"Hello the house!"

Nobody answered the call, though Arlington could have sworn he heard suppressed voices within. It flashed upon him that the place might be a trap for travellers, and the sign-board a decoy. His two heavy pistols, each more than a foot long, hung strapped to his belt. The priming was fresh; the flints were accurately set.

"Hello, there, within!"

Still no answer, yet again the sound of voices—women's voices. The stranger left the front portal to investigate the rear end of the long cabin. Loopholes in the log walls permitted air and light to enter the rooms. Through one of these openings, an aperture which might very likely conceal the muzzle of an aimed rifle, Arlington heard—not the report of a gun, but what surprised him more—his own name shrieked by Evaleen Hale. The hurried, excited appeal of the captives made clear the prompt and only course for the man to take. He hastened to the front door again, and now saw a reason why the strong bolts on the outside had been fastened. These he drew, and almost heaving the door off its hinges, rushed into the den. Mex stood on guard in the first partition door, a butcher knife in her hand. Slight parley did the athletic, impetuous Virginian ranger hold with the dragon who interposed between him and his lady-love. "Drop the knife! Throw up your hands!" he demanded, with an emphasis of desperation, which left no doubt of his intentions. Mex knew the meaning of pistols; she was cowed; the knife fell and her hands went up. Secretly she was glad to be foiled. She wished to be rid of the woman Palafox admired, and she could think of but two modes of disposing of her—killing her or letting her escape. Slowly walking backward, menaced by a cocked pistol, Mex retreated to the door of the room in which the ladies were locked up. The bolts were unfastened by her, the door swung inward, and the prisoners sprang to freedom. Now again Mex showed fight. She flashed Pepillo's poignard from a hidden sheath and made at Arlington, who struck the weapon down, shoved the savage woman back into the room, and bolted the door.

XX.: MOSTLY LOVE MATTERS.

Captain Winslow and those with him in the yawl at the time of the sinking of the barge, intent on their work of landing and of managing the cordelle, did not witness the rescue of Miss Hale and her companion. The place where the yawl came to shore, was overhung by bushes, and shut from view in the direction of the mouth of the bayou by trees and branches just blown down. Throughout the disastrous half-hour, only Dr. Deville thought less of self-preservation than of the safety of others. Constantly he tried not to lose sight of his daughter and of Evaleen, and he felt sure he had seen the girls going ashore in a skiff, rowed by two men. The boatman, who escaped by swimming when his fellows went down in the whirl of the eddy, could not believe but that the women were drowned.

Winslow and his drenched crew followed Dr. Deville down to the angle formed by the river and the bayou, where stood those of the wreckers not employed with oar or boat-hook. And now the conclusion of the sailor who swam to shore was confirmed by other testimony. These fellows swore they had seen the lost women struggling in the water. Another declared he saw them sink while he was making a desperate effort, against wave and gale, to reach them in his boat. Notwithstanding the assertions of the watermen, Deville did not relinquish faith in his own eyes. He suspected foul play. So did Winslow, who began to discover the spurious quality of the pretended salvage corps. The vigilant exertions of these hookers-in of flotsam could be accounted for only on the supposition that here, at the outlet of Cypress Bayou, Captain Winslow had fallen into the hands of a gang such as he had described to his passengers.

Palafox and his confederate made haste to return from their thieves' den to the scene of the wreck. Deville's pleading inquiry concerning the missing girls drew from the abductors feigned expressions of surprise and regret. Turning to Winslow, Palafox said:

"I'm 'stonished, captain, that you risked takin' women on board a freight boat."

"Yes," added Sheldrake. "You'll blame y'rself 's long 's you live. Them bodies will come up as floaters, down about Baton Rouge."

Doctor Deville groaned.

"No, no! Say not that. My dear daughter shall not be lost! Ah! Mon dieu!"

"Daughter? Was one of 'em your daughter, grand-daddy?" exclaimed Sheldrake. "Think of that, Burke! His daughter drownded!"

"Je suis fachè de votre malheur, père," said Palafox, in a tone of affected commiseration. Then turning to Sheldrake with a grin, "Better not devil the old man any more, Shel; he's gone crazy. Hello, there comes another boat!"

The craft sighted was a transport, flying the Stripes and Stars, and bearing a detachment of soldiers from St. Louis to Natchez. On being vociferously hailed by Winslow and his men, the batteau headed for the shore. During the slow and laborious process of landing, the wreckers, observing uniformed soldiers, with guns, furtively slipped away, one by one, disappearing in the bush; all excepting Palafox, who, with brazen audacity, still held his ground, acting his part as succorer of the unfortunate.

"I mean to join the army myself," said he to Winslow, as a lieutenant and several men came ashore. "I'd enlist now if it wasn't for my family at home—two sick babies."

A yell of delight from Dr. Deville startled all on shore and on the boat. His vigilant eye, ever enfilading the tangled copse to the eastward, had caught through an opening in the bushes the flutter of a blue gown, which he recognized as the kirtle of his idolized Lucrèce. She presently emerged from the thicket, accompanied by Arlington and Evaleen. Palafox was much disconcerted. He forgot his role of public benefactor, and was casting about to slip away as his fellows had done, when Arlington, rushing forward, pistol in hand, savagely confronted him.

"Stop!" thundered the Virginian, covering the desperado with his pistol, and glaring upon him with determined eye. Palafox, unable to escape, nonchalantly bit a chew of tobacco and nodded insolently.

"Take this man prisoner!" demanded the Virginian, keeping his eye and his pistol on the boatman.

"You've no warrant to take me," sneered Palafox.

"No warrant is required. Seize him, soldiers—he is a robber, an outlaw!"

To the accusation of Arlington, Miss Hale added her entreaties in terms so urgent that Palafox was arrested with little ceremony.

While the soldiers were hustling the kidnapper aboard the boat, the officer in command, Captain Warren Danvers, hastened to the shore, having recognized the voice of Evaleen. Neither Lucrèce, who loved Danvers, nor Chester, who loved Evaleen, could hear what passed, in rapid speech, between the affectionate couple. The story of the voyage, the wreck, the abduction, Evaleen imparted in a breath. She told as briefly the circumstances of the rescue.

"Oh, Warren, is it really you? A divine Providence guards us. Such a coincidence is not blind chance. Who could guess when we parted that we should come together under these circumstances. The hand of Heaven saved us."

"My dear girl, will you give no credit to human saviors? It appears you owe special gratitude to a mortal. I can't claim any merit for saving you, but I am extremely happy that we are once more together. Who is your travelling companion? We must look after her."

"Are you tired of me already," she playfully chided, "and curious to make a new friend? They are French people from Gallipolis."

"French? Is she French?" asked Danvers, gazing toward Lucrèce.

"French? Is she French?" tenderly mocked Evaleen. "I told you they were French. Now I am jealous. Do you know any French girl in Gallipolis?"

"Nonsense, Evaleen! I am not a woman's man. Pardon, I don't mean that I don't like you, of course—"

"Like—don't you love me? I love you with all my heart, you dear fellow! But I love Lucrèce also, and maybe I'll let you love her just a little."

Danvers seemed embarrassed. Evaleen went on:

"We are forgetting our friends. Come, you must thank the man who saved us."

The pair hurried to where Arlington stood.

"Mr. Arlington, this is Captain Danvers."
"I have met Captain Danvers."
"How, what? Have you, Warren, formed the acquaintance of—?"
"I have seen Mr. Arlington once before."
"Where?"
"In Marietta."
"When?"
"A good while ago. On the day I left for St. Louis."
"You never told me." Danvers looked hard at Arlington, who felt called upon to explain.
"Madam, I challenged Captain Danvers to fight."
Evaleen's blue eyes opened wide.
"Challenged Warren!"
"Yes."
"And you accepted the challenge?"
"Yes."
"Why, brother!"
Arlington's heart leapt within him. "Brother?" he stammered. "Captain Danvers your brother?"
"He is my half brother."
Danvers laughed out. Putting his arm around Evaleen, he said, "Mr. Arlington, if you are still disposed to fight me, we may meet when you please. But I am of the opinion you will learn from Evaleen that you have more cause to cherish hard feelings against the man you champion than against me."

"At any rate," said Arlington, as the two shook hands, "whatever you may think concerning Colonel Burr, this is not the place nor time for quarrelling. You have the Spaniards to fight—I must fight a rash temper."

Lucrèce, pale and sad-eyed, was leaning upon her father's shoulder. Evaleen hastened to her, and the doctor went up to Arlington to pour out endless thanks.

"Are you sick, Lucrèce? Shall we go to the boat?"
"Sick, sick at heart."
"There is a way to cure that."
"No, my Evaleen, there is no cure. But you shall it all forgive. How could I know? You say you sometime tell me the story I read, alas, too late."
"Story? What story?"
"Ah, my sweet friend—pardon me—pity Lucrèce. Mon soldat—mon capitaine, you love heem—he love you—how shall we not hate us?"

The captain made bold to approach the ladies. When his eyes met those of Lucrèce, Evaleen interpreted the silent language exchanged.

"Lucrèce, your soldier is my brother, you jealous little tigress! But," she added in a whisper, "don't let him kiss you again."

Danvers, without delay, gave directions for all to embark, and himself conducted Lucrèce and her jubilant father on board.

Arlington, escorting the Lady of the Violets, asked her, in an undertone, "Did you get my last letter from Virginia?"

"Yes," answered Evaleen. "Did you receive mine, in which I explained the mistakes of Byle?"

"No; I did not get such a letter. Tell me all the contents."

"That will require time."

"Did you answer my—my question?"

"Wait until you see the letter."

"I don't think I can wait."

"Then until we can talk on the boat."

Danvers proposed to take the crew and passengers of the wrecked barge Buckeye aboard his transport and carry them as far south as Natchez, where a family boat could be procured for the continuance of their voyage to New Orleans. Arlington, of course, was accommodated; also his faithful horse, Jetty, which had followed him down the margin of the bayou. The understanding was that Winslow should conduct the doctor and the ladies from Natchez to New Orleans, leaving Danvers free to march his troops to Natchitoches, while Arlington remained in Natchez to transact the business intrusted to him by Burr.

The transport was soon afloat. Monsieur Deville, quickly recovering his habitual gaiety, chirruped:

"Have I not said, Mees Hale, to your father that hees gairl sall be safe as ze baby in ze cradle? Have I not keep my word? Ze leetle blow of ze wind, it is all ovair. What we care now for ze boat-wreckair, ze bad robbair? Voila! have we not brush away ze mosquito? But say to me, my daughter's dear friend, am I myself Eloy Deville? Ze Captain Danvers, is he a lunatic?"

"No, doctor, not a lunatic, but a lover. My brother and your daughter have been sweethearts for many moons."

"Now I am sure you also, Mees Hale, have lost your head. You also are in ze delirium."

Danvers, attempting to ingratiate himself with pere Eloy, was called away by an occurrence which caused him chagrin. The sentinel to whom was assigned the duty of keeping watch over Palafox was not sufficiently vigilant to foil his cunning. The amphibious athlete managing deftly to loosen the cords which bound his wrists, slipped like an eel from the boat into the river, and, diving deep, swam awhile under water, then on the surface, and finally reached the eastern shore of the Mississippi, a few miles south of the point at which the boat had landed. Long, toilsome, exhausting, was his return tramp toward the sole haunt in which he could expect sympathy or command protection. He did not rely on honor among thieves, but he had confidence in Mex, who was bound to him, he believed, by two strong ties, love and fear.

Night had fallen before Palafox reached the southern edge of the bayou at the point opposite his only house and home, and it was pitchy dark, when, having swam across the stagnant channel, he trudged, wet and weary, to the barred door of Cacosotte's Tavern, and knocked. Mex undid the bolts and let her master in, her sagacious eyes swiftly taking note of his bodily plight and desperate mood. To her demonstration of savage tenderness he returned a ferocious growl, and shoved her from him roughly.

"Fetch me the brandy, quick! Don't you see I'm drowned?"

He swallowed at a gulp the potation she poured out, and stepping into a dark recess christened "The Captain's Corner," where hung various stolen articles of men's apparel, he exchanged his soaked garments for dry ones.

Meanwhile, Mex sullenly placed upon a table such food as her cupboard could supply. Palafox emerged, mollified in temper, but still irascible. In his hand he held the long leathern pocket-book containing the alleged evidence of Wilkinson's complicity with the Spanish government. It was creased and dripping, and before eating he opened it, carefully took out the papers, and spread them on the counter of the bar to dry.

"You wouldn't guess there might be a fortune in these, would you, Blackey?"

"Not Blackey! No negar-wool!" She shook her long black hair, and her blacker eyes glittered. "No Mexicano, no red squaw—your woman."

Palafox was wont to amuse himself by provoking the pride and jealousy of this caged creature of untamed affections.

"Where is Sott? Did he come home? He ought to be burnt alive for letting my game escape. Where is he?"

Mex, standing behind her lord and watching him as he ate and drank, explained that Nine Eyes had been badly hurt in a fight with one of the band; a bullet had shivered the bones of his arm; the sufferer had groaned and howled, but she soothed him, she said, by a charm, and he at last slept.

Sott's nondescript nurse had in fact, administered an opiate. In addition to the arts of the hoodoo and medicine man, she possessed unusual knowledge of the virtue of wild plants, including those of dangerous quality. There was never race or tribe so primitive as to be ignorant of deadly herbs. This scarcely half-civilized daughter of miscegenation was a Hecate in the skilful decoction of potent leaves, roots and berries.

"You charmed him to sleep?" sneered Palafox, glancing back threateningly, and speaking in Spanish. "Be careful who you charm. Best not be coddling Nine Eyes, or any other man, while I'm livin'. Bring another bottle. You could have kept those girls here for me, if you'd tried. You allowed that strutting dandy to carry them off before your eyes. This makes the second time he got away from me. The third time is the charm. Not your kind of charm, Mex, but one that acts quicker."

"What charm?" asked Mex, who had gone behind the bar, and was busy with bottles and cups. She decanted some drops into a flask.

"What charm! Copper-cheeks! You don't recollect how I dosed Pepillo that night!"

"Yes, that night me save your life. Me your wife then! Me kill dandy?"

Palafox chuckled at the question.

"No, señora, no. I'll do that part of the business, and you see after the charming. You might have captivated the dandy for all I care, and kept him to yourself. It isn't him I want. I want her. And I'll have her yet. I've set my heart on getting ahold of that woman."

The hand of Mex could not have been steady; she let fall something that broke like glass.

"What are you spilling, there? Don't break my bottles. Bring me more drink."

Mex started up confusedly from behind the bar, brought a flagon, sat down on the bench beside Palafox, and looked into his face. A furious resentment was raging in her heart.

Palafox enjoyed his temporary wife's manifestations of jealousy. He laughed, took a deep draught from the flagon, and said:

"You are infernal particular, Mex. I never heard of another woman of your pedigree who was opposed to polygamy."

She did not understand all the words he used, but gathered the chief import, and replied with impetuous wrath:

"No Mex—not Choctaw—me Castiliano—me Señora Palafox." The desperado sat still several minutes, drank again from a bowl which Mex had mixed.

"You're all right, señora—I couldn't keep house without you. Look ye here, bring all those papers and I'll put 'em safe back in the pocket book." The papers were folded up and enclosed carefully into the leathern wallet. Palafox, with trembling hand, thrust the package in his pocket, and then staggered to his feet.

"There's a queer pain in the back of my neck and in my chest, Mex; I can't stand up—help me." He leaned on the bar, and the woman hastily drew to the middle of the floor the great buffalo robe which was her usual bed. She also brought a panther's hide rolled up to serve as a pillow. The horribly staring eyes of Palafox followed her motions.

"There's something ails my heart, I tell you."

He stumbled upon the bed of pelts and lay sprawling.

"More drink! water! brandy! quick!"

With difficulty Mex turned the man upon his back. A while he lay still. His breathing was labored and he twitched convulsively. The entire nervous system was suddenly depressed. Mex stood motionless beside the pallet, her eyes riveted upon him. Presently his livid lips opened, and he spoke gaspingly, "I'm done for."

His hand fumbled about his heart. He was falling into syncope. He did not feel the sweep and tickle of downfalling hair which, for a moment, enmeshed and covered his face, when Mex knelt at his side and took from his bosom the pocket-book he had told her contained a fortune.

Having secured this treasure, the slighted mistress of a dying robber slid noiseless as a shadow to her accustomed covert behind the bar. When she came thence her feet and ankles were encased in high buckskin moccasins adorned in bright colors. About her shoulders she drew an Indian blanket decorated in richest style of barbaric elegance. She paused to bestow a parting look on the distorted face of him she had loved and poisoned. A feeble moan came from his lips. She knew it meant death, for wolf's-bane was mixed with the last draughts he had taken.

Like a shadow Mex passed from the cabin into the darkness of the woods. She had prevented the man from pursuing any other woman.

The hours of night wore slowly away, and Cacosotte, returning to consciousness after his anæsthetic sleep, felt renewed pain in his disabled arm. As soon as he realized his condition, he sat up in bed and shouted for his nurse. "Mex!" No answer.

"Mex, for God's sake come and fix my arm."

No answer. No sound whatever was to be heard in the lonely cabin.

"Mex, O Mex!"

No response. Cacosotte waited half an hour and again called out. Finally he got up, and in the gray light of a cloudy November dawn made his way from his remote couch in "Heaven" to the glimmering twilight of "Hell." Mex was not in her lair, nor was the couch itself in the usual place.

Cacosotte bent over Palafox and saw a corpse.

XXI.: PRO AND CON.

"No, sir, no, sir! I deny the statement. Burr is not getting justice. Daviess is a persecutor, not a prosecutor. He hates Burr as he hates every Republican. He rakes up all the filthy lies of the past, concerning Burr and Wilkinson, and peddles them round in that dung-cart, The Western World, which his man Friday, John Wood, drives."

"You'd best not talk too loud, Hadley; Wood is at the door."

"Who wants John Wood?" bawled the bearer of that name. "Hadley, you?"

"No; I avoid you and your paper. You ought to be sued for libel. I say to you as I just now said to Ogden, that Jo Hamilton Daviess is making this fuss, not for furtherance of law and justice, but to blacken the name of Burr."

"Burr blackened it himself," retorted Wood, "with the blood of Hamilton."

"Black blood it was, from a black heart. Don't say anything against that duel here in Kentucky!" said Hadley.

The wrangle, of which the foregoing speeches were a part, took place in Frankfort, Kentucky, on the morning of December 2, 1806. The town was thronged with zealous partisans, Federalists and Republicans, from near and far. Scores of sturdy ploughmen and cavalcades of stock-raisers had ridden from their Blue Grass farms to the State capital, on horses of a breed and beauty unsurpassed in the world. Every tavern, blacksmith-shop, and grocery drew its crowd, for the weather was cold, and the country folks were glad of a chance to warm themselves while they boisterously discussed the latest phases of the legal proceeding then in progress, involving the reputation of Aaron Burr, and threatening his personal liberty.

Daviess, a staunch Federalist, controlled a political newspaper, the avowed purpose of which was "to drag to light the men who had been concerned with Miro in the Spanish conspiracy of 1787." Daviess had written to Jefferson accusing General Wilkinson of having been in Spanish pay, and later had charged both Wilkinson and Burr with the grossest disloyalty. These two men were openly and repeatedly attacked in the paper, a copy of which Wood held in hand when he confronted Hadley.

"You can't smutch the character of Daviess," said Wood. "His name is above suspicion. He performs his duty as United States District Attorney without fear or favor."

"You are not competent to give an unbiased opinion; your bread-and-butter depends upon the man who set you up in business."

The sneer drew applause from a majority of those in the store. Burr had won the heart of the populace. Wood returned a sharp rejoinder.

"What a pity that some good man has not set Hadley up in a better business than pettifogging. Apply to your patron, Judge Innes. Lick his foot. There's an immaculate judge for you! Talk of corruption! I've been present at every session of the court whenever the case of Burr came up. Away back as early as the beginning of November Daviess moved for a process to compel the attendance of Burr in court to answer charges of treason. Daviess made affidavit that he had positive evidence of Burr's plotting to wage war against Spain, invade Mexico, and break up the

Union. What was the action of Judge Hary Innes? He overruled the motion—denied the course of justice."

"No," broke in the other, "he denied the motion because there were no grounds for the charge."

"Hold on, Mr. Hadley, till I am through. I want these young men from the Blue Grass and from Lexington to know the truth, the whole truth, and nothing but the truth."

"Fust time truth ever come from the editor of The Western World!" growled a backwoodsman in buckskin breeches. "I'll bet my money on Burr. Burr ought to be President 'stid of Jefferson. He was cheated out of the Presidency."

"That's the talk!" put in a squeaky-voiced old man, wiping his lips with the back of his hand, after having taken a drink of cheap whiskey, for a dram went gratis with every purchase, and old Jim Sweet had bought a long woollen "comfort" for his scrawny neck. "That's the talk, gen'l'men. I say, hurrah for Wilkinson and Burr and Harry Clay! I wisht Clay had popped a hole in Daviess, jest like Burr did in Hamilton. Why didn't they fight? They say Daviess sent a challenge. Wonder why that dool 'tween Jo and Harry never come off?"

Hadley shrugged his shoulders.

"That gits me," continued Jim. "Reckon it were a case of one askeert and an' t'other da'sn't, eh, Hen?"

"Skeert nothin'!" mumbled the backwoodsman. "Clay's a dead shot."

The man of the newspaper here put in. "Daviess sent Clay a challenge; that's certain."

"Yes! an' there's another fack what's durn certain, my friend, or I'm a liar!" The backwoodsman roused himself from his stooping posture and sat glaring at the editor. "Harry Clay done accepted Daviess's challenge; an' if matters was arranged satisfactory to both parties without no pluggin', I reckon there ain't no need of comments from outsiders."

Editor Wood, aware that the public sentiment was against him, prudently withdrew, leaving the floor to Hadley, which zealous Democrat, addressing sympathetic auditors, voiced their feelings and his own.

"I was in the court room, and I saw some of you there when first Daviess tried to calumniate Burr; and I was there when Innes overruled the motion. That was a great day. The judge had scarcely finished speaking when Burr himself, just from Lexington, entered the court-house. He made the neatest speech ever I heard—perfectly calm and dignified—and he asked for a full and free investigation—the sooner the better, he said—now, if possible. You heard that speech, Jim, didn't you?"

Old Jim, who, with trembling hands, was in the act of adjusting his new comfort, swore he had heard all the great preachers and lawyers of his day, but Burr knocked the persimmons.

"Do you recamember, Hen," said he, familiarly addressing Hadley. "Do you recamember how Daviess hopped up and snarled out, 'You shall have all the investigation you want!' He said it in jest that tantulatin' style. 'All the in-ves-ti-gation you want.' I was riled. I hissed."

"Like an old snappin' turtle," said the backwoodsman.

"I recollect," resumed Hadley, "the judge fixed the next Wednesday for the hearing, as Burr desired. Wednesday came, but Daviess wasn't ready. One of his witnesses absent. What could the judge do but discharge the jury? He did discharge the jury, and then, gentlemen, we had another surprise! No sooner had those jurymen left the box than in marched Burr once again, and said he regretted that the jury had been discharged, and asked the reason. Daviess buzzed up, like a mad hornet, and explained that one of his principal witnesses, Davis Floyd, was in Indiana attending a territorial legislature. Everybody burst out laughing, and the judge had to call the court to order. You ought to have seen Burr! Without cracking a smile, he desires that the cause of Floyd's absence be entered upon record. Then he makes another address, partly to the court and partly to the people, denying in toto the charges against him, and insisting on a fair investigation. There is not a franker, more open-and-above-board soul living than this same Aaron Burr of New York! They can't catch him by any tricks of law or lying. He won't be downed. To-day comes the last tug of war. I never saw such another crowd in this town as we have now to attend court. All Frankfort is here, all Lexington, and pretty much all Kentucky."

"I'll be danged," piped old Jim, "if I don't start right away and try to git a bench. An ailin' man, like me, can't scrouge, as I used to could."

"Go 'long wi' me; I'll jam you through the crowd, or mash you, Jim," offered the backwoodsman. "Fetch out the jug, Sanders, it's my treat. Come up to the counter, neighbors, 'less you mean to insult me. Here, use this dipper, Jim. All must drink—yes, you too, Solly." These last words were addressed to a ghost-like man with a long white beard and insane eyes, who had glided into the store. He was recognized by all present under the name of "Solly," an abbreviation of Solitarius. The demented fanatic sadly shook his head.

"Peace be with you all. Amen!"

"Amen, Solly; how's the Halcyon Itinerary?" asked Hadley, in playful irony. "Where's your revelations?"

"Awake from your dreams." This monition, uttered in a slow, solemn tone, was received by the loafers good-naturedly, being advice they had often heard from the same lips.

"This whiskey'll wake 'em up, Solly, if anything this side of liquid fire can. Here's a tinful for you."

The crazy prophet waved the offering away, raised his palms in silent benediction, and glided out as noiselessly as he had entered.

"Badly cracked," said the grocery-keeper.

"Religion done it," exclaimed Old Jim, between swallows.

The drinks having been paid for, the entire company, led by the backwoodsman, left the store and hurried to the court-house.

XXII.: NOT A TRUE BILL.

The oft-deferred and eagerly expected hour came, in which the charges brought against Aaron Burr by the United States District Attorney of Kentucky were to be investigated before a Grand Jury, Judge Hary Innes presiding. The court-room was crammed from wall to wall with a crowd of men impatiently awaiting the first move in the anticipated war of words between two famous lawyers, who were known to be not only political antagonists, but also personal enemies. The cause of the impending battle was worthy of the contestants. On the result of that day's testimony and debate hung the fortunes of the conspirator and his federaries. This Burr realized, though few of his devoted adherents in that crowded room had suspicion that the charges against him were true. In the minds of most of them he figured as a martyr, a patriotic citizen maligned and traduced. There were many in that assemblage who, had they believed his designs traitorous, would have greeted him not with applause, but with a volley of rotten eggs.

When Judge Innes stepped behind the high desk of justice, and took his official seat, a buzz of expectation went round. The clerk of the court bustled in with an air of importance, and shook hands with the District Attorney, whose troubled, anxious eye shot piercing glances in every direction. Daviess appeared to be seeking for somebody he hardly hoped to find. Old Jim, standing in a corner, craned his neck to get a better view, wheezily murmuring in the ear of his friend, the backwoodsman, "Jo looks cross. I reckon he has lost somethin'."

"'Spect he has lost his case," remarked Buckskin Breeches, stooping to spit tobacco juice on the floor. At this moment a cheer, seconded by general handclapping, announced the coming of Burr and his counsel, Clay and Allen. The judge did not check the demonstration; on the contrary, he smiled a beaming welcome and was unjudicial enough to nod familiarly from his high bench.

The case was called with the usual forms of procedure, when, to the disgust of Old Jim and the auditors generally, Daviess asked a further postponement owing to the absence of an indispensable witness, John Adair. The judge hesitated, Burr had nothing to say, and the spectators manifested signs of democratic protest against being disappointed in their hopes of a forensic entertainment. Burr's lawyers were very willing to treat the populace to a taste of oratory, which, in the guise of legal discussion, might produce remote political effects, for office-seeking was a fine art in the good old days of Jackson and Clay. Colonel Allen arose to insist that the investigation go on or else be abandoned finally and entirely, and to this the judge seemed to assent. Daviess, fearful that the court and the balance of public opinion were against him, felt the difficulty of his position, but determined to summon all his power of argument and persuasion, hoping to turn the tide in his favor. A bold man, ready in debate, sharp at repartee, the leader of his party, the District Attorney was considered a match for any member of the Kentucky bar. The judge, the assembled lawyers, and the waiting audience perceived in the very attitude of Daviess, when he rose to plead for postponement, that he was loaded with a great speech. They were not mistaken. For more than an hour he held the absorbed attention of every listener. He set forth clearly and forcibly the fundamental reasons why the accusation of treason against a prominent citizen should be fully investigated.

"Your Honor," said he, in conclusion, "I appear before you and before the people of this State and county, and before the throne of Almighty God; I come in the discharge of an imperative duty, as a servant of the United States, to which I am bound by a sacred oath; I come to lay before you damning evidence that the accused is guilty of treason to his country. Only give me time—grant me another day. I shall produce unwilling witnesses whose testimony will convince even the most prejudiced politician, will persuade even his own deluded followers that Aaron Burr is engaged in machinations to destroy this Federal Union which the men of Lexington and Bunker Hill fought and died to establish. Behold the Brutus who would stab, not a despotic Cæsar, but the nourishing bosom of his native country. We have here, in loyal Kentucky, a Lexington, our most populous city. Remember that it was named in commemoration of the first battle of the Revolution. Shall our Lexington be suffered to become a hot-bed of sedition? No, your Honor—a thousand times, no!"

The effect of this peroration was for the moment overwhelming. A dead silence prevailed throughout the court-room. Garrulous Old Jim attempted no sarcastic criticism; he rolled his blear eyes in the direction of the backwoodsman and shook his head as if to say, "I give it up." The climax of the day's oratory, however, was yet to come. Daviess took his seat and Clay instantly sprang up to answer him. "Harry of the West," already a popular idol, was the most celebrated speaker in Kentucky. Not yet thirty years of age, he had just been chosen to represent his State in the Senate of the nation. Burr, soliciting his professional aid, had written a note denying either treasonable intentions or complicity with traitors. "You may be satisfied," wrote he, "that you have not espoused the cause of a man any way unfriendly to the laws, the government, or the interest of his country." Relying on this assurance, Clay gave his services without fee, perhaps in anticipation of the satisfaction he would enjoy in vanquishing with the tongue the man who had once challenged him to mortal combat with pistols. His resolute mien, tall, graceful figure, expressive gestures, flashing eye, and mellifluous voice captivated independently of the substance of his discourse. Clay was eloquent by nature. There was no resisting the flood of his impassioned speech.

In the course of his address, which was meant as much for the public ear as for that of the judge, he said: "These paltry charges, may it please your Honor, these foul and slanderous charges, the filthy ooze of an irresponsible newspaper, are incredible, preposterous—nay, mendacious! They are not made in good faith. The purpose of those who are fomenting mischief, under the pretence of performing public duty, is not what it professes to be. The motives underlying this show of public virtue are sinister and selfish."

"Do you mean to cast reflections on my character, sir?" demanded Daviess.

"Not at all. You are brilliant enough to shine by your own light. Look, sir, a moment, at the history of this illustrious American citizen whom you are called upon to vex and vilify; remember his heroic conduct in war, his splendid services in peace; recall the story of his public sacrifices and his private misfortunes; who, I ask, is worthy of a generous people's gratitude and confidence if Aaron Burr be not worthy? Do you charge him with disloyalty? him the hero of Quebec, of Long Island, and of Monmouth? him the very sword hand of Washington?" This flourish of rhetoric added an extra inch to the length of Jim Sweet's craned neck.

"Sock it to 'em!" he tried to shout, but his phthisicky effort ended in a spell of coughing.

"Order in the court!" shouted the clerk, fixing the disturber with threatening eye.

"They tell us Republics are ungrateful, and it seems that my learned friend, the district attorney, would have you believe that miserable maxim. Out upon such a sentiment! We boast, sir, of the hospitality of Old Kentucky, especially of the Blue Grass region, and well we may boast. Our people are magnanimous—their hearts are great. But what shall be said of the unspeakable meanness, baseness, perfidy, of that man or that community which would betray the stranger at the gates, that would traduce and malign a high-minded, unsuspecting guest? What, your Honor, is the hospitality of that section or city in this vast Republic, the function of whose tribunals is to protect the rights of the individual; what is the hospitality of a neighborhood which permits a citizen to lie in wait to assassinate a pilgrim of peace? That, your Honor, is what the prosecutor purposes. He would blacken the reputation of his brother who happens to be of a different political complexion. He would filch from the ex-Vice-President of the United States his good name."

"He'd flitch his own mother," ventured Jim, on whose brain the dipperful of whiskey was producing mixed results.

"Hold yer gab," said the backwoodsman, hoarsely. "Listen!"

The orator turned full upon the district attorney and thundered: "Has it come to such a pass that a private citizen cannot make a tour of observation through this free country without being dragged before a court to answer trumped-up accusations as preposterous as they are malignant? What will become of your rights and mine? Will some prosecuting attorney arrest me on my way to Washington, because I have somewhere, at some time, expressed private opinions from which he dissents! I would like Mr. Daviess to tell us what the Constitution means? Does it not insure to us all the right of habeas corpus?"

The outcome of the day's debate was a substantial victory for Burr, though a technical one for Daviess. The court adjourned to the following morning. Again the officers of the county, the jury, the lawyers, and the great concourse of citizens, assembled. The district attorney submitted his indictment and sent his evidence to the jury. The jury heard witnesses and returned the presentment, "Not a true bill."

On hearing the foreman announce this decision, the partisans of Burr and his counsel broke out in tumultuous rejoicing. Hadley stood up on a bench and shouted:

"Three cheers for Aaron Burr; Hip, hip, hurrah!"

The judge could not or did not check the enthusiasm.

"Three and a tiger for Clay!" squeaked Old Jim, and the cheers were repeated.

Burr, escorted by his attorneys, made his way through the crowd, shaking hands right and left. On the sidewalk, near the court-house, the three gentlemen were accosted by the ghostly Solitarius.

"Awake from your dreams!" said the mild lunatic, in his peculiar, hollow, monotonous voice—and he rolled his overlustrous eyes upon Burr.

"Brethren, be not forgetful to entertain the stranger! I am that Solitarius, to whom this new gospel was revealed, by an angel of God, while I dwelt in a cell at the foot of the Alleghany Mountains, in the year of our Lord 1799."

Clay drew his client forward by the arm, but not before "Solly" had thrust into Burr's hand a copy of the "Millennial Prophecy."

"Awake from your dreams!" These repeated parting words of the crazy prophet stuck in Burr's memory.

The ordeal of a legal investigation had been endured, apparently without scath to the accused. The grand jury, not satisfied with acquitting Burr, pressed upon him a written declaration, signed by every member, exonerating him completely. A public ball was given in his honor. Exulting in his triumph, he danced and made merry, admired by the chivalry and adored by the beauty of the choicest society in Frankfort and Lexington.

On the very day in which Daviess moved for a process to compel Burr's appearance before the Frankfort court, a woman clothed in black and closely veiled was granted an interview with the President of the United States, in his private office at Washington City. She came from Philadelphia, and appeared to have no acquaintance in the new capital on the Potomac. She declined to unveil her face or to impart her name.

"I am here to put into the hands of the President a written statement, accompanied by copies of letters and other documents, revealing the secret plans of a conspirator, who, if not quickly arrested in his career of treason, will disrupt this Union and establish a rival government in the Southwest."

The President mechanically accepted the package handed him, and the mysterious woman left his apartment, re-entered her carriage, and ordered the driver to take the road back toward Philadelphia.

XXIII.: THE FATAL CIPHER.

The disgruntled Spaniards continued to threaten war. Governor Claiborne ordered Casco Calvo and Intendant Morales to quit the territory of New Orleans. Soon after this a body of Spanish troops, supported by Indian allies, assembled on the Sabine to menace the American borders. In August a force actually crossed the Sabine and advanced to Bayou Pierre, near Natchitoches, a hundred and twenty miles west of Natchez.

General Wilkinson came from St. Louis to Natchez, and presently advanced to Natchitoches at the head of a body of one hundred regulars and five hundred militia. Late one afternoon in October word was brought to Wilkinson in his tent that a young man of fine appearance had arrived in camp, desiring to enlist as a volunteer. The general gave orders to bring the man into his presence. The would-be soldier was conducted immediately to headquarters, and there he imparted his name and the real cause of his coming, his representation to the sentinel being a ruse.

"Ah, you are Colonel Burr's confidential secretary; you have travelled far and must be exhausted. You bring documents for me?"

"Yes, sir; my credentials are included with matters more important."

"You know the contents of the enclosure?"

"Only the general import. The sender of these missives has divulged much to me. You may trust me."

"I trust you implicitly, Mr. Swartwout. The embassy on which you come is of a delicate character, requiring discretion—as secret service always does."

The general opened the package, and found that it contained three separate papers. The first was a letter introducing Samuel Swartwout, and vouching for his prudence, courage and trustworthiness. The other two papers were in hieroglyphics. Wilkinson, smiling graciously, turned to the messenger.

"Perhaps I had best be alone while I examine the other documents. I will see that you are made comfortable."

An officer was summoned. "Captain Danvers, this gentleman is my guest. Please see that he is suitably quartered and provided with a seat at my table. He is the son of an old military acquaintance of mine."

The cipher agreed upon by Wilkinson and Burr was a composite of arbitrary signs and of numerals representing letters of the alphabet. The first riddle read by Wilkinson was a private letter to Burr from General Dayton. Part of the contents ran thus: "Under the auspices of Burr and Wilkinson, I shall be happy to engage, and when the time arrives, you will find me near you. Write and inform me, by first mail, what may be expected from you and your associates.... Wealth and honor, courage and union, Burr and Wilkinson! Adieu."

The other communication was from Burr himself.

"Your letter, postmarked 13th May, is received. At length I have obtained funds and have actually commenced. The eastern detachments from different points, and under different pretences, will rendezvous on the Ohio, 1st of November. Everything internal and external favors our views. Naval protection of England is secured. Truxton is going to Jamaica, to arrange with the admiral on that station. It will meet us at the Mississippi. England, a navy of the United States, are ready to join, and final orders are given to my friends and followers. It will be a host of choice spirits. Wilkinson shall be second to Burr only, and Wilkinson shall dictate the rank and promotion of his officers. Burr will proceed westward 1st of August, never to return. With him go daughter and grandson. The husband will follow in October, with a corps of worthies. Send forwith an intelligent friend, with whom Burr may confer. He shall return immediately with further interesting details; this is essential to harmony and concert of movement. Send a list of all persons known to Wilkinson west of the Alleghany Mountains, who could be useful, with a note delineating their character. By your messenger send me four or five of the commissions of your officers, which you can borrow under any pretence you please. They shall be returned faithfully. Already are orders given to the contractor to forward six months' provisions to points Wilkinson may name; this shall not be used until the last moment, and then under proper injunctions. Our project, my dear friend, is brought to a point so long desired. Burr guarantees the result with his life and honor, with the lives and honor and the fortunes of hundreds, the best blood of our country. Burr's plan of operation is to move down rapidly, from the falls, on the 15th of November, with the first five hundred or thousand men, in light boats now constructing for that purpose, to be at Natchez between the 5th and 15th of December, there to meet you, there to determine whether it will be expedient in the first instance to seize on, or pass by, Baton Rouge ... on receipt of this send Burr an answer ... draw on Burr for all expenses, etc. The people of the country to which we are going are prepared to receive us; their agents, now with Burr, say that if we will protect their religion and will not subject them to a foreign power, that in three weeks all will be settled. The gods invite us to glory and fortune; it remains to be seen whether we deserve the boon. The bearer of this goes express to you; he will hand a formal letter of introduction to you, from Burr; he is a man of inviolable honor and perfect discretion, formed to execute rather than project, capable of relating facts with fidelity, and incapable of relating them otherwise. He is thoroughly informed of the plans and intentions of ———, and will disclose to you, as far as you inquire, and no further; he has imbibed a reverence for your character, and may be embarrassed in your presence; put him at ease, and he will satisfy you."

The eastern sky was flushed faintly with morning red before the general finished deciphering this long message. Wilkinson saw that he could no longer maintain an equivocal attitude, but must either yield positively to Burr's proposals or denounce them. Early in the day he summoned the messenger to his tent for a private interview.

"My dear sir," said the general, "you should be proud to be recommended by such a man, in such language. Burr has absolute confidence in your honor, fidelity, veracity and courage."

Swartwout answered with feeling and dignity.

"I hope I may prove myself worthy of his confidence and of yours. I would not hesitate to risk my life for Colonel Burr or for his best friend, General Wilkinson."

"That is very noble of you. Tell me, now that you are rested and refreshed after your long journey, by what route did you come?"

"I came straight from Pittsburg, thence westward through Ohio and Kentucky to Louisville, and from there on to St. Louis, expecting to find you at that post. Learning that you had gone down the Mississippi I followed in a skiff. I have been more than two months on the way from Philadelphia to Natchitoches and have travelled fully fifteen hundred miles."

"The document in your custody justified the difficult journey, Mr. Swartwout. What information did you gather in the progress of your trip, concerning our preparations?"

"I learned that, with the support of a powerful association extending from New York to New Orleans, Colonel Burr is levying an armed body of seven thousand men, with the view of carrying an expedition against the Mexican provinces. Five hundred men are to descend the Alleghany, for whose accommodation boats are ready."

"What will be the course of action?"

"This territory will be revolutionized. Some property will be seized in New Orleans, I suppose. Our boats will be ready to leave in February for Vera Cruz; the troops will march from there to the City of Mexico."

"Does Colonel Burr know there are several millions of dollars in the Bank of New Orleans?"

"We know that full well."

"Is it the intention to seize upon the deposits of private individuals?"

"We mean to borrow, not to violate private property. We must equip ourselves in New Orleans; we expect naval protection from Great Britain. Of course, general, everything depends upon your co-operation."

"Mr. Swartwout, the plans set forth in Colonel Burr's schedule are admirable! You will readily perceive, however, that my part in carrying them into effect must be manipulated with caution. I am surrounded, as you see, by officers whom I must manage discreetly. It is impossible that I should ever dishonor my commission. If I cannot join in the expedition, the engagements which the Spaniards have prepared for me in my front might prevent my opposing your operations. Do you understand me?"

Burr's agent understood. He interpreted Wilkinson's language to mean much more than it said, attributing to the commander a profound sagacity which imposed reticence for causes beyond an ordinary man's ken. His unsuspicious mind had been schooled by Burr to believe implicitly in Wilkinson.

Swartwout was under engagement to join Burr at Nashville, and he pressed for a letter which he might deliver to his chief. This request Wilkinson evaded. Promising to return Burr a speedy answer, he detained the envoy under various pretexts, bestowing upon him every hospitable attention, and finally dismissed him with oral messages, after having consumed ten days of his time.

Three days subsequent to the departure of Swartwout another messenger, as secret and more swift, was dispatched from Natchitoches, bearing to Washington City from the commander-in-chief, a full disclosure of the plans of conspiracy, and fastening the charge of treason on Aaron Burr. All the machinery of civil and military executive power was put in motion in the districts over which Wilkinson's authority extended.

The information forwarded by Wilkinson's messenger reached Washington City November 25, 1806. It was by no means the only evidence the President had received, impeaching the loyalty of the eminent politician. Daviess had written, and Morgan had written, and the veiled witness in black had come in person with the facts reiterated in Wilkinson's letter of exposure.

The President issued a proclamation, "warning and enjoining those who had been led to participate in the unlawful enterprise, to withdraw without delay, and requiring all officers, civil and military, of any one of the States or Territories, to be vigilant, each within his respective department, in searching out and bringing to punishment all persons engaged or concerned in the undertaking."

XXIV.: THE MIDNIGHT DEPARTURE.

The first snowstorm of early winter was whirling its flaky showers over the frozen fields and through the naked woods of Bacchus Island. The short day was nearing a dismal close. Harman Blennerhassett paced uneasily to and fro within the narrow confines of his study. His face was haggard, his general aspect that of a man harassed and hopeless. Yet he seemed idle and without sense of responsibility for the future. His air indicated irresolution, ennui, mild disgust of the world and of himself. He took down Homer, brushed the dust from the covers, and then replaced the volume on its shelf. He gave the glass cylinder of his electrical machine a turn or two, and was for the moment gratified to elicit a faint spark, a feeble snap of blue fire, which clicked from the "receiver" to his knuckles. His eye dwelt fondly for a few seconds on the air-pump, but wandered from that to the telescope, and finally took cognizance of an apparatus for weighing heavy articles. This was provided with a small platform, upon which the recluse philosopher stepped, to determine his exact weight. He was busied in this personal experiment, when a visitor was announced and ushered into his sanctum sanctorum.

"I beg pardon! Do I intrude?" said the caller, a man of official bearing, who gave the name of Graham.

"Not in the least, Mr. Graham. I have been taking my weight, and I beg you to excuse me until I note the precise number of pounds and ounces. My memory is treacherous. I make it a rule to ascertain my weight and my height several times a year, but I can never remember either, an hour after. I actually forget the date of my own birthday and how old I am."

"That is owing, doubtless, to the fact that your mind is absorbed in important things," said Graham, not very tactfully. "I make bold to come to your house, Mr. Blennerhassett, uninvited, but not without warrant. You are, I am informed, a partner of Aaron Burr in certain enterprises now much talked of. It is of this Wachita expedition that I wish to speak with you."

"Speak freely, Mr. Graham. Colonel Burr intimated that you would probably join us. Here are letters giving recent information. Read for yourself."

Graham glanced over a number of communications containing secrets that Blennerhassett, had he been a man of ordinary forethought, would not have trusted out of his own hands. Among the letters was one from Burr, giving a brief account of his troubles in Frankfort. "You perceive, my dear sir," so ran the lines, "that this step will embarrass me in my project of the Wachita settlement, and will deprive me of the pleasure of seeing you at your own house." Graham smiled gravely at the guileless simplicity of the man who had not hesitated to take a stranger into his confidence, unquestioned and unsuspected.

"It is my duty, as a man of honor, to undeceive you, Mr. Blennerhassett. I have no intention of joining your expedition. The fact is, I am here, not to aid and abet you, but the reverse. I come commissioned, as the agent of the Federal Government, and my duty is to prevent the execution of Burr's designs. Do you not know that orders have been issued for the civil authorities to interfere with your plans?"

Blennerhassett opened his eyes wide, with a stupefied stare.

"Then you are not one of us? I was told that you were a leader in the New Orleans Association for the invasion of Mexico. The printer of the Gazette d'Orleans informed me that three hundred men had joined the company."

"There is not a word of truth in the report. I am an officer of the Government, but I have no desire to molest misguided people. My motive in coming through this snowstorm to you to-day is friendly. I want to save your family and you from disaster. I hope to dissuade you from your present purpose. You are misinformed—deluded."

The lord of the isle plucked up spirit and replied haughtily:

"I thank you for your good intentions toward me and my family, though your coming is inopportune, not to say impertinent. We know our own affairs. Colonel Burr and myself are, I conceive, sufficiently experienced in business, and well enough informed in law, to know what we are about. The interference of local officials I shall resent, and if necessary, prosecute. As for yourself, you have not shown your credentials. I trust you will have the honor not to magnify or distort any information I may have inadvertently exposed to your scrutiny. I wish you farewell. Shall I send one of my servants to conduct you to the wharf?"

The official, who was really sincere in all that he had said, left the house and the premises in rather bad temper, yet he cherished no resentment on account of the rebuff.

No sooner was Graham gone than Blennerhassett's courage collapsed. He flung himself into a big chair, and yielded to the pressure of despondency. His wife came into the study and discovered him with his head bowed upon his hands.

"Husband, what ails you?"

"Oh, Maggie, Maggie—we have been deceived. I fear Colonel Burr has not told me all he should have told. We must go no farther in this enterprise." He went on to tell what had passed between himself and Graham, and ended his lament by saying: "I am worried to death! Half my fortune is already squandered! We must think of the boys; we must stop further expenditure, before we have lost all."

The wife stood erect, unshaken, firm almost to rigidity. A white heat of resolute energy burnt in every capillary of her nerved body.

"Give up nothing! Carry out the original plans decided upon here in this library. We expected difficulties—we shall overcome them. All great enterprises are difficult. What do we care for the prattling of this Graham? Now is our time to act. We must do our own thinking. Burr is not here to direct, and if he were, I would not trouble him with details. Why play a secondary part? You are as wise a man as he is, and you are my husband. You have spent money—spend more! To abandon the enterprise is to throw away your chances, all your past expenditures, and all your labor."

"But, my dear wife—"

"Harman, this is not a time for ifs and buts. Hasten your preparations. Bring the boats down from Marietta. Keep every engagement with Burr, and join him at the mouth of the Cumberland at the appointed time. Whoever weakens, let not you and me do so. Remember the pledges made to and by us, and bear yourself as becomes the man chosen to be Minister to the Court of St.

James."

   What spur more sharp than a beautiful woman's appeal to a proud man's vanity? Blennerhassett hastened every preparation for the forwarding of provisions, ammunition, arms, and men. Night and day the busy work went on. Skiffs flitted in and out of the secluded cove, fetching and carrying supplies or recruits. Skilful hands folded cartridges and manipulated the bullet-mould in the light and heat of the kitchen fire—even the slender fingers of the mistress shared in this significant task.

   The time came for bringing the fifteen batteaux from the shipyard on the Muskingum, where Byle had heard the clatter of saw and hammer. But when Blennerhassett's tardy employees made an attempt to get the boats, they were frustrated by the civil and military authorities of Marietta. Only a single batteau was brought down. Jefferson's proclamation was producing its intended effect. The country had awakened to a sense of public danger. The militia was called out in Ohio and a rumor came to Blennerhassett that Colonel Phelps, at the head of the militia of Wood County, Virginia, was about to cross over to the island, seize whatever supplies might be found there, and arrest the proprietor.

   The islanders were alarmed. There was no time to waste. Nevertheless, the head of the household hesitated—dawdled. The crisis paralyzed his energy. It was an imperative duty, now, for his wife to make up his mind and to make it up strong. Her will was adequate. She took command of the domestic ship, captain and crew. Peter Taylor hung around his master deprecatingly; she sent him to Belpre on an errand. Albright, the dairyman, spoke disparagingly; she ordered him to look after the cows. She put an arm round her wavering lord, and drew him into his favorite retreat, the library.

   "You must embark to-night or lose your liberty, possibly your life. The trunks are packed—everything is ready! We must be brave, as an example to the children." While she spoke Dominick knocked at the door. "May I come in, mamma? I want to go along with papa; I want to go along to Mexico!" The mother gently pushed him from the room. Tears were in the eyes of both parents.

   "Margaret, ought I leave them and you unprotected?" She kissed him on the forehead and pressed his tremulous hand.

   "Have no fear. I shall be safe. To-morrow we will follow you. Now make haste and complete your final preparations. Tell your men just what to do. We know not the instant that Colonel Phelps may come to arrest you." Blennerhassett assured his wife that everything had been attended to, and that he was ready, at a moment's warning, to start for his boat, which lay waiting by the shore. Night came on, however, and still the fond husband and father lingered. The snow was falling in the outer darkness, and the wind howled through the long avenue of the portico. No wonder the easy-going devotee of luxury shrank from stepping into the bleak night, to navigate a scow down the rough, icy current of the Ohio. Against his wife's protest he took up the violincello and began to tune up its three remaining strings. Touching the chords lightly with the bow, he attempted to play "Auld Lang Syne." A confused noise in the direction of the river stopped the plaintive music.

"Now you must start; I will go along to the river's edge, and see you safe aboard."

Blennerhassett hurried to the bedroom of his boys. Little Harman was asleep. The father kissed the favorite child, and then embraced Dominick.

"Be a good boy, Nicky. Mamma will soon bring you to me again."

Voices were heard shouting, somewhere, in the distance. When Madam Blennerhassett opened the hall door to go forth with her husband, a dash of snow was driven into her face by the insolent wind. Arm in arm went the pair, through the drift which heaped the dooryard path and covered the flower beds. They saw a fire which a squad of the recruits had kindled near the river, to warm their numb hands. The flickering blaze made fantastic lights and shadows among the gaunt bare trees. Just beyond the limits of the snow could be seen the broad Ohio.

"How sullen the black flood looks!" thought the woman.

"Do you hear the water swash against the logs along the shore?" said Blennerhassett.

The couple made straight for the camp-fire, breaking a track. The dry leaves under the snow, when trodden on, gave back a muffled rustle. Near the fire stood a group of a dozen men, with guns in their hands.

"Who are these? Are they militiamen? Will they arrest you? O Harman, my dearest!"

"They are my own people!" answered the husband.

The words had scarcely passed his lips when a figure emerged from the hollow of a huge sycamore, and advanced to intercept the coming party. A powerful man clapped his hand on Blennerhassett's shoulder.

"Harman Blennerhassett, I arrest you in the name and by the authority of the State of Ohio."

"The hell you do!" a gruff voice responded from the group of armed men, who instantly levelled their guns at the intruder.

"Take your hands off that man, and take yourself away, or we will blow your damned brains out!"

"Don't shoot! don't shoot!" cried the foiled agent of the State of Ohio, taken by surprise. "You won't be rash enough to kill an old army officer, will you?"

"We will be rash enough to shoot any man who interferes with our affairs. Who the devil are you?"

"I am General Tupper."

He came forward, into the light of the fire, and was recognized by several.

"You say you represent the State of Ohio," Blennerhassett faltered. "This island belongs to the State of Virginia; you have no business here."

"Blow his head off!" growled one of the guards, and again the recruits covered the spy with their muskets.

"For God's sake, men, don't fire! Upon my word and honor, I came here with good intent. All Marietta is friendly to you, Mr. Blennerhassett. Can't you be persuaded to give up your rash design? You are rushing to your own ruin."

"Put down your guns," commanded Blennerhassett.

"Time is flying," whispered the wife, impatiently. "Let them scare him away."

"If you delay us longer, General Tupper, I cannot be answerable for what my men may do."

The cocking of a gun warned the well-intentioned officer to hurry away.

"Farewell," he shouted back, "I wish you a safe escape down the river, and a fortunate adventure."

The speech was answered by a yell of derision from the boatmen as they leapt on board the batteau, muskets in hand.

"Good-bye, my love," whispered Blennerhassett, clasping his wife in a parting embrace.

"Good-bye, dear!" she said, and kissed him. "Be strong! Be brave! All will end well. God bless you! Think of a glorious future!"

She turned to go, looked back, turned again from the icy margin of the river, and started homeward; but, after taking a few steps, she again stopped and stood a minute, shivering, and weeping under the bare boughs of the great oak tree beneath which Burr had read aloud to her one of her own sentimental poems. Groaning in spirit, and heart-stung by pangs of self-reproach, she hurried up the slope of the carriage road alone.

Through the drifting snow the brave woman returned to her house, which, seen dimly through a veil of falling flakes, had looked to her from a distance like an unsubstantial pile—a phantom habitation for spectres. As she entered its dark hall the Geneva clock struck twelve.

XXV.: HEROINE AND HERO.

Blennerhassett was afloat to join Burr. The management of the affairs of the island devolved upon his wife. In the sole care of one woman were left houses and land, man and beast, domestic duties at home and business transactions abroad. Her children required constant attention, and the servants, bond and free, for the most part lazy, evasive, and insubordinate—spoilt by the inefficiency of a vacillating master—were hard to govern or to please. Peter Taylor was insidious, but plausible; Albright, obstinate; the negroes, with few exceptions, "something between a hindrance and a help."

On returning to her house at midnight, having just seen her husband embark, the vigilant wife and mother did not bury her troubles in sleep. The urgent demands of a crisis not to be postponed forbade slumber. The words of General Tupper rang in her ears: "I arrest you by the authority of the State of Ohio." That her peace and liberty would soon be threatened, if not taken from her, by civil or by military force, she had much reason to fear; that her island retreat was already invaded by scouts from the Virginia militia she did not surmise. "How I wish I were a man," she said to herself, and sat down to think how a man in her situation would act. Whatever may have been the sex of her brain, her mind worked swiftly, both to decide and to will. "I shall go to Marietta," was her mental conclusion, "and make another effort to secure the family boat for my children and myself. It belongs to my husband; he paid for it from his own private purse; I will claim that boat."

The tardy sun, peering through the dense fog of the following morning, caught a first glimpse of Madam Blennerhassett when she dismounted near Fort Harmar, and asked to be ferried across the Muskingum, to the boatyard on the eastern shore. The resolute lady sought the town authorities of Marietta—magistrates, lawyers, generals, merchants, common laborers—whom she importuned to intercede in her behalf. She argued, she coaxed, she threatened, she tried the persuasive influence of bribes, and as a last resort, she summoned tears to plead her cause—but of no avail—she failed to obtain the boat. Enraged, disappointed, filled with anxious forebodings, she recrossed the Muskingum, and started back over the road which leads to Belpre, following the windings of the Ohio.

During her absence from home a very disagreeable surprise was preparing for her. The militia of Wood County, Virginia, crossed over to the island and camped on the most eligible grounds they could find, the premises nearest Blennerhassett's buildings. The commander of this reckless and undisciplined infantry, Colonel Hugh Phelps, did not appear at the place of rendezvous until late in the day, having gone on a reconnoitering errand, to the mouth of the Kanawha, hoping to intercept Blennerhassett. The soldiers, if a name so honorable can be applied to the raw levy, mustered on the spur of the moment, assumed all the boisterous swagger which, as they imagined, was the prerogative of the citizen dressed in uniform and armed with musket. It was their idea that a soldier's privilege is insolence, and the badge of his superiority, self-importance. The captain and lieutenants exercised slight control over the men in the ranks, who conceived that the offices had gone to the wrong men. The Wood County militia regarded itself as an "army of occupation," by law and precedent warranted in abusing a brief authority. Instead of guarding and protecting property not their own, the men showed their patriotic zeal by mutilating or demolishing the results of Blennerhassett's labor. They took malicious pleasure in wantonly defacing whatever was elegant or ornamental. They tore off the fence-palings to build their camp-fires; they broke down young fruit trees and pulled up evergreen shrubs; they ransacked barns and outhouses, stole hoarded apples, killed chickens, and frightened the negro slaves out of their small wits. Peter Taylor protested in vain; the roysterers threatened to put Peter in the guard-house and gag him, or even to "string him up," if he didn't hold his tongue.

The butler was forced to produce the keys to the wine-cellar, and the consequences of his surrender were what might have been expected. The mischief already perpetrated in coarse fun— the horseplay of backwoods big boys cut loose from restraint, though rude and destructive, was harmless compared with the orgies to which it was a prelude. The rich and abundant liquors stored away to supply the family demand for twenty years were in a day poured down the throats of the pseudo-soldiers. Under the influence of drink many of the privates, and not a few officers, lost all sense of decency. Some of the bolder among them entered the house, roamed through kitchen, parlor, library, bedrooms. One drunken lout smashed the rare violincello, another brought the gilded harp out into the barnyard and used it as a gridiron on which to roast a confiscated pig. The oil portrait of Blennerhassett, set up as a target, was riddled with bullets.

Dominick made a frantic effort to rescue his father's picture from so ignominious a fate, but, cuffed on the ear by a bully, the boy had no recourse except to hide away in his mother's room with Harman and the black housemaid, Juno.

Such were the scenes enacting in and around her beautiful mansion, while the disappointed mistress was hurrying homeward. A heavy fog still hung over the valley and almost hid the sullen waters of the river from view. As Madam Blennerhassett urged her horse along the river road, her vigilant eye kept her aware of a small boat, which, soon after her starting back from Marietta, she had seen glide out of the mouth of the Muskingum and drift down the Ohio, hugging close to the north shore. Indistinctly, through the mist, she could make out the shape of a man rowing the boat. Whenever she quickened the pace of her horse, the man plied his oars rapidly; whenever she slackened reins, the man slowed up; he kept opposite her and was watching her. Madam Blennerhassett was a courageous woman; but she was a woman, and she began to be afraid. Why was that man furtively following her down the river? Why did he keep her constantly in sight? What might be his evil design? Her terror increased as she neared the ferry, where she had ordered Peter Taylor and Ransom, the negro, to await her return. Striking her steed smartly with the riding whip, she galloped fast. She reached the ferry landing, the boat was there, but Peter Taylor, in whose face she read distressful tidings, was reluctant to carry her over.

"Maybe, mum, you'd best stay in Belpre; there's a rough set on the island."

"The militia, I suppose," said she. "Make haste! Take me to my children."

Hesitatingly, the rowers obeyed their mistress, whose eyes watchfully pierced the fog, in every direction, though nothing could she see of the sneaking river-spy or of his canoe. She drew a long breath of relief, and turned inquiringly to Peter Taylor.

"Has anything gone wrong?"

"Heverything 'as gone wrong!"

He told her a dismal tale of the doings of the militia, dwelling on his own inglorious sufferings. A flush reddened his mistress's cheeks, her eyes flashed and her heart was on fire. "Go faster! Work with all your might!"

The white man and his black helper bent hard to their poles, and brought the boat speedily to the landing. The horse was led ashore and its rider sprang into the saddle, and galloped to the door of her house. The soldiers, bivouacking in the front yard, stared in amazement as she rode past. In a minute, in a second, she alighted and swept into the parlor, where six or eight brawling intruders sat on mahogany chairs and upholstered sofas, drinking wine and singing filthy songs. One fellow, maudlin from liquor, rolled on the Smyrna rug. Another was in the act of firing a bullet at the frescoed ceiling.

"Robbers! Cowards! Beasts! Begone! Where is your commanding officer? By whose permission are you here? Young man"—this to a captain—"you wear a sword—draw it and drive these ruffians out! This is my house. You have no warrant to break in, like a band of thieves."

This speech and the imperious bearing of the offended woman checked, but did not stop the orgies of the irresponsible men. A few slunk from the room, ashamed and overawed. But the mob spirit was not to be quenched by an angry lady's lofty speech. The brutal element prevailed. What cared those intoxicated revellers for a scolding tongue? The young captain, his head swimming in the fumes of whiskey, impudently replied, "I'm in command here myself, my dear. When Phelps comes back, I'll interduce you to him." The soldiers yawped applause. In the midst of the uproar, Juno, the house servant, ventured to come in by way of the library, with Harman. The child ran to his mother where she stood in the centre of the room. A saucy corporal broke out with obscene speech and plucked at the dress of the negro girl, imitating the affrighted child.

Again the mistress made a vain appeal:

"Do American soldiers abuse women?"

"A nigger's not a woman!" hiccoughed the corporal, and his words were applauded by a general guffaw.

"Think of your own sisters and mothers and wives!"

"Wives! That's good! How many wives do you s'pose I've got? I wish to hell I had a bloomin' wife like yerself. Yer man's run away, how will I do for a substitute?"

"Shouldn't wonder," interrupted the captain, "if the damned Irish traitor was lynched by this time."

Madam Blennerhassett looked around imploringly and supplicated:

"I am alone here with my poor children. Will no one take our part? Is there not one man here who will defend me?"

A drawling voice responded:

"By ginger-root, there is sich a man. Blast you, you forward skunks, git out of this! Say, you woods-colt with the humps on your shoulders and a stalk-knife by your side, help drive these hogs into the Ohio River. They've got more devils in 'em than what's-his-name, in the Holy Scripture, cast into all the swine of Jerusalem. Git out, I say, you knock-kneed jackasses!"

Loquacity was Byle's riches, but he could transmute speech into action. Instead of wasting words, he began to deliver convincing blows. His first stroke sent the obscene corporal to the floor, minus front teeth and consciousness. The amazed captain labored to unsheath his sword, but Byle snatched the rusty weapon and thwacked the young scapegrace over the pate with it. A rash rustic drew up musket and fired; the ball grazed Plutarch's right thumb, bringing blood. This enraged the doughty champion to the highest pitch of his fighting compass. Rushing upon the dismayed private, he seized the offending musket with both hands, and snapped stock from barrel by suddenly pressing the piece against his bent knee. So impetuous and so violent and so general was the onslaught of Plutarch, that the untried militiamen, "flown with insolence and wine," were taken aback, surprised and confounded. Seeing his advantage, the gaunt giant resumed bellicose speech, like a Greek taunting the Trojans.

"Bust my buttons, bimeby I'll get mad, and hurt some of you 'fore I know what I'm about! What the Holy Moses did you shoot my thumb for? durn you! Don't you guess I've any feelin', you onery idiot? Needn't be skeered, Margaret, I'll make ground mustard out of anybody that dares touch a hair of your head with his sass!"

The rout, ignominiously driven from the parlor by the vigorous assaults of Byle, immediately rallied, in the yard, ashamed of their precipitate panic and retreat. The humiliated captain gave orders to a file of men to enter the house and take the champion, alive or dead. This command might have been executed had not Colonel Phelps come upon the scene unexpectedly. A rapid survey of the premises, a few inquiries, revealed to him the shameful misbehavior of his officers and men. Byle freely imparted his version of how matters stood.

"Colonel, these scandalous boys of yourn are guilty of burglary in open daylight! yes, and of unprovoked 'sault and batter, prepense. The law is on our side, all round. The citizen has an inalienable right to defend his home and family, and we did, didn't we, Harman?"

Phelps admitted the correctness of Plutarch's views. To the captain the colonel said sternly:

"Consider yourself under arrest. You have disgraced your temporary commission." Addressing the derelict soldiery, he added:

"You are not fit to carry muskets! Shame upon you, men, shame! You have soiled the name of Virginia, and stained the honor of your homes."

"Say, cap'n," resumed Byle, staunching his bloody thumb with the fringe of his buckskin doublet, "you'd best trade your side arms for this young un's tin sword; git it for him, bub; and I'll make him a pop-gun of elder-wood. Colonel Hugh Phelps, of Parkurgberg, how are you? Excuse my not shaking hands sooner."

Phelps assumed a haughty military attitude, which displayed to advantage his large and imposing form. "Who is this person?" he asked the captain.

"Jersey cranberries! Don't you know me? I've heard of the Phelpses ever since I was knee-high to a duck. They are folks nobody need feel ticklish about shaking hands with. You're the only swelled up one of the stock. I never knowed but one wuthless Phelp, and he was a good enough fisher when he was sober. Colonel, were you ever picked up by puttin' out your paw to the wrong man? Want to see inside the 'stablishment? Come right in, I'll introduce you to Mrs. Blennerhassett."

The colonel pushed forward through the open door and accosted the dignified lady, who was taking an inventory of the ruined household effects. Byle stalked into the room at the officer's side.

In the stately manner of the gentry of the period, Phelps made his compliments and solicited a brief interview. He apologized as well as he could for the outrageous behavior of the militia, and offered to do anything in his power to make amends. The only favor which the proud woman asked was the privilege of embarking as soon as practicable, on a down-river boat that would carry her and her children to the South.

"Can you procure for me the family boat which my husband provided for us at Marietta?"

The colonel feared not. Marietta was out of his jurisdiction.

"Is there any boat that I can borrow here, or buy? I must join my husband; I promised him that I would not delay."

"I'd lend you my big piroque, but you'll overset before you get as far as Farmer's Castle," said Byle.

"Pardon me," responded Madam Blennerhassett, in tones of apology, bestowing looks of infinite gratitude on her zealous guardian; "I cannot put in words my sense of obligation to you, sir. Colonel Phelps, I owe to this gentleman more than money can repay! It was he who protected me and my servants from the drunken soldiers; he drove them out, risking his life; he was wounded defending us!"

"You don't owe me a fip. It is no trouble at all to me to do a little chore for you. It was fool's luck, anyway. I saw you in town this morning, skiting about, from pillar to post, and says I to myself, 'There's uneasiness under that fine bonnet!' I noticed you dodge in at the court-house and at Squire Hale's, and everywhere, and something told me to investigate. So I went in wherever I saw you come out, in reg'lar order, and larnt, I guess, just about as much as you did, about your disappointment and your worry. Then I thought, 'as like as not that woman is having more trouble down upon the island than I know anything about. So, true as calamus is sweet-flag, as soon as you was on your white horse, like the old lady of Banbury Cross, I was in my everyday skiff, and I didn't lose you out of my sight from the minute you started to the minute Peter and Ransom took you on the ferry—but I slid along where you couldn't spy me."

"I did see you, sir, and I confess I imagined you might be some river-ruffian watching me with no good intention. I did you great injustice."

"I looked like a river pirate, did I? No, ma'am, I was a privateer, but not a pirate. I was sailing under your colors, unbeknown to you. Is that correct military language, Phelps? To make a long story short, Scipio told me in his charcoal style what happened last night, and all about Harman's sudden going away. Well, sir—ma'am, I mean—it struck me of a heap. I never was worse doubled up by news in my life. I'm not a praying man, as a rule—I only remember praying out loud once—that was when brother Euc was near 'bout dead with cholera morbus—I began to pray, and he says, 'Don't be fooling with the Lord now, but give me some more camphire.' That speech of Euc's sort of cured me of praying out loud, though I'm orthodox. Let's see; where was I? Oh, yes, I felt so dangnation sorry for the family, that I says, in my mind, or I reckon it was in my soul, I says to God, 'Don't forget to keep your all-seeing eye on Margaret.' Well, Colonel Phelps; I leave you in charge of the widow and the fatherless. If you have any trouble with the militia, just send for Plutarch Byle. Good-bye, Mrs. B. I never seen you lookin' handsomer since the day I first met you and Evaleen, last May a year ago, when I was up here investigating that hunk of raw beef in the puddle."

Notwithstanding his precipitate farewell, Plutarch lingered at the door, and kept nervously wiping the blood off his thumb upon the fringe of his doublet. Mrs. Blennerhassett, with gracious solicitude, insisted upon wrapping a small linen handkerchief about the wounded member. The gawky hero looked very sheepish while she tied the soft bandage fast.

"Is this yourn?" he asked.

"It was mine," she answered, smiling amusedly, "but it now belongs to the knight who came to fight my battle when I was in great distress."

"By gum, I'm obliged to you."

Uttering these elegant parting words, Byle bolted out of the room to the long porch. He stood a moment, then turned his face toward the door, where stood the lady, smiling her embarrassed thanks and adieux. Big tears were trickling down Plutarch's cheeks. The awkward giant gulped, wheeled round, and with long strides made a bee-line for his boat, followed as he left the yard by cheers from the Wood County militia.

Fortunately, a party of youths, including Morgan Neville, William Robinson, young Brackenridge, and a dozen others, who had attached themselves to Burr and Arlington in Pittsburg, came down the Ohio, in a flatboat belonging to one of their associates, Thomas Butler. These adventurous voyagers, suspected of complicity with Burr, were arraigned before three justices of the peace, of the Dogberry caliber, and after a ludicrous examination were acquitted. The best room of their boat was fitted up with carpets, hangings, and a suite of furniture taken from the chambers of the White House, soon to be deserted. The unplaned, unpainted cabin, perfumed by the sour odor of oaken planks and the scent of pine resin, was transformed into an Eastern boudoir—couches, divans, gorgeous colors and all, for the accommodation of Mrs. Blennerhassett.

The ill-starred gentlewoman whose passion for the magnificent prompted her to adorn her floating bower thus luxuriously, and who, like Cleopatra, was attended on her barge by Ethiop slaves, had not relinquished her faith in Burr's dream of conquest and empire.

"Where are we going," asked Harman, when the boat which was to convey the family to Bayou Pierre had been pushed off from their island, and the mother and her children realized that they were afloat upon the river.

"We are going to meet your father in a splendid city far away in the South."

"Will Colonel Burr be there?"

"Yes, but we shall not then call him Colonel; he will be Emperor."

"And what will you be, mamma?"

"A duchess, my son."

The weary mother sank back upon her oriental divan, which was piled with cushions, and closed her eyes in fragrant slumber, a luxury she had foregone for many days and nights.

XXVI.: OUT OF THE NET INTO THE TRAP.

December was well-nigh spent when Blennerhassett's bateau reached the mouth of the Cumberland and joined Burr's flotilla of a dozen similar boats. The number of men ready to embark for the Wachita counted only three or four score. This informidable showing discouraged Blennerhassett, but the "general," for so Burr was now styled, saw fleet and men with the multiplying eye of faith, and he rejoiced to have actually begun the campaign. Followers yet unseen were surely on their way to join his resolute band. The miscarriage of plans at the island imposed only a temporary delay on the five hundred expected to descend from the Alleghany country. That recruits would flock the Mississippi shores to look for the coming of the leader, and to offer themselves—blanket, gun and soul—for the bold venture, was to be expected of men whose names were written in the "Roster of the Faithful."

The motley forces drawn up on the bank of the Cumberland for review and instruction made up in fantastic variety for what they lacked in number. There was much of the grotesque and somewhat of the pitiful in the spectacle presented by the straggling ranks of boatmen and backwoods farmers. Many wore garments of butternut linsey; others had on buckskin breeches and coats of bear's pelts; some, in imitation of Boone and the pioneers, had donned moccasins and wolf's skin caps, ornamented with foxtails. Some of these picturesque resolutes leaned on their long rifles, displaying to advantage tomahawk and scalping knife.

To this nucleus of an expected great army Burr made a brief speech: "There can be no failure in any enterprise backed up by patriots of such stock as I see before me. You have the muscle and the sinew, the blood and the brains, the heart and the soul, of Western heroes. Your officers, while expecting obedience, give in return their friendship and protection. We are to share common hardships and dangers, putting up with things as they are to-day, in certainty of reward to-morrow."

The progress of the unwieldy batteaux was impeded by perils of winter navigation. Burr exercised his best generalship in directing his men how to overcome the difficulties they must encounter. He now thought he knew the river in its two siren moods, its summer singing hour and its winter rage of hunger for decoyed victims. His royal progress in Wilkinson's barge he recollected as an event so long ago as to seem an impression revived in the brain, of a voyage enjoyed in some previous state of existence.

The flotilla had passed New Madrid, when, one afternoon, Burr standing near the stern of his boat—amused himself by contemplating a procession of flying clouds in distorted shapes of dragons, hippogrifs, witches, and ghosts. The boat was close to shore, skirting a low bluff, covered with shrubs and trees. A majestic poplar standing on the river's edge drew the colonel's attention by its noble aspect. At the very moment when the prow drove opposite the monarch tree, its lofty top trembled, the towering trunk reeled and fell into the river with a terrific plunge. The twenty-foot long steering pole, to which was attached a rudder like the blade of a huge oar, was struck and splintered by the falling trunk. The seemingly firm-rooted and defiant poplar had been undermined by the incessant erosion of the flood.

"Good Heaven!" exclaimed Burr, involuntarily. "Am I the tree or the undercurrent?"

That he had far less to dread from winds, waves, and falling trees than from ominous storm gatherings of human element, menacing the fleet from the shore, the adventurer discovered full soon. He was prepared to battle with the Mississippi, but had not anticipated collision with the territorial militia, for he was in ignorance of the fact that his plans had been exposed, and that a thunderbolt from the hand of national authority had been hurled. His flotilla, as it proceeded southward, instead of being hailed and boarded by eager recruits, was bayed by the watch-dogs of the law, civil and martial. Intrusive messengers from the courts and officious colonels of raw militia regiments pestered and threatened; those, with paper warrants from local magistrates, these, with flintlock muskets in reserve.

Not until his boat arrived at Bayou Pierre, near Natchez, and landed in Petite Gulf, was Burr fully informed of the action taken by the National Government and the several States. The situation was disclosed to him by Major Flaharty of the Second Regiment, who, acting under the authority of the territorial governor of Mississippi, ordered Burr to appear at the village of Washington to undergo examination. The order was not promptly enforced, and the boats were permitted to cross the river to a point on the western shore, a few miles lower down.

Before Burr's boat pushed out from Petite Gulf, Blennerhassett hurried to his superior, and with many apologies, handed him a letter, crumpled from having been carried long in the bearer's pocket.

"This came by mail to the island, addressed, as you see, in my care. Margaret warned me to deliver it to you promptly; but the commission escaped my mind." The superscription on the letter, written in fine hand, ran thus: "To Colonel Aaron Burr, care of Mr. Harman Blennerhassett, Blennerhassett's Island, opposite Belpre, Ohio, U. S. A." Burr waited until the boat was in motion before entering his cabin to open and read the belated billet-doux, for such he judged the missive to be. The news he had just heard of Wilkinson's changed attitude, and the prospect of his own arrest, left him in a state of mind not favorable to playing the capricious game of flirtation, with pen or tongue. He cast the sealed epistle on the table provided for his use, and sat down on a wooden stool to ponder. The only illumination of his rude quarters came from a tallow candle stuck in a socket made by boring an auger-hole in a block of wood. Night had fallen, the wind blew in violent gusts and the timbers of the flatboat creaked and shuddered. Burr sat in meditation, his face buried in his hands, his elbows resting on the table, a foiled conspirator—frustrated, trapped, as he conjectured, by his suave confederate. He had drifted into the eelpot prepared for him. No mode of escape could he devise. He thought of Madam Blennerhassett, of Theodosia, of glorious visions seen and royal assurances given, in the secluded library of the White House on the lonely island in the Ohio. Vividly he remembered his first voyage down the beautiful river, the conversations with Arlington, the serio-comic encounter with Plutarch Byle, the reverie on deck of the ark, the evening in the ladies' bower. Slowly he raised his head from his hands, and moved by the automatism of habit drew a cigar from its case, lit the solacing weed at the blue-yellow cone of the candle flame, and smoked. He now felt not disinclined to take up the neglected billet-doux. He broke the seal and read.

Philadelphia, Nov. 31, 1806.

"Forgive—forgive me, if you can—I am dying of remorse. You deceived me, betrayed me, in my girlhood, but I pardoned that, for I loved you more than any other woman ever loved a man. When we met in Ohio, by strange accident, all was reconciled. How happy I was! But when I learned of your perfidy; when I was forced to realize that I was not only your jilted victim, but your hoodwinked dupe; that your object in coaxing from me my fortune was wholly selfish; that you never meant to restore either my property or my good name; while your kisses were warm upon my lips your heart was planning proposals to another woman to become your wife that I, your discarded tool, could not claim even to be regarded as your mistress; when I felt sure of all this, I was frantic with grief and rage. I went to Washington, saw the President, gave him all the facts and papers you had intrusted to me. I did this in hatred, for revenge. In my madness I wanted to crush you, to blast your hopes, to kill you, if I could. But anger gave way to remorse. I would undo what I have done, but it is too late. I know you cannot love me—you cannot pity or forgive. I never shall forgive myself. There is nothing for me to live for—I am wretched, wretched, ruined—abandoned by you and despised by the world. When this reaches you, if it ever reaches your dear hand, I will be out of this awful misery and free from shame.

"I send enclosed the diamond ring you gave me in Princeton—the one you took from my finger in that farmhouse on the Miami, to write with it on the window-pane your name, dear Aaron, my first love, and underneath it my own.

"Salome."

The unhappy trifler having reread the reproachful lines, took up the ring which had fallen upon the table when the letter was unfolded. There was a small window in the side of the cabin, opening on hinges. Burr rose, stepped to the rude casement, unfastened the bolt, thrust his arm out as far as he could reach, holding betwixt his thumb and finger the sparkling gem, and was about to cast it into the water; but he checked the impulse, drew back his hand and slipped the love-token on his little finger.

"Poor Salome!" he murmured, closing the sash. "Foolish Salome! She thinks she is the cause of my ruin; but she is not. I wish to God I could say I am not the cause of hers."

The fickle lover, rousing from his remorseful reverie, became the man of action. His boat was freighted, in part, with military stores, proof positive of warlike designs. This objective evidence must not come to the knowledge of judge or militia-man. Burr seized an axe, and calling one of the boatmen to his assistance, led the way to the main storage room, where guns and ammunition, packed in chests, lay piled. The place was closely boarded up, having no openings whatever in the sides.

"Here, Gilpin, take the axe, while I hold the light. Cut a hole in the side of the boat, between these two upright braces. Hurry up! Make the space large enough to let these boxes pass through."

The boatman chopped with lusty strokes and soon hewed an opening sufficiently long and wide through the plank siding.

"Now, take hold; help lift this, and slide it overboard."

Rapidly the two worked with might and main, casting chest after chest overboard to sink plumb to the muddy bottom of the Mississippi. By the time the steersman gave orders for landing on the Arkansas shore, the telltale cargo had all been unloaded. The innocent vessel was brought to harbor in a bend and made fast to some friendly trees.

Military officers, acting for the governor of Mississippi Territory, lay in wait to seize Burr and Blennerhassett. To the governor's aide-de-camp the chief conspirator said with bitter resentment:

"As to any projects or plans which may have been formed between General Wilkinson and myself, heretofore, they are now completely frustrated by the treacherous conduct of Wilkinson; and the world must pronounce him a perfidious villain. If I am sacrificed, my portfolio will prove him such."

This petulant outburst was of no avail to stave off the minions of the law. Burr was again in the toils. He, the distinguished attorney who had won so many cases before the New York bench, and who had presided over the Senate of the United States, was summoned to a hearing before a grand jury in the obscure village of Washington. What a descent from Washington, the capital, to Washington, the frontier hamlet; from presidency of the Senate to a prisoner's box in a backwoods court-house!

The good genius of Burr did not desert him at the hour of this, his second humiliating ordeal. Fortune, who had rescued him in Kentucky, again favored him in Mississippi. The grand jury, to the chagrin of judge and territorial governor, brought in the unexpected presentment that Aaron Burr was not guilty of any crime or misdemeanor. The jury was dismissed, but the prisoner was not discharged. Burr, who had many secret friends, was advised that the governor intended to seize on his person the moment the court should release him. The conspirator resolved to elude judiciary and executive by flight. Prudence and dignity, however, forbade precipitate action. Never was fugitive so intrepid, so calm. No valet had ever regarded him less than a hero. But how would Madam Blennerhassett judge him? She had arrived at Bayou Pierre—that Burr knew—and the first tidings she heard of her husband told her that he and Burr had been arrested. Burr sat down, and penned the following:

"Washington, Miss., Jan. 31, 1807.

"Mrs. M. Blennerhassett.

"Dear Madam: Your good husband has informed you of the miscarriage of our plans, and of our humiliating detention by Government officials. This temporary delay on the road to Beulah is wholly chargeable to the treachery of one individual in whom I placed absolute trust. No fit abiding place is yet provided for you on the Wachita acres. And Orleans is a port closed against us. How mortifying! Let not these tidings distress you, but draw upon the infinite resources of a determined will. I am not discouraged—only pestered and stung by a swarm of mosquitoes in the shape of magistrates, militia colonels, and false witnesses. Doubtless, Mr. Blennerhassett will be restored to you soon; as for myself, I take all the responsibility for his misfortunes upon my shoulders. Circumstances compel me, for the present, to move with circumspection, but you shall hear from me in good time.

"Last night, in my sleep, I had a delightful experience. I dreamed we were all sailing the

Mediterranean, in a silken-sailed barge, bound for Egypt, Syria, Arabia, and every spicy, flowery land. I awoke to the 'slumbery agitation' of today's evil chances. However, 'there's nothing either good or bad, but thinking makes it so.' The Kingdom is within us. You recollect old Shirley's solemn lines,

'The glories of our blood and state
Are shadows, not substantial things.'

The only substantial world is comprised within the two hemispheres of the human heart.

"Dear madam, will you console Theodosia with one of your brave, loving, womanly letters? She is the one who will suffer most from the miserable collapse of our plans—she and poor little Gampy.

"I presume you will return to the Enchanted Ground! 'Tis a heavenly retreat. I enclose a sprig of Spanish moss from a cypress-tree near the village jail. Adieu,

"A. B."

The gallant traitor did not linger for the governor's catchpoll to seize him. French leave was better than a sheriff's hospitality. Three of Burr's faithful adherents agreed to convey him secretly, in a skiff, to a point twenty miles from Bayou Pierre, and there to provide him with a horse and a mounted guide, to facilitate his escape from the Territory. In pursuance of his project, he was about to leave Washington, on foot, to join his clandestine abettors, when he was curtly accosted by a young man whom he was startled to recognize at that time and place. Burr put out his hand, but the young man haughtily withheld his own. He spoke vehemently.

"Colonel Burr, I challenged a brave man, a patriotic soldier, to fight a duel with me, because he spoke severe words about you. He wronged you a little, but you have wronged me much—my friends more. You called Hamilton to the field for traducing you; I demand satisfaction from you for treacherously involving me and my family name with your own, in charges of disloyalty to the Government. You lied to me!"

Burr compressed his lips and filled his lungs with a quick-drawn breath. His cheeks purpled and his eyes shot dark fire.

"Mr. Arlington, you go too far. I cannot brook insult."

"Do not brook it. Resent it. You have smutched my honor. You have ruined the Blennerhassetts. You have betrayed a host of confiding people. You have endeavored to destroy the Union. I can right myself before the country and in my own estimation only by calling you to personal account. Will you meet me with pistol or with sword?"

Burr quenched the resentful fires that burnt in his heart, and replied calmly:

"My friend, I decline to meet you in any form of duel. You cannot provoke me to accept your challenge. I respect you too much to kill you. You demand satisfaction. Arlington, no satisfaction comes to either party in a fatal conflict. The dead man is indifferent to the boast of honor vindicated. I have fought my last duel. But don't imagine me afraid of threats, or bullets, or swords."

The Virginian responded in milder tones.

"Can you justify your deceptions, practised on me, or make amends for the injury done the

Blennerhassetts?"

"I justify nothing. I promise no reform. My plan failed. I did my best. I am no traitor. I meant to benefit everybody. I shall be vindicated. Good-bye. Go, Arlington, marry the belle of Marietta, and be a happy man."

Arlington's nostrils quivered. A second surge of anger swept over him. Burr continued:

"I advise seriously. Win Miss Hale. I know she likes you. She is the finest woman west of the Appalachians—or east of them. I had matrimonial inclinings toward the paragon myself."

"That I know," said the young man, with crabbed acrimony.

"Yes, you know that. That is an additional reason, you think, for wishing to meet me in dudgeon. A lover hates a rival, even an unsuccessful one, and cherishes hotter resentment against the man who steals a kiss from his lady love than against him who violates a dozen federal constitutions, and breaks all the apron strings of his mother country."

The flippancy of this speech renewed Arlington's animosity.

"You will not, then, permit me to right myself by the code of honor?"

"No, Arlington, as I told you, I fought my last duel on the bank of the Hudson. Good-bye. I am not the bad man you believe me to be. But I am under a cloud. My hopes are darkened. I would like to keep your friendship, but cannot demand it. It was in our plans to make you a 'belted knight, a marquis, duke, and a' that,' but the Creator anticipated me by making you a true gentleman, which is the highest title of nobility."

Burr started on the path which led to the covert where his three faithful friends awaited his coming, to row him down the river. Halting for a minute, he looked back at Arlington wistfully, and said:

"I am an outcast and an outlaw. Farewell."

Burr followed the path which he hoped would extricate him from the labyrinth of his troubles, and Arlington left the village of Washington, and was soon on the way to New Orleans, where Evaleen Hale expected him at the house of her uncle.

XXVII.: FLIGHT AND SURRENDER.

Disguised in the borrowed clothes of a boatman—pantaloons of coarse stuff, dyed in copperas, a drab-colored roundabout, a broad-brimmed slouch hat much the worse for hard usage in rain and sun—Aaron Burr fled. He deemed it impossible that any detective could recognize him. One precaution, however, he neglected to take; his genteel feet disdained the boatman's cowhide shoes, nor would he put on the pair of big Suarrow boots proffered by one of his followers. He insisted on wearing, as usual, his tight-fitting, neat, elegant city-boots of polished calfskin.

Clad and accoutred for flight through a wild country, mounted upon a spirited horse provided by devoted accessories for the severe journey, and accompanied by a guide who knew the forest ways, he set out, a fugitive from justice. Both he and his pilot carried pistols in holster and provisions in saddle-bags. Their route lay through a desolate region sparsely settled by pioneers, and not yet relinquished by wandering aborigines, nor by the bear and the catamount. The month of February was spent before they reached the valley of the Tombigbee, a distance of two hundred miles from the Mississippi River.

Late one evening the weary travellers drew rein at the door of a log tavern in Alabama. A bright fire was crackling within, and several guests sat conversing before the broad hearth.

"Hello the house!" shouted Burr's attendant. Not hearing a prompt response to the call, the guide dismounted, rapped on the deal door, at the same time jerking a stout leathern bobbin which drew up the wooden latch inside. The door flew open, disclosing a puncheon floor, a bar with bulging decanters of whiskey, and the group of talkers sitting in the ruddy glow of the wide fireplace. The landlord came to the threshold.

"Alight and come in, stranger. I have good beds."

"We are obliged to you, landlord," said Burr from the saddle, "but we can't stop. We hailed the house only to inquire the way to Colonel Hinson's. How far is it?"

"A long seven miles, and all that isn't stump is mud hole. Better put up here till morning. A bite of pork and pone, washed down with a cup of hot coffee, will make a new man of you."

"Thank you, my friend, but we are in some hurry. What direction shall we take?" The tavern-keeper gave the desired information, with tedious minuteness. Meanwhile the party at the fireside took sharp notice of the man on horseback, whom they could plainly see in the outshining light of the fire. A tall gentleman, whom the host called "colonel," inspected the strangers with comprehensive scrutiny.

"Neighbors," said he, listening to the receding hoof-beats of the horses, "did you notice that man's face and his feet? He don't look like a common man. Our backwoodsmen don't wear shiny boots." Leaving his companions mystified by this speech, the colonel hurried from the inn, and bent his steps toward a cabin, from the single small window of which a lard-lamp levelled its faint ray. This was the lodge of the district sheriff. The tall colonel called the officer out and described the appearance and actions of the two travellers.

"Brightwell, I have my suspicions. Hadn't we better go—you and I—to Hinson's, and learn who these parties are and what they want? I doubt if your cousin, Mrs. Hinson, knows that her husband sympathizes with a certain individual who falls under the charges of Jefferson's proclamation."

Colonel Perkins easily persuaded the sheriff it was their duty to follow the suspected persons, and the self-constituted spies saddled horses and spurred through the woods, along a solitary road, to Hinson's lonely cottage. Perkins remained outside, holding the horses and shivering under the gusty pines. The sheriff knocked at the back door of the cabin; the mistress of the house received him kinswomanly in the kitchen. From this rear apartment Brightwell could peep into the front room, where sat the object of his curiosity. Having exchanged a few familiar remarks and inquiries with Mrs. Hinson, the sheriff asked, in a whisper:

"Who is that man—the small man with black eyes and white hands?"

"He calls himself Hodge—Jeremiah Hodge—and claims acquaintance with my husband. He says he came by request to have a talk with Hinson about raft-building on the Tombigbee."

"Do you believe this?"

"I don't know what to think. He is a civil man—very civil—as soft spoken as a girl, and he has the nicest table manners I ever seen in a man. I couldn't turn strangers away on such a raw night."

"No," said the sheriff, "you could not; we must be neighborly; but I have my doubts of Jeremiah Hodge. Good-bye, Jane. Drop over and see Fanny and the new baby."

The officer, highly satisfied with his cunning detective work, slipped out and joined his impatient companion, Perkins, who agreed to communicate straightway with Lieutenant Gaines, commandant at Fort Stoddart, a post on the Tombigbee. Having secured a canoe and a colored boy to paddle it, Colonel Perkins, on the following morning, descended the river, and told Gaines his story.

While Perkins was floating down the Tombigbee, the polite boatman, Jeremiah Hodge, was writing letters, eating breakfast, and chatting most agreeably with his admiring hostess. At about nine-o'clock he requested his fellow-traveller to saddle the horses, and within the few minutes required for this to be done he surprised Mrs. Hinson by disclosing his real name.

"Madam, if you should ever chance to meet a boatman by the name of Jeremiah Hodge, which is not probable, please make my apologies to him for borrowing his name, as I have borrowed also another man's clothes. I am Aaron Burr, of New York, a name pretty widely known and much bandied about in these scandalmongering days. I know your husband well; Colonel Hinson and myself are old friends; I saw him lately in Natchez, and he was kind enough to invite me to make his house my home, in case I had need of a comrade soldier's hospitality. Under the circumstances now existing I cannot remain longer."

Mrs. Hinson looked incredulous and scared.

"Mercy me!" was her suppressed interjection.

"Pardon me for giving a false name, and not a pretty one, either. A reward of two thousand dollars is offered to any one who will give information leading to my arrest. Such a snug sum might serve you for pin-money." This was jocularly said and with a smile. Mrs. Hinson found a tongue to protest.

"Don't fear I'll blab. I wish I could help you to get out of danger. Now I see why cousin

Brightwell was Paul Prying here last night. There's your horse saddled and bridled. Take keer of yourself."

"Good-bye, my dear madam. I cannot, of course, offer to pay you for your generous entertainment of me and my follower. But you must not deny me one small favor—take this ring as a keepsake from Jeremiah Hodge."

He waited not for a reply, but gently raising her hand, which was a very pretty one, he placed on her finger Salome Rosemary's diamond ring! Bowing a graceful adieu, the versatile fugitive rode away at his faithful servant's side.

The brace of horsemen had not trotted a mile before they were overtaken on the highway by a rider who accosted them very cordially. His sorrel steed kept even pace with the other two horses.

"A nice frosty morning," chirpped the friendly bore. "I hope I don't intrude. I like company myself when I am on the road. Which way are you bound? Pensacola?"

Burr made no reply, but his attaché answered freely:

"Yes, Pensacola. Which is the best road from here to Carson's Ferry?"

"The best road and the shortest is by way of the cut-off. I am going that way—I'll show you the road."

All three cantered forward. In half an hour they came to a place where the road made an abrupt turn, and just at this bend a file of mounted and armed soldiers stopped their progress. Lieutenant Gaines and Colonel Perkins rode at the head of the troopers. The lieutenant waved a military salute and spoke.

"Have I the honor of addressing Colonel Burr?"

"You have that honor; I am Aaron Burr."

"You are my prisoner."

"By what authority do you detain me, a private citizen, attending peaceably to my own affairs, on a public thoroughfare?"

"I arrest you, Aaron Burr, in the name and at the instance of the United States of America. I hold in my hand the proclamation of President Jefferson. I am a lieutenant in the United States Army. The gentleman at your side is Theodore Brightwell, a sheriff, and the officer accompanying me is Colonel Nicholas Perkins, who detected you last evening when you rode up to the Piny Woods Tavern."

Burr surrendered. That night he slept, a prisoner, in Fort Stoddart.

XXVIII.: WHAT BECAME OF THEM.

Almost eight years had elapsed since the date of Burr's arrest and imprisonment, when on the first day of May, 1815, two young families loitered away an afternoon in picnic outing on Blennerhassett Island. The party consisted of eight persons—Colonel Warren Danvers, his wife and a small daughter; and Mr. and Mrs. Arlington, their two pretty little girls and a boy-baby. The children, excepting the infant, were old enough to enjoy gathering wild-flowers. They kept within call of the parents, who, conversing on events familiar to them all, strolled over the deserted grounds of an estate rendered sadly famous by the misfortunes of its former possessors. Amid scenes associated with the disastrous failure of a treasonable conspiracy, it was natural to speak of Burr.

"He is paying a bitter penalty for his crime," Danvers commented. "Though acquitted by the Federal Court at Richmond, in spite of Wirt's arraignment, the traitor will not recover the people's good-will. He lives in New York City, a man forbid. His four years' self-exile in Europe, I am told, was a humiliating banishment from the loyal and patriotic. No country can be a "Sweet Home" to the man who repudiates his own nation's flag. Burr declares himself severed from the human race, and so he is."

"You are relentless, Warren," said his sister. "I feel much pity for the man, since his heart-breaking experience of two or three years ago."

"Ah, yes; yes," Lucrèce impulsively said; "Theodosia was her father's incentive and his happiness. It was bad enough to lose the little grandson. Think how you would grieve if your dear little boy should die."

"We don't ever think of dying, do we, Dicky?" Evaleen cooed, making mother eyes at her baby. "The world must have seemed a blank to Burr after Theodosia was drowned."

"Was she drowned?" questioned Arlington. "That was a mysterious affair—the disappearance of the schooner—what was the vessel's name, Danvers?"

"The Patriot. She sailed from Charleston for New York in the winter of 1812. I remember reading of the disaster just before marching with General Harrison to Fort Meigs."

"The boat may have foundered or wrecked," said Arlington. "Some believe it was captured by pirates, who carried Theodosia away to a foreign port."

"That's an absurd theory!" declared Danvers.

"But not impossible, my dear," put in Lucrèce. "I hope the poor lady was not carried away; drowning is preferable," said Evaleen.

"You two wouldn't drown when you had a chance at Cypress Bayou," laughed the husband. "You chose to be carried away by one robber and brought back by another."

Lucrèce snugged close to her soldier, and he gave her a playful kiss.

"Spoony," sang Evaleen, whereupon her prim younger daughter, whose plump fist tightly held a bunch of spring-beauties, looked up in wonder and lisped:

"Mamma, what is spoony?"

The elder sister, some seven years old, came running to her mother's side.

"There's a man by the well!"

"I saw him first," chimed in the smaller child. "Didn't I see him first, Eva?"

The rambling party had returned from the woodland to the cleared tract, in the midst of which the White House of Blennerhassett formerly stood. The mansion, never occupied after the ill-starred family left it, was destroyed by fire a few years before the time of the picnic excursion. Near the low foundation walls of blackened stone stood the wooden curb surrounding the mouth of a deep well. The old windlass, below which a leaky bucket still swung, was kept in repair by unknown hands. Upon looking for the man whom Eva had discovered, Mrs. Arlington saw leaning upon the curb, in a posture of meditation, a figure which both she and her husband recognized. There was no possibility of avoiding or of evading a meeting with the meddlesome babbler who had volunteered to prescribe "cowcumber bitters" as a sure cure for Chester's love. Within the ten years since the revelation on the summit of the mound, and the piroque tour to the island, Arlington had seen and heard a good deal of Plutarch Byle. Though it was always more or less of a social annoyance, and at times an intolerable bore, to encounter the gossipy humorist, his numberless acquaintances, far from wishing him ill, admired his honesty and lauded his goodness of heart.

Byle heard the children's voices, and straightening up his awkward form, turned to observe the advancing group. His wide mouth opened with a grin of pleasure; he came forward with gangling strides.

"By crackey, if it isn't the Arlingtons! Home from Virginia, Evaleen, to old Marietta, on a visit to the folks? You're looking peart. How do you all do?"

Arlington, out of regard for his wife and kinsfolk, made some dignified efforts to stem the tide of Byle's familiarity, but his polite formality was not noticed by the associable democrat, who shook hands with every one, beginning with the baby.

"So these is your offspring, as the preacher says, are they, Chester? I knowed you'd have a lot of 'em when I recommended the match. Here's the suckin' kid; let Uncle Byle heft him once. Gosh, baby, you want to grab uncle's nose, do you? Well, then, pull away till the cows come home. What's 'is name?"

"Richard," answered the mother.

"Why didn't you name him after me? P. B. Arlington would sound sort of uppercrusty, eh? 'Richard,' you say? Oh, I see. Named for your daddy's Orleens brother, the cripple! Yes! yes! Did Richard leave you as big a pile of money as folks say? It must have been a heavy slam on you, Evaleen, when he dropped off. Lucky, too, in another pint of view; he's better off, and so are you—lots better off."

Danvers and Lucrèce, wishing to prevent posthumous comments on Uncle Richard, came to Evaleen's rescue.

"You are a frequent comer to this island. You know its products and topography?"

"Topography, yarbography, bugology and the dickens knows wot ology. The ground is jest kivered, in places with Injun arrers, and pipes and stone hatchets, and I've dug up some of the durndest queer-shaped arthen pots you ever sot eyes on. Yes, I reckon I know Bacchus Island, major."

"Not major," interrupted Arlington. "He was promoted after the battle of New Orleans. He is now Colonel Danvers."

"Jehoshaphat! Let's shake hands on that, Danvers. No resk this time, Arlington, is there? You recollect, don't you? the day I first seed you and Hoopsnake on the roof of his flatboat? I read t'other day in the noospaper that Harry Clay met the aforesaid in the court-house in New York. The sarpent put out his hand, but Harry wouldn't tech it. By gum, Clay was smarter than me."

Danvers and Lucrèce looked mystified. Byle winked at Arlington.

"Don't tell 'em my disgrace. So cap's a colonel? This is a surprise. I'm just back from a jant to Cinc'natti. Stayed there a coon's age with brother Virgil, who moved down from the Yok, last fall, and went into the pork trade. Virgil's married, same as you four, but I'll be dadbanged if he wasn't fooled in his woman. I tell you, Mrs. Danvers, matrimony ain't always sich honey in the comb as Warren is swallerin'. Virgil's wife looks nice, but Spanish flies! how he enjoys her going away from home. Well, that's that. I went down on the Enterprise. You've rid in a steamboat, I dare say, going to see your pa, in Orleens? How's he? I forgot to ask. They say the old man's got to be stylisher than ever. Jest run slap bang into rich relations. How much is the doctor wuth? He never met me, but they say Deville is a choice mackerel, for a Frenchman. I was about to say, I went down to Cinc'natti on the Enterprise last December. Best boat on the river, Captain Shreve says, and the fourth one built. I have saw the Orleens, the Comet and the Vesuvius, but the Enterprise knocks 'em all. Keelboats and barges is clean cut out."

To check the deluge of Byle's conversation, the picnickers soon took occasion to shift their ground from the well to the beautiful green plot which had been the carefully kept lawn of the Blennerhassett premises.

Raised flowerbeds, of various forms, circular, crescent, and diamond, could still be traced, though overgrown with grass and weeds. These abandoned garden beds furnished convenient seating space for the excursionists, while they ate lunch and drank water fetched from the old well by Plutarch. The conversation reverted to Burr and his alleged associates, involving the name of Wilkinson. Danvers defended the general from severe animadversions. Arlington had no patience with his brother-in-law's lenient judgment.

"Why, Warren, you, a colonel in the regulars, must know Wilkinson to have been a failure every way. Wasn't he court-martialed last spring, after holding the command of the Northern army less than a year? He blundered in all he undertook. He was, in effect, discharged for want of generalship and for excess in wine."

"I admit he lost laurels in the late war. So did many others. Jackson and Harrison are our heroes now. General Wilkinson was acquitted by the court-martial, as he was acquitted in 1811 of charges accusing him of complicity with Burr."

"Acquitted! I know he was acquitted; so was Burr; but public opinion condemns the decision of the courts. Before the bar of history both stand accused and sentenced. They are guilty alike. Wilkinson seems to me no better than Burr. Perhaps he is worse, for he betrayed his comrade."

"Did he betray Burr, or did he only find him out? I was in Wilkinson's tent when Burr's cipher letter was exposed. Wilkinson was outspoken in denouncing Burr."

"Hold yer hosses. Let me put in a word edgeways, Captain Danvers—'scuse me, I mean colonel. You spoke of Andy Jackson. He's not my stripe—I'm a Federalist yist'day, to-day and forever—but Old Hickory is a truth teller. What did Jackson say? I give you his upside dixit, word for word, ex litteratum, as they say. Andrew Jackson says, says he, 'Whatever may have been the project of Burr, James Wilkinson has went hand in hand with him.'"

Mrs. Arlington introduced a new topic of conversation by saying, "I'll not believe that Mr. Blennerhassett was consciously guilty."

"No, my dear, he was deluded. Mr. Wirt is right in contending that Blennerhassett was comparatively innocent, 'a mere accessory.'"

Here Mr. Byle stood up and began rummaging in his pockets. The mention of the name of Blennerhassett had altered his mood and changed his manner. A shade of seriousness bordering on melancholy came over his features. He slowly drew from the poke of his warmus a white cambric handkerchief, which he blinked at for a minute, and then replaced, venting an audible sigh. Long he listened in silence to remarks about the islanders and their untoward fate. At length he broke in with:

"I told Harman before he sot out for Eternal Smash what he was comin' to. He wouldn't take my advice. But, gentlemen and ladies, in my opinion, the near-sighted was about as much to blame for what happened, as a pewee is for being swallered by a black snake. Harman lost everything, as I told him he would. Fust in debt heels over head—then the house burns—then he sells the plantation. Now he's tryin' to run a cotton-gin down about Natchez. The boys are growin' up no account. And she—Jerusalem artichokes! What a shame it war for Margaret to throw herself away!"

The amused expression of Arlington indicated his appreciation of Byle's sentiments, but Evaleen could not smile when the distress of her much-beloved friend was the theme of conversation. The rich, beautiful, commanding lady, who had presided like an Eastern princess, in her luxurious island palace, was now struggling with adverse fate, on a cotton plantation, near Port Gibson, Mississippi. Recollecting the downfall and humiliation of Madam Blennerhassett, Evaleen sighed and cast her gaze mournfully toward the spot upon which had stood the stately mansion, which had been to her a second home. But on that May day in 1815, could she have lifted the veil of the future, events far more depressing would have been disclosed. She would have beheld the former lord of the isle, landless, harassed by debts, now in Natchez, now in New York, and now in Canada, unsuccessfully attempting the practice of the law. He made a voyage to Ireland, returned to Montreal, and then again crossed the ocean to reside with his maiden sister, Avis, on the Isle of Jersey. His wife shared his disappointments and sorrows, and it was on her faithful bosom that he breathed his last at Port Prerie, Guernsey, in 1831. Ten years later, the widow, having returned to the United States destitute, forlorn, her health gone, her beauty faded, took up lodgings in a poor tenement-house in the city of New York—and it was here that she died, forsaken by fortune and by friends. Such were the crown of thorns and the crucifixion of Margaret Blennerhassett, who aspired to wear the coronet of a duchess in the court of Aaron the

Emperor.

The sons, Dominick and Harman, were reserved to fates not less abortive and wretched. The first entered the navy as surgeon-mate, but was discharged for drunkenness. He died in penury, an outcast. Harman became a portrait painter in New York, but he lost his strength of body and mind, and finally perished in an almshouse on Blackwell's Island. His body lies buried beside that of his mother, in the family vault of Emmet, the Irish patriot, in the "Marble Cemetery," New York.

Well was it that the Book of Fate, in which was written the story of the House of Blennerhassett, was not opened to Evaleen, for had she read therein, the revelation would have turned the day's pensive melancholy into poignant grief.

Moved by a common impulse of commiseration, and by reverential regard akin to such as one feels when standing beside the tomb of a dear friend, the married couples and the lank bachelor bent their steps from the lawn to the rubble-strown site of the burnt mansion-house. The foundation stones indicated the size and location of the several rooms formerly occupying the ground floor. Danvers and his wife sat down upon the sandstone steps leading, in bygone days, to the wide hall door. The three little girls were at play in the paths of the ruined shrubbery; Evaleen's baby boy lay asleep on the lap of Lucrèce.

Arlington and Evaleen stepped across the crumbling foundation wall, and a few short paces brought them to the middle of the square area once covered by the floor of the reception room. A bunch of wild violets, in bloom, grew in the charred leaf mould at their feet. The wife plucked one of the flowers, and gave it into the hand of her constant lover.

"Here is just where you stood when we met for the first time, love; do you remember? And look, Chester," she pointed upward to the empty space once enclosed in the walls of Lady Blennerhassett's bower, "right up there is the window through which we watched you go away in the moonlight."

"Yes, darling; there you stood, caring very little whether or not we should ever meet again. It is exactly ten years since the day you—didn't kiss me. Do it now."

"Hold on for about three shakes of a sheep's tail. Then fire away when I'm gone. I want to tell you, Chester, here is just the spot where I stood when I fit for her—"

"Fought for my wife?"

"No, for Harman's wife." Byle took out the handkerchief again, and Evaleen thought he intended to tell its history.

"That is a fine piece of cambric. It looks like a lady's token."

"This hankercher?"

"Yes."

Plutarch gulped down a big emotion.

"It's a thumb-stall."

THE END.